I prided myself on my courage, my temperament under duress. I had never known comfort. My safety had been that which I could forge with my own two hands, by fist and violence. A life like that forged a person hard. Or it destroyed them.

Imagine my dismay then, the first time I saw her. It was the closest thing to fear I had felt in a long time. The place unfamiliar, the building cold and confusing, the colour of her skin foreign. If I had never known a place like this existed, why was I here?

No, I knew exactly why I was here.

The nature of sleep was thus: the body rested, and the spirit wandered. I had heard tell of people who could do amazing things in the spirit; run faster than any beast, ride clouds, even fly. I was always bound by what my flesh and blood body could do, as irrelevant as that was while in the spirit. I could never appear oceans away, not on purpose. Yet that is exactly where I found myself, the first night I saw her.

To think that, even though every night while I slept this girl was all I saw, that we would never meet…

*   *   *

"I saw her again."

Rahim sighed audibly from his bunk across the room.

"Again?" He replied, not attempting to hide the disdain from his weary voice. "Does this mean I have to hear about her all today as well?"

Jonah, masking the very real hurt at his cousin's emotional betrayal, lobbed a boot. It bounced satisfyingly off Rahim's forehead as he leapt from his bedroll.

"Pitts of disgrace, Jonah, relax!" He exclaimed, barely stifling a laugh. "You're crazier than two tied at the tail!"

Jonah paused from dressing.

"Maybe." Brushing aside the tent flap as he exited caused a loud clap. He had to admit, he was affected. Turning his long stride into one full of purpose, he sought the familiar to still his nerves.

The desert air was already full of heat and dirt, sweat and fire. It enveloped him as it did every day; as it always had. Though it was mere moments since first call, an explosion of activity surrounded him, like a bomb going off in slow motion. The war camp spread for maybe a 'fist' in every direction, tightly group tents snuggled into the valleys between the dunes. A chorus of flint and blade met his ears, soldiers and the sun meeting as per their daily routine. It was the song of the young man's life.

"Was it the same place?" Rahim called as he jogged to catch up.

"Now you want to hear about her?" Jonah laughed as he accepted a bowl of oats. He did not slow, just began to eat as he walked on. Rahim glanced back at the cook fire, but kept stride.

"If you're going to moon over this girl all day I might as well benefit. Tell me a story. Tell me of beauty, grace, and the haunted look in her big brown eyes." His hands waved through the air in a mock display.

"They're not brown, they're blue. Mostly. They have a green tint that only becomes visible as the light grows in the morning…"

"Pitts of disgrace, Jonah!" Rahim cursed again, this time not hiding the laughter that followed. "Did you spend your entire sleep watching her?"

"And what did you do last night while you slept?" Jonah turned accusingly.

"I," He began, pausing for effect, "am learning Bassk."

"Bassk? I thought you were learning Engsam."

"I have learned Engsam. I am now learning Bassk. As I have learned Fallst, and Remane."

"Peace, Rahim, how many languages do you need to know?"

"It's about bettering yourself, my old friend. Can't drink, smoke, or play Scon while you sleep. You may as well fill the spirit hours doing something productive."

Jonah's eyes turned suddenly cold, distant.

"I have not the patience to read or study during my sleep. I am always wandering."

"Until now, it seems." Rahim corrected him.

Jonah stopped. "Yes. Until now." He smiled suddenly, a smile full of joy and promise. Thrusting the remainder of his oats at his bemused friend and with a clap on his shoulder, the young captain entered the command tent.

*   *   *

Assara opened her eyes. Beside her, her younger sister Tamra still breathed the deep, even breaths of one well away from waking. The mist that escaped her lips told her daylight was well away. Why had she woken?

For a time, she lay perfectly still, trying to bring the details of the young man's face back to memory. She had no idea what had taken her so far from home. Usually when she slept, she could not bring herself to wander far; her constant fear for Tamra's safety prevented it. Instead she spent the many hours gazing out over the Hold, wondering what would become of the many inhabitants who called it home.

Home. It was a strange word for such a place.

Prison would be more apt.

Last night however… She had no memory of being here at all. As soon as she fell asleep, she was on the other side of the world. Well, she assumed it was the other side of the world, based on what she had found there. Although her spirit self could not feel the desert heat in her sleep, she was aware of it, as she was aware of the sand whisking over the dunes and the moonlight casting long shadows on burnt, barren earth.

As she was perfectly aware that whatever, or whoever, had pulled her here had been inside that tent.

The place had indeed felt far away. It was night here, so did that mean she was sleeping during the day? Instinctively she had reached to pull back the tent flaps, and then caught herself as her fingers passed through them. Her heart had pounded in her sleeping chest. She shouldn't have been able to feel it, but she could.

Inside she found him, stark naked and mouth agape in a deep sleep. He was not alone; on the other side of the spacious tent another fellow slept, all but buried in thin brown sheets. Despite herself she had crept, knowing full well that they could not see her, could in no way be aware of her presence. Her head told her she was an intruder; that this was wrong and that she should leave.

Her attention however remained fixed on this one sleeping figure. She remembered clearly leaning closer, fascinated by the curve of his cheek and jaw. His skin was a strange colour, auburn where it should be pale. Perhaps all people here were the same. Perhaps he was special. His dark hair had just enough curve in it to follow the edge of his brow line on its way to his cheek. She longed to see his eyes. Were they brown, or grey, or something she had never seen before? Were they strong, or soft, or somewhere in-between?

She was not sure how long she had watched his face waiting for his eyes to open. Time often moved oddly while you slept, just as travelling distance never seemed linear. All she knew was one moment she was with him, the next, she was awake.

Guilt washed over her. She was needed at home, needed by her sister.

And yet, she lay.

Trying to remember his face.

*   *   *

Jonah absently watched the great wall in the valley ahead. Somewhere in his mind he was aware that the guard was changing, periodically doubling the number of men on patrol. The thought was passive, secondary.

"If Falan's line breaks, we will have to get out of here fast." Rahim was saying. Jonah didn't respond. "No-one can survive an assault of that many undergarments."

Jonah murmured non-committedly.

"Peace, Jonah!" Rahim said, backhanding his distant friend's shoulder. "Where is your focus? I need you!"

Jonah paused then shook his head. "I'm sorry cousin. I'm here. I'm just..."

"Don't say it. We need to bring the company up. Just promise me you will keep your thoughts present. I don't fancy fishing bullets from your shoulder because you were too busy day-sleeping!"

"I'm here, Rahim. Let it go already."

Rahim's glare spoke of words repressed as he turned from the hilltop.

Behind them, hidden in the depression between dunes, thirty armed men waited silently. The sun was an hour past rising, which meant in moments it would be casting considerable glare from behind them, straight into the eyes of the sentries on the wall.

Jonah walked among the men, silently urging them to readiness, steadying them with nods and pats on the shoulder. Any moment now.

A 'twang' gave the signal they were waiting for. The projectile whistled louder and louder as it neared its target. Now back on the crest, prone above his weapon, Jonah saw men on the wall begin shouting orders before the burning missile landed well inside the town. Following the subsequent explosion, a great gate opened, and soldiers emerged. As expected, men appeared from all directions to line the wall at each side of the gate, preparing armaments in defence of the now vulnerable opening.

Jonah's company rested low on the hilltop, rifles at the ready. He picked his target - a newcomer who had taken authority. Lungs full, he relaxed his chest, letting the air seep steadily through his pursed lips, and pulled the trigger.

His gunshot signalled his companions. Fifteen barrels erupted. Men on the wall dropped, pierced by one, two or three bullets, their cries of pain and alarm clear in the warm morning air. Jonah dropped behind the crest along with the first half of the attack to reload as another fifteen shots rang out.

"Captain!"

A pointed finger led his eyes to a gap in the dunes to his left. Falan's horsemen were advancing already.

"Pitt stained fool!" Jonah said to himself as he turned his barrel back to the wall. "Let them have it!" He called. "Give those men some cover!"

Falan may have been arrogant, but Jonah's riflemen were formidable. The horsemen's advance along the city wall went unchecked. Stationary cannons sat unmanned and useless as the operators lay fallen or fled to safety. The large group of soldiers who had passed through the gate turned at the sound of cavalry. Smart, he thought. They had lost the advantage of the high ground, and had no idea that Jonah's allies operating the catapult were, by now, advancing and would soon surround them.

Small groups of reinforcements emerged from the gate sporadically but Jonah and his men were ready, their systematic firing system keeping a constant stream of death on any who risked exiting. In mere minutes the enemy were dead or retreating, the unmanned gate now defenseless.

Falan raised his curved blade above his head. Jonah drew his own sword, repeating the gesture. He would lead the assault on the town, and Falan's horse would hold formation behind, ready to charge should the resistance build.

As soon as he crested the dune an impact took him from his feet. He felt the punch of steel before he heard the gunshot, then rolled backward clutching at his shoulder.

"Jonah!"

*   *   *

Assara was aware of the desert before she opened her sleeping eyes. It had a feeling so far removed from anything she had ever known; it was tangible beyond sight, already familiar beyond memory. She was outside his tent again, despite being able to sleep herself straight inside. Did she want to feel the sensation of entering his private space? Or was it respect of his private space that kept her from going straight there, as if waiting for an invitation that would never come?

Her hand went to her mouth as she passed through the tent wall and noticed the bandage and sling, red with blood, around his left shoulder. She was on her knees and reaching for the wound before she realised there was nothing she could do, no comfort she could offer. Instead she sat, allowing worry to crease her forehead.

Her day had been exciting, more exciting than any she could remember. Her work hours flew by as she routinely performed the assembly line tasks that paid for food and board for her and her sister. In the hour before dark she and Tamra had visited Sivvel, one of the oldest surviving workers in the Hold.

"Yes, I know some of the countries of the world." He had said. "I was lucky enough to go to school, for a few years at least. We learned all sorts of things then you know, not just how to work here in the Hold. We learned of countries and cultures, some remaining, some long gone. We also learned how to manipulate numbers on paper, how to write to people who spoke different languages, how to cook, even how to hunt."

"Do you know of a desert land, where people of auburn skin live?" She had asked, trying not to let her heartbeat tremble her voice.

"The East? I know some. I'm not sure there is much to know about the East. It was a place of constant war as I recall, and a place like that squashes culture, and burns history like a fire that cannot be put out. Death consumes all, body and knowledge alike."

Those words rang in her mind now. A land of death, consuming all. His bandaged shoulder began to look more and more life threatening. How long would he live, one like him, in a land like this?

"I should like to go there one day." Tamra had said innocently. "It sounds exciting!"

"I would hope, my dear girl," Sivvel had replied, "that you never know excitement of that kind."

The next morning began as any other for Assara. Up at bells, in line for slop, then on to her station for the day's work. Her quiet jubilation of the previous day had quickly turned to constant fear. Fear for a strange man in a distant land, fated to live and die by the sword. Not that her life was much better. He could run if he chose, hide and live a hard life, but a free life nonetheless. At least he had the luxury of a slim chance at freedom.

A distant boom shook the racks and shelves. A murmur rose through the busy workers.

"Back to work! Get back to work!" The authority seemed not to notice, so Assara bent once more to her tasks, eager to avoid notice.

Another boom, closer this time, shook an empty jar from a shelf nearby. Assara jumped, but did not scream. She was well practised.

"I said back to work!"

Assara's fingers moved automatically at her post as she dared quick glances here and there. Wide eyes darted this way and that, but no-one left their place. Tense minutes turned to long hours, and finally the day was over.

As she and Tamra wound their way to Sivvel before dark, the hushed tones told fragments of rumours about the days' events. War, uprising, and invasion were bandied about and argued for. One word rose repeatedly from the huddled crowd: revolution.

"What's a revolution, Assara?" Tamra asked as they walked. She didn't answer. She had no answer.

*   *   *

"You will be fine, young one." The doctor said in his sharp cut-off manner. "Lucky Rahim got the bullet out straight away."

"Lucky?" Jonah grunted as he sat. "He carved me up like an old goat."

"Nonsense!" Rahim shouted in mock offense. "I have the utmost respect for goats."

As they exited the dirty medical tent, Jonah's tone became sincere.

"In truth Rahim, had you not been there I may have lost my arm, or worse. Thank you."

Silence, accompanied by dark eyes, was the only response offered.

"Really Rahim, I mean it. I – "

"You were careless Jonah, and it nearly cost you your life!" Angry fingers pulled at the tie which had held his long hair back during the battlefield surgery. "By my death, I told you to focus!"

Rahim noticed his finger suddenly underneath Jonah's chin. People were starting to stare. Embarrassed, he walked on. Jonah jogged to catch up.

"I have learned my lesson, cousin. I am back. Focused. Ready."

Rahim turned but did not slow.

"We shall see. We shall see how many bullets I have to fish out of you tomorrow."

"My Captains?"

A familiar messenger waved for them to follow. The Shareef wanted to see them.

In minutes they were inside his large tent. All the Captains were present; this must be important.

Falan jeered at them openly. Rahim rolled his eyes; Jonah blatantly ignored him.

"My Captains." The Shareef began. The two youths dropped to their knees. He was certainly an imposing fellow. Strong, despite his years of success showing in his waistline. Adorning his head was a crown combining bronze, gem and bone; around his neck, various trophies hung over a bare chest.

"Honour, Shareef."

"How is your shoulder Jonah?" He questioned, leaning forward in his decorated chair. "Lucky shot, huh?"

"There are no lucky shots, Shareef. I was foolish enough to walk in front of his fire line. It won't happen again."

"It will, but you will fight on. You will all fight on for the honour of your Shareef, yes Captains?"

"Honour, Shareef." They said as one. He gestured the young men to their feet.

"This latest victory has been even more prosperous than we had imagined. As such, we will now move on Bandarat."

Had they been less stalwart men, they would have gasped. As it was, a stunned silence settled on the normally cocky group of veterans. Bandarat was the greatest city in the nation and, despite recent campaigns pushing them deeper and deeper into the territory, taking the well-fortified, and high walled, location would be extremely dangerous.

Not to mention the fact it had never been done.

"Honour, Shareef." One of the other Captains began haltingly. "Bandarat has not fallen in seven generations, and never to an outsider. How will we accomplish such a task?"

"In seven generations, Captain, none of the hill tribes has come close to taking as much territory as I have in four years. Bandarat has become lax in its uncontested comfort, while we in the wilds are forged hard and sharp. I have arisen from these lands strongest, tempered through the fires of conflict, now harder and sharper than ever before. I will cut through the soft rulers of the great city as the bullet slices the air!"

If the Shareef did have a plan, Jonah mused, he was keeping it to himself for the time being.

"War council, first call tomorrow." The Shareef stood signalling the end of the meeting. Jonah turned to leave. A call caused him to pause.

"Yes, Shareef?"

"Despite your untimely exit from the battle yesterday, the town is ours." Standing to approach caused a rattling of accoutrements. "You can sleep with a solid roof over your head tonight."

"Honour Shareef, but I will return to camp."

"Walls are good for you, youth. They keep the bugs from your bed and the enemy from your back." He squeezed Jonah's good shoulder warmly.

"No enemy is brave enough to approach my back, and no bug my bed."

"Ah! The ignorance of the young; how I miss it! Very well Captain, I will feel better knowing you watch over the camps."

As the Shareef departed, Rahim spoke under his breath.

"Some of us like walls at our backs."

*   *   *

Nightfall saw the two captains sharing a meal around a cook fire. Though there were many in the camp at the edge of the captured town, Jonah and Rahim dined relatively privately, given a respectable distance due to their rank.

Rahim broached the subject first, his fire lit eyes going from black to brown with each breath of flame. "What do you think the Shareef has planned for tomorrow?"

Jonah finished his mouthful before replying with shrugged shoulders. "I don't know. I can imagine several ways with which to attack a fortified city like Bandarat, but none I wish to try."

Rahim went suddenly from eating to stirring his stew. He spoke without looking up.

"Do you still trust him? I know he has not let us down before, but this time…"

"Don't even finish that thought, cousin." Jonah pointed his spoon. "You could be executed for voicing such things."

"You must think it though!" He replied, hissed tones escaping through clenched teeth. "Maybe the victories have finally gone to his head. I mean, Bandarat? How many armies have beat against its walls only to fade like ocean spray in the wind?"

Jonah met his gaze, but had no reply.

The two ate on in tense silence. A shrill, high call from a hunting owl raced between the cold dunes.

Rahim smiled. "Do you remember hunting owl when we were young?"

Jonah laughed. "I didn't think you would ever learn to shoot straight!"

"Neither did the Shareef!" The unexpected mirth lightened Jonah's heart. "He was just a warlord then, and we simple orphans." Distant eyes turned skyward. "Did you ever think back then we would be where we are today?"

"Of course!" Rahim bellowed proudly. "I was going to be a great warlord myself by now, with as many rifles, horses and wives as I could count!"

Jonah's laughter slowed. "I was just grateful to have a full belly."

"That was always your problem, cousin. Afraid to imagine for yourself something greater!" Rahim punctuated his point with a raised fist.

"Afraid? Well, perhaps you're right. Imagining anything better for myself, for us, always seemed to me to be too dangerous."

"Is that why we still sleep in a tent with no wall or bed, while good women go wasted?" His old friend replied astutely.

Jonah looked about to apologise.

"Save it cousin." Rahim cut him off, standing. "Wouldn't want to know how good it can be before we go into a battle tomorrow that we cannot win, yes?"

With a warm pat on Jonah's head he wandered off in search of a drink, leaving his cousin to search the flames for solace.

*   *   *

Assara took a break from her bedside vigil to explore the new camp, then the nearby town where she had found him today. Though the moon was high, there was movement everywhere, all of it new and fascinating. Cooks were hard at work soaking oats for the morning, adding strange looking spices she dearly wished she could smell.

Leather workers repaired strips and thongs for seats on horses, something she herself had never seen, but recognised from Sivvels stories. For the first time she saw women, working at looms, carrying food, being grabbed and groped all the while. She did not linger where they were. She knew enough to fear those men and those gestures.

A larger structure was lit up brightly and, despite the hour, bustled with activity. Assara wandered closer, hugging the walls and shadows despite herself. Bangs and hisses emanated from inside. People ran to and fro carrying metal cylinders and lengths of smooth wood, strange things all.

Of course. They were all weapon parts. Assara lived a very sheltered life, but she knew what a gun was. She had seen people in the hold executed with them. These were strange though, fatter in the middle than normal and longer in the end. There were hundreds of them, and many more boxes full of what she assumed were the bullets that went with them.

A land of death indeed.

She could not hear clearly the words from the workers as they yelled at each other, muted and strange as noise was while you slept, but the gestures and constant attention from an educated few suggested that these weapons were unfamiliar to the majority of hands that worked on them. Many questions were asked, the responses loud and annoyed, judging by the set of tooth and jaw that formed them. Some new invention perhaps? Or something gained through conquest?

She suddenly felt very exposed. Her skin crawled. She longed to clutch herself, but her fingers passed frustratingly through her shoulders. She moved to run, but no sooner had she turned when she was stopped in her tracks by someone in the street.

In the wide pathway between houses stood a small boy, wearing only a cloth about his loins. He was darker of skin than others she had seen, brown eyes deep and staring. A long lock of white hair hung conspicuously down one side of his face, looking very out of place amid his otherwise dark brown tresses.

He was staring straight at her.

I'm being paranoid, she told herself. No-one can see you while you sleep. Such a thing is unheard of. She made no move though, and neither did the boy. People ran past them on their busy way, coming and going. Neither of them moved a muscle.

This is ridiculous, Assara thought. In defiance she raised her hand in a slow wave.

Did she perceive a shift in his eye? A change in his posture? The boy's hand began to rise…

The next thing she knew she was sitting up in bed. Her breathing was heavy, her brow moist.

"Assara? What is it?"

"Oh, Tamra. I'm sorry." Assara regained her composure. "It's nothing. Everything is fine." She reached over, smoothing some of her sister's dusty blond hair, a familiar motion to settle both their nerves. "Go back to sleep."

"I don't want to sleep, I'm bored."

"You must, Tamra, or you'll be tired all day tomorrow. Your body needs to rest."

"Fine."

Assara waited until she was certain her sister was once again resting before lying back down.

Surely not. Surely…

She visited the sleeping young man with the wounded shoulder again that night, but did not venture into the town again.

*   *   *

A cool breeze tickled at the open space between Jonah's leather breastplate and the leather straps wrapped around his shoulder and upper arm. Winter would come soon, which meant rain. It would be a good time to hold the city of Bandarat. Plenty of room and shelter for the Shareef's army to recover and resupply while the elements took their toll on his enemies.

The clouds parted, allowing the moon to cast a sliver of wan light on the plains before the city walls. Streaks of charcoal down Jonah's face and arms distorted his outline, but only to a point. An army could be cut to pieces on that plain, Jonah thought. We should have waited till there was a moonless night.

No, the Shareef had his reasons for attacking immediately. It was wrong to question. Nevertheless, thirty men with unusually large rifles lay nervously on the cool ground until the clouds returned, gifting them once again with the cover of night.

Murmurs from behind alerted him to movement. He rolled to his side to look back over his prone ranks. A small boy weaved closer, slightly hunched but running, bearing the distinctive arm band of a messenger. No doubt he bore word from the other captains. Carelessly he trotted, silent and direct, and without pause presented Jonah with a slip of paper that had been sealed with a stamp. Jonah accepted and began to open it. The boy remained.

"Go boy, it is not safe."

The child made to leave, but hesitated.

"Boy, go!" Jonah said with as much urgency as his hushed voice could muster.

The boy finally departed. Jonah turned his attention to the letter.

In moments Rahim, birthed from the darkness, joined him in his reconnaissance.

"We are still clear of the scouts, but their circuits are getting wider. They obviously work their way outward from the city as they go. They will be on us on their next sweep."

"It doesn't matter, we have word. I don't know how he plans to do it, but the Shareef has instructed us to advance when the wall defenses fall."

"So, no word on what is going to make the defences fall?" Rahim questioned, not hiding the concern in his voice.

"None."

"Then this will either be our greatest victory, or our shortest assault."

"Faith, Rahim. The Shareef will see it done, and so will we."

Jonah's face showed only calm, hiding the turmoil inside. Absent thoughts had nearly gotten him killed two days ago. This should have shocked him back to reality, and yet his focus remained split: one half on the world in front of him, the other on the world he visited while he slept.

This afternoon all had rested in preparation for the night assault. Sleeping during the day meant seeing her while she was awake, watching her move around her world. The excitement had nearly prevented him from getting to sleep. That excitement had soon turned to confusion upon discovering her standing over a steam-powered conveyor, placing lids on jars of pickled food. It wasn't the action, or the surroundings that had so shocked him. It was the look in her eyes. Jonah was well familiar with that look. He had seen slaves before. There was nothing unusual about slaves, or women working while the men managed the war. It was just the way things were done. The way things had always been done.

It shouldn't have affected him. It wouldn't have affected him had they been someone else's eyes.

But they weren't someone else's eyes. They were her eyes.

An insect-like clicking snapped his attention back to the present. The noise came from a device they all carried; one that mimicked the call of a locust. The patrol would be on them in moments.

Silhouettes formed out of the murky landscape, each step closer peeling the thin veil of night from their outline. Jonah silently drew his sword. Rahim already held his alongside his body, making sure to keep the moonlight from the blade.

Great orange flashes revealed prowler and prey alike, as the wall of the city began to explode in sections. Jonah reacted first, leaping on the confused patrol. Their surprise at the distant eruptions gained him the vital seconds needed for a strike, and in mere heartbeats he and his men had felled the few startled enemies.

Rahim stood expectantly, head facing Jonah, body facing the burning wall. At his nod, Rahim bellowed an order, clear and fierce, three times into the burning night.

"To war! To war! To war!"

Thirty men at his back rose up from the scrub, already moving. Hundreds more behind them broke cover and rushed toward the fire and flame. Jonah battled with his mind. How did The Shareef manage a sabotage of this scale? No, it mattered not, so long as it had worked. His sword now sheathed, he readied the first round in the unfamiliar and unusually weighty rifle as he ran, as hundreds around him readied and ran.

Faith, he told himself. Faith and victory in the Shareef.

*   *   *

Assara's spirit form jumped from here to there in a panic. One moment she was running alongside Jonah as he charged headlong into the maelstrom, the next she was atop the burning wall, fearful as to what awaited him once he breached it. She shouldn't even be asleep now; it was, she had discovered, well into daylight where she rested.

Behind the wrecked cannons and ramparts where she now stood, large groups of men were arriving with swords and rifles, preparing to repel the invaders.

Preparing to repel him.

She shook her hands in frustration. It was too much; too much fire, too much confusion. Riflemen found spaces atop the city wall not burning, then levelled their barrels at their attackers.

Assara was once again running alongside Jonah, screaming despite herself. She felt her lungs lose air but no sound escaped her lips, no hint of warning. Pops and cracks escaped from small brilliant flashes ahead. Men around them began to fall.

It took her a few steps to realise he had fallen behind. By the time she looked back he had already raised a familiar looking weapon to his shoulder. A muffled, barely contained boom nearly took him off balance despite him kneeling. Others around him also paused to fire, some falling under the force of the shot.

Sections of the wall ahead popped and exploded. Cries followed. Assara realised her hands were over her mouth. The rifles caused explosions wherever they struck, destructive force making up for lack of accuracy at this distance. He ran past her, reloading as he went.

Assara took a step toward him and was instantly back on the broken, blazing wall. She stomped her feet in frustration, she was all over the place! Guilt mingled with relief as, behind the wall, she saw those firing outward fall to men on horseback, pouring in from somewhere to the east. Screams of agony brought tears she could not feel to her eyes. She wanted to run and hide but was too anxious, too fearful for the approaching man's safety.

The warrior and his party entered the beleaguered city, meeting with the force on horseback just behind the wrecked gates.

"Orders from the Shareef, Jonah!" One called from atop his mount, obviously in command. Was he talking to –? "You will take your force west and take the harbour."

"West? My orders were to push south and secure the storehouses."

Jonah. His name was Jonah.

"Do you question the wisdom of the Shareef?" The man on horseback called down arrogantly.

Jonah paused, still breathing heavily. He turned, raising a gloved hand.

"To me! To me!" Jonah glanced defiantly back at the man who had issued his command before moving off into the streets, his men already at his back.

As he did, Assara noticed a small smile push its way into the messenger's face. One of secrets and betrayal.

She moved, sometimes running, sometimes appearing streets and blocks ahead of Jonah and his force, searching for the trap her heart told her he was walking into. There was strangely little resistance. The few soldiers she did see seemed to be retreating to some point of perceived safety. Women darted this way and that, gathering animals and children, emanating a terror that to her felt so strong as to be unbearable.

She saw the small boy from the previous night at the same time as he saw her. Both froze dead in place. What was he doing here? His eyes darted from her to the street ahead and back again. Was he a messenger of some sort, young though he was? A spy?

A rolling, clanking sound from behind him caused him to turn. He wrung his hands and took a step toward her, toward the direction from which she had come. Forgetting the unusual nature of the situation for a second she raced past him, clearly startling him with her passing.

Around the corner, two cannons were setting up in a wide street. Riflemen crouched behind stacked debris. She did not understand the language, but she recognised Jonah's enemies from their clothing and weaponry. She turned, desperate. The small boy was already disappearing around a pile of crates.

A step took her to his heels. Another and she appeared right in front of him. The boy fell in confusion, mouth flapping strange uncertain words. Assara screamed soundlessly for help, waving her hands in panic, desperately trying to communicate to the boy that her friends were coming, that they were in danger. The boy sat on the ground, shaking his head, his eyes flicking between her and his escape route.

Jonah and his men emerged from the street at a trot, large rifles levelled. They only glanced at the boy on the ground as they continued on. In moments they would face the cannons.

Assara's gesturing had stopped. She was frozen in panic. Jonah was only moments away now. She was going to watch him die, powerless to stop it. Why had this happened? What force dreams up a torment for a person this perfect?

"AAAAaaaaaahhhh!!" The boy yelled. It was a strange sound, not filled with panic but with a loss for words.

Jonah halted. The boy was looking at him. His men paused with him. Jonah looked ahead at the blind corner, then back at the boy. The boy shook his head.

For a moment no-one moved. Man and child gazed respectively, trying each to communicate through the silence. Finally, with a signal from his gloved hand Jonah and his force began to backpedal, his eyes fixed still on the boy.. Long seconds passed as the order reached each member of the party, instigating the retreat.

The small boy turned back to face Assara. She knelt, reaching her hands out to cup his cheeks.

"Assara!"

What? Who was calling -?

"Assara, wake up!"

She sat up in bed, numbly wiping fresh tears from her cheeks. Tamra was clutching her arm.

"You were crying in your sleep! What's wrong? Did you see something bad?"

"No, I ah.... It's fine Tamra, I just, what time is it?"

"It's nearly lunch time. The guard has changed."

"Okay Tamra, I'm up, I'm up." Although the question in her eyes was obvious, Assara did not feel she could burden her sister with the terrible events she had just witnessed. She dressed and washed water over her face, the familiar movements deliberately used to settle both Tamra and herself.

Jonah. He was somewhere out there, in the thick of battle, right now. She had no idea whether he would be alive or dead by the time she slept next. All she knew was his name.

A bell rang out, though not the one she had been expecting. This one was smaller, and meant specifically for the few who shared her section of the Hold. A message was up, one that must be read immediately. Tamra looked intrigued. Assara felt panic.

Don't be silly, she thought. It could be a change to meal time. It could be a new addition to our section.

Her anxiety persisted.

By the time she and Tamra arrived at the notice board it was crowded, the mood electric and tense. She found Sivvel and immediately chose to approach him rather than push for the notice itself.

"Sivvel?"

"Assara, Tamra. How are you, my children?"

"What is all this about?" Assara asked, trying to keep the uncertainty from her voice. "Are they changing something?"

"It seems we will no longer be assembling jars." His tone was unusual, the set to his eyes heavy with an old sorrow. She considered pressing him, then decided instead to see the message for herself.

Because so many in the Hold were illiterate, the message was less writing, more pictures. At the top of the paper were drawings of the jars of food on which she would normally place glass lids. There were red crosses over them. Below that...

Below that were pictures of rifles. Long barrelled rifles, with stout looking cylindrical sections in their centre sections. The same rifles she had seen in the hands of Jonah and his compatriots only minutes ago.

How could this be?

"All workers to their stations for training! Rest day is over! All workers to their stations! Come on!"

The stern voice of the authority stopped the hushed murmuring. Soon they would all be shown the small parts they would play in assembling these weapons of war; weapons from a distant land.

Weapons she had just seen in devastating action.

*   *   *

It was barely past midnight by the time the city fell. Jonah's revelry was only stifled by his disbelief. Bandarat, the city whose walls had stood against ten wars, a hundred earthquakes and a thousand tempests, had fallen in mere hours. Enemy defences had been crippled before he even faced them. Then there was the cry from the servant boy that had saved him from ambush. It all seemed too easy, too good to be true.

Perhaps that was why he couldn't quite relax. In his experience if something felt too good to be true, then it was too good to be true.

Rahim prodded him, gesturing toward the approaching horses. It was the Shareef, Falan as always at his side.

"Honour Shareef!" They said in unison, each falling to a knee.

"Honour to you, my Captains! A great victory for our nation this night! Rise, both." As Jonah stood, he saw the sneer in Falan's expression. His arse must be stitched to that horse's back, he mused.

"I expected to find you in the city's south quarter." The Shareef spoke as he dismounted, his hand immediately on Jonah's shoulder. "How is it that I find you dancing on the ashes of the harbour?"

"Falan issued me an order - which he assured me came from you, Honoured - that I should push west upon breaching the gate."

"A mistake by the messenger boy." Falan called nonchalantly. "He has already been dealt with."

Killed more like. Jonah's face grew dark. "I would not be so callous with the lives of our messengers, Falan. Entire campaigns often depend on their loyalty."

"Well said, Captain." The Shareef added without turning. "You would do well to listen to Jonah's advice, Falan."

Falan said nothing, only turned his mount and left.

"Come!" He continued. "Let us celebrate the spoils of war!"

*   *   *

Jonah's mind raced at the implications of what he was seeing while he slept that night. These high calibre rifles and their explosive ammunition had been pivotal in last night's battle. It was like having every man armed with a cannon. The effective range and damage potential of his riflemen tripled easily while wielding these devastating weapons. Jonah had been certain it was the addition of these rifles to the army that had not only prompted the Shareef's decision to move on Bandarat, but had also sealed the victory.

Now, here they were, quite literally a world away. And being assembled by none other than the woman who, for the past week, had been captivating his thoughts.

It couldn't be a coincidence. Some force was surely at work here.

He had finally learned her name. Every few hours someone would walk past the workers offering water. She had been so lost in her thoughts, her name had been called three times before she noticed. Even through the haze of the spirit he heard.

Assara.

It sounded exotic, and yet strangely similar to names he would hear in his own country.

Assara.

She wiped hair from her forehead with the back of a greasy hand. She was tired. Maybe she wasn't resting well. Her lips pursed momentarily with the strain of lifting the heavy barrel, sliding it into the wooden stock. Colour flooded them, rushing like a blood red wave from the centre of her mouth to her cheeks.

He knew daylight was approaching. He could feel his body stirring like a distant responsibility he was desperate to avoid. He wasn't ready to wake, not yet. Just a few more minutes…

"Just a few more minutes."

"Peace, cousin. If you sleep any longer the meeting will start without you!"

Ice cold water ripped him from his rest, sending him flying to his feet.

"Rahim! You son of a lame rat! That's a good way to get yourself stabbed!"

Rahim just laughed and threw clothes at him, already on his way out the door. Jonah pretended to be good natured, but inside he was seething.

Pitts, he thought. What I wouldn't do for more time with her.

What has she done to me?

Outside, the city was already hectic. Jonah rested his hand on the sword at his belt, still considering this to be enemy territory. Those set to oversee such matters were organising groups of women, children and animals, sending them this way and that. In mere days Bandarat would run under the Shareef's direction as if it always had been, and his victory would be complete. This meeting would be about what he planned to do next.

Jonah was the last to arrive at the pre-appointed building. No sooner had he bowed his respects, The Shareef began.

"The mighty city of Bandarat has fallen to my name!" Shouts and calls arose. After sufficient time had passed, a gentle gesture quieted the revelry.. "Our control of this nation is all but assured, and come next season, on the heels of the rains, our steam wagons will push ever deeper into the far reaches of these lands. All will bow as one to my authority." More cheers followed. This time he patiently waited for them to die down. "However, our enemies rise against us from over the seas. War waits not on the season, nor heeds the wind nor seizes the sun. War rages on."

The Captains were less jubilant now. Doubtless they had been looking forward to taking it easy behind Bandarats still formidable fortifications, resting until fairer weather opened up the Eastern Fold. They hadn't imagined that they could be sent on campaigns in foreign countries.

"Alliances have been made that have been profitable for us, and we must now reciprocate. Those who have provided for us must now be provided for." Jonah started putting the pieces together. "By securing major trade routes and sea ways my reign, and your prosperity, will be assured for a hundred generations!"

More unconvincing claps and cheers emanated from the uncertain captains. Rahim and Jonah shared a knowing look.

"Who then will be my champions, and conquer the far reaches of the world in my name? For whom is this glory pre-destined?"

"In your name, Shareef." Jonah spoke so quickly that Rahim jumped.

"Thank you, Faithful." He replied, obviously not surprised by the response. Rahim sighed audibly.

"In your name, Shareef." The confidence in his voice surprised Jonah. With raised eyebrows he silently questioned his old friend, who shrugged his shoulders in response.

"You will carry my name to the corners of the world with glory at your back and conquest in your hands. Remain now, and learn what you will face in these strange lands. All others may leave us."

It was not a choice. Presently the crowd departed, revealing a stranger in their midst.

"Captains, this is Lord Fauld."

He stepped forward, but kept his hands clasped behind his back. He wore several layers of clothing, coloured in pale blue and white. Gold tassels ran around his neck and down a plunging neck line.

Uh oh, Jonah thought.

"He will be your Honoured while you serve me in this new land. Treat him as you would me, and his orders as you would my own. He will teach you some of the language, and assign you your missions."

Lord Fauld didn't speak. Jonah was relieved. Something told him he would like him less if he did.

"We leave at first light tomorrow morning. A ship waits at the harbour. Return as heroes, alive or dead, Captains."

The Shareef left then, Lord Fauld right on his heels.

"What in the Pitt are we doing, Jonah?" Rahim punched him in the chest.

"Come on, Rahim!" Jonah said good naturedly to hide his true intentions. "Sounds exciting! More exciting than spending all of the wet here, getting fat and slow."

"There's more to it than that. I know you Jonah. What's going on?"

Jonah paused. "Look, there's more to all this than we know." He scanned the room, and then dropped his voice. "This 'Lord Fauld' must be the one who sabotaged Bandarat's defences, and sold out the ruling powers. My guess is he was trading here, which is how he got his saboteurs in in the first place."

"Okay, so?"

"So…" Jonah paused, his mind making justifications even as the connections came. "I want to find out what he got out of the bargain. Besides which, I don't trust him. What he's done before, he can do again."

Rahim took a long look at the comfortable city just outside the door.

"Fine, I'm with you. I don't like this, but I'm with you."

*   *   *

Assara woke with a smile that morning for the first time in, maybe ever. She had spent the night following Jonah and his friend as they rested in the conquered city. She watched them eat, see their weapons to maintenance, and she had left them playing at dice together in a room attached to an inn.

He survived.

For the first time Assara allowed words like fate and destiny to wander into her thoughts. Ideas like that had once been too painful, too cruel to consider, even for a moment. Now they carried with them impossible promises, fanciful dreams and boundless possibilities.

She longed to discuss with someone how the child had seen her in her sleep, and how she had communicated with him, to see what people would say. The expected taunts and disbelief kept her silent.

"What did you do last night?" Tamra asked as she crawled over to her bed to pull at a thread on her blanket.

"Well, I…" Assara's smile widened. "I explored. What did you do last night, my sister?"

Tamra's eyes remained fixed on the thread. "I explored too."

Assara tilted her head, curiosity suddenly piqued. "Where did you go, Tamra?"

"Um… I went to see where the funny things I make go."

Assara took urgent hold of her sister's arms. "Tamra, you know better than to spy! If the Authority finds out, you can be sent out of the Hold! What were you thinking?"

Tamra still hadn't met her eyes.

"Sister…. what did you see?"

"I don't want to get in trouble…."

"Please Tamra." Assara's voice dropped. "You must tell me."

"Um, the boxes all went onto a train, and then the train was leaving so I rode it for a while, and then it blew up, and some men started to – "Tamra stopped abruptly.

"Started to what?"

"Some men with swords… cut the men on the train… then they were dead… then they took the boxes… with the stuff we made yesterday… I didn't follow them after that…"

Assara clutched her sister close. "Don't tell anyone what you saw! Do you understand? Even if they ask you! Forget it all!"

The call went out for breakfast. A stern glance told of the seriousness of the situation. Tamra nodded in understanding.

She dropped four barrels that morning at the assembly line. As Tamra's work station was within eyeshot of hers, constantly checking that her sister was still there made it hard for her to focus. Hours passed though, and despite her concern the day progressed as usual.

Maybe she was being irrational, she thought..

Two men appeared from the upper gangway, and approached the guard on duty. Assara's heart dropped. They couldn't know. How could they possibly know? They exchanged a few hushed words, then the guard raised a hand and pointed.

No. No it was impossible!

The three then walked over to Tamra. She was close enough to hear them.

"Come with us please."

Tamra looked over at her sister, eyes wide with panic.

"No!" Assara called. "Please, let me come with you! She is my sister, please!"

"Stay at your station!" The guard yelled. Assara approached anyway.

"Please, I must – "

"I said stay at your station!" The guard produced a long narrow baton from his belt and raised it overhead.

The air shuddered. For a moment all went dark. Cold steel on her cheek told Assara she was on the ground. At first she assumed she had been struck, but as her vision cleared she saw the guard struggling to stand just in front of her.

"Tamra!" She called, only to discover her throat was full of dust. Her words sounded muffled, her head like it had been clapped on both sides by a giant.

"Tamra!"

Where had all the smoke come from? She could see her sister sitting stunned just a few feet from her. Had she been at her station still, the haze would have surely blocked her from view.

As her hearing began to return, panicked yelling and screaming that had been a distant impression now became frighteningly real. Her sister, now abandoned by the two men who had only moments ago singled her out, spied Assara and reached out her hands.

"I have you, I have you!" She repeated over and over, covering Tamra's small ears against the tumult. Sivvel appeared, moving as fast as his age would allow.

"Girls, thank goodness you're alright. You must come with me, right now!"

Assara nodded and, carrying Tamra, began following the elderly man back towards the beds. The unmistakable sound of gunfire pierced the din. The screaming increased.

"Quickly!" Sivvel yelled, despite the fact he was slowing them down. People were running everywhere, or cowering in corners. The gunfire was getting louder and more frequent.

In the sleeping area groups of women huddled together, crying. Sivvel hobbled straight past them, moving a little slower with every step. He led them to a nook, barely big enough to be called a room, picking up their sleeping pallets along the way.

"Against the wall, girls! Hurry!"

Assara crawled into the corner as deep as she could go. Tamra's face was still buried into her chest. Sivvel followed them in, dragging the beds and blankets along behind him.

"Quietly now, it'll be alright. No noise."

The screaming and gunfire was getting louder still. Assara pressed her hand tighter over her younger sister's ear, pushing her other harder into her chest. Sivvel was struggling to regain his breathing. It wheezed in and out, bellying barely contained panic with each exhale.

Shots rang out, alarmingly close. Assara could hear the women in the sleeping chamber yell in terror, could hear them run mere feet in front of them. Amid the terrible cracks of rifle fire, she heard screams cut short, heard bodies fall awkwardly to the floor. Sivvel squeezed her arm. She was certain her trembling would give them away, but she could not stop. She struggled to breathe. The footsteps seemed endless, the shouts, the relentless gunfire.

Oh God, she thought over and over. Oh God! Oh God! Oh God!

Agonising minutes passed. Tamra began to sob. Whispering soothing noises to her began to calm Assara's own nerves.

In the black of the shadow of their bedding they waited. They waited until the noise stopped. They waited until the footsteps ceased. Other noises, as of things being moved and carried, followed and they waited until those ceased also. Without the familiar clanging of the Hold signalling the movements of the day, Assara lost all track of time. The only clue she had was the grumbling of her stomach.

Finally Sivvel shifted. He stifled well the pain of moving his joints after being stationary for what must have been hours. After a very careful series of glances he nodded, then peered out from behind the bedding.

Assara waited until he beckoned her to follow. Tamra looked up from the safety of her sister's arms for only a moment then returned her face to Assara's chest. The constant dark of their Hold saved her from some of the finer details of the horror scene before them. Bodies lay strewn amongst the ruined mattresses and burned blankets. Assara tried not to let her gaze linger on the faces, but watching where she stood inevitably revealed more distant eyes, now forever lifeless.

She stayed close to the still stiffly moving man who was gathering up scattered items and placing them in a sheet. From the nearby kitchen they found some intact foodstuffs, and a water bottle. Neither of them said a word, they just worked in silence. Tamra slept despite the constant movement. In mere minutes the three survivors were on their way clear of the Hold that had been Assara's entire universe until a week ago.

She did not look back.

* * *

"You must tell me something, Jonah. You look like you're about to breathe fire."

To his credit Rahim did seem genuinely concerned, despite his attempts at humour. An overpowering stench of salt and mangroves assaulted his unfamiliar senses. Hands too long clenched into fists began to ache. He regarded them as he forced himself to relax his hands, working out the tension and stress.

"She is alive. That is all that matters."

Thick ropes fell wet and heavy against the deck. Shirtless men grunted as they guided the large ship off the dock.

"Fine then." Rahim exclaimed, patience obviously running thin. "Shall we begin with the Engsam then? We have six weeks at sea, and I can tell you right now, I'm not spending the whole time translating for you."

A new breeze came, fresh from the open sea. For a moment the stink of fish and sweat abated. Jonah breathed deeply, willing the purity of that air into his being. His focus cleared.

I am coming, he thought to himself.

"Yes, Rahim. Let's begin."

*   *   *

The world outside the Hold was cold and hard, much as the Hold itself had been. Ruined buildings that must have once been three or four times as tall stood defiantly, clawing on to whatever life was left in them. It was up on the third floor of one of these that the three companions rested, albeit fitfully, through their first night of freedom. There was little shelter to be found between the broken walls and patchy floor, but at least up high there was less chance of being robbed, assaulted or worse. Sivvel had changed dramatically from the man Assara had grown up with. He spoke little and smiled less. When groups of men passed, he pressed her and Tamra into a corner and waited with his face behind a hood. Even now, after everything that had happened that day, whenever she was awake so was he; his strangely hard eyes surveying all around them.

Although she slept in fits and spurts, each visit to Jonah lifted her spirits immeasurably. She had been in absolute disbelief to discover him not only on a ship, but learning to speak her language! It seemed to her, more and more, that some unseen force was pulling them together. It gave her faith, hope. If whatever it was that brought her to him had kept them both alive so far, it would surely keep on keeping them both alive. Surely….

A slow drizzle greeted them with the sunrise. Together they shared in some of the food they had brought with them. Tamra was so quiet. It was like her body was there but her mind was somewhere else. Assara brushed some dirt from her cheek, and offered her a smile, which was not returned.

"Where will we go, Sivvel?" She asked as she returned the lid to a jar of pickled fruit.

"I am afraid I do not know." He replied slowly. "It has been many years since I was free of the Hold. I do not know which colonies are still where, and who rules who. We will have to tread carefully, and glean information from wherever we can."

From several blocks away a commotion rose. Shouting became increasingly aggressive, then shots echoed between the destitute walls and buildings.

"Come children. It is past time we were gone from this place."

*   *   *

Lord Fauld adjusted his coat against the vest and shirt beneath. The oppressive heat of this place made his uniform exceedingly uncomfortable, but he persisted with it, fearing a lapse in decorum would somehow lower him to a level more in line with the savages. The way they behaved, constantly yelling and gesticulating. It was barbaric.

The guards outside the Shareef's quarters weren't even standing, although to their credit they did prevent him from entering until they had asked permission. Fauld gritted his teeth against their disdainful looks.

Barbarians indeed.

"My Lord Fauld." The Shareef called with a relaxed manner. A scantily dressed and veiled woman was feeding him grapes. How dreadfully cliché, he mused.

"Honoured, word from the King. He needs more artillery."

"Are his factories not already making good use of the plans we gave him?"

Fauld hesitated. "The Kings factories are… presently out of commission."

The Shareef harrumphed. Fauld suspected he saw through his careful use of words.

"Our bargain was for plans, not guns. New request, new bargain."

Fauld had expected as much. "Very well. The King offers one hundred slaves in exchange for one hundred artillery."

"Two hundred slaves for fifty artillery."

"One hundred slaves for one hundred artillery, and free trade through the port of Safar for a year."

"The King couldn't tax me through Safar if his life depended on it." The Shareef chuckled.

Imbecile.

"Very well, free trade for the duration of The Shareef's rule."

"You presume to give me what I already have? You are new at this, Fauld!"

"Free trade means we will not one day come looking for what is already owed, Honoured."

The reclining ruler raised an eyebrow at the veiled threat. He sighed dismissively.

"Very well, tell your King he will have his hundred artillery. But tell him if he sends me cripples and widows for slaves, I will find recompense in his children!"

Fauld clenched his hands behind his back. He barely managed a nod before turning quickly on his heel and exiting the building.

One day he would pay for his callous indifference to the monarchy. In the meantime, he could play the diplomat. Bide his time.

He would be the one to cut the tongue from this insolent mouth.

That night before he slept, he wrote a note and left it on the nightstand. It read:

One hundred artillery for one hundred able slaves. First ship bound for South Harbour left yesterday with half the Banji riflemen. Ship with artillery leaves in one week.

First his tongue, then his head.

*   *   *

Rain fell in sheets as Assara, Tamra and Sivvel made their way through the ruined streets of the city. Its relentless flow carried with it an unusual sense of relief; fewer people noticed their passing in the deluge. Wicked men with dark leering glances stayed indoors or huddled in corners, their savage desires quelled by the misery of the ceaseless wet.

It had been dark for hours, but with no safe lodgings Sivvel insisted they march on. They took turns carrying Tamra, who had been all but silent since the fall of the Hold. Assara longed to sleep and visit with Jonah, to draw strength from being near him, even if only in the spirit. Her feet ached with every step. She had never walked for more than a few minutes anywhere in her life. Now her legs felt as if they would give out from under her.

Sivvel stumbled, catching himself on a wall. Tamra nearly fell from his arms and the sudden awakening caused her to yell.

"Are you alright?" She asked him, as he panted on one knee.

"I think we should rest." He said between breaths.

Together they huddled against a door frame with a small ledge above, affording them some respite from the downpour. Assara knew one of them should stay awake just in case, but exhaustion took her before she could contemplate voicing her concern.

She immediately found Jonah on the deck of a large boat, sitting behind a railing to hide some papers from the wind. His constant companion was watching him make some crude markings with a pencil.

He was writing the alphabet.

Badly.

Jonah's hair was getting longer, he hadn't cut it once since she had met him. Well, since she had started watching him. His lips pursed with concentration. He shuffled from one knee to the next, before presenting his work to his friend who, upon scrutinising it, promptly fell over laughing.

Assara folded her arms. Brute.

The unsympathetic teacher returned to his haunches and began to point out the errors with Jonah's work. Jonah lightly pushed against his shoulder, and he fell again.

Assara shared in their laughter. She was almost with them for a moment. Almost with him. The burden of her desperate situation became lighter, for a second.

How would she find him? Could she trust in whatever force was at work, be it fate or something else, to see it done? The thought was too painful so she let it go, allowing her mind to settle as she watched Jonah return again to his work.

*　　*　　*

"You haven't talked about her much lately." Rahim said casually as he worked on his writing. "Do you still see her while you sleep?"

He paused, lifting his eyes to gage Rahim's hidden questions.

"I do."

"And?" The question was laden with suspicion.

"And... she is alive." He replied, cryptically.

"Alive? Why wouldn't she be alive?"

His gaze remained fixed on the page, but the writing slowed. He wasn't completely sure why he didn't want to share with Rahim all that he had witnessed in his sleep – the rifles appearing in a factory halfway around the world, the attack on that factory that had nearly gotten Assara killed, the knowledge that he was almost certainly on his way to that place – he knew it would make Rahim angry, although he did not understand how. All things considered it just seemed easier to keep him in the dark.

"No reason. There's just not that much more to say, other than she still lives."

Folded arms accompanied Rahim's frustrated tone. "First you can't stop talking about her, and now all you can say is whether or not she still draws breath. Something's up, cousin."

"Look, maybe I'm just a little tired of you sighing and rolling your eyes, okay?"

Rahim raised his hands. "Okay, okay. I'll let it go." Standing dismissively, he began walking to the stern of the large ship.

Jonah returned to his work. She would be alright, he told himself. She had made it this far, she will make it until I can get to her.

And then what? A voice from inside asked him. You'll rush up to her and tell her you've been stalking her in her sleep for the past three months? The pencil in his hand sat frozen between letters.

Rahim stayed cold toward him for the rest of the day, and they had spoken little by the time they were both asleep that night. Jonah was patrolling from the rooftops around where Assara and her party were walking, his spirit-self flitting from building to building.

As if there was anything I could do, he admitted to himself in frustration. Powerlessness was not a trait he wore lightly. He was learning a lot about the strange place she called home, however. Landmarks were becoming familiar and, despite still not understanding her language enough to read the words on her lips, the way they moved around others spoke volumes about the social climate and what he could expect. The city was more or less in a state of martial law; it was no wonder the agreement with the Shareef had included soldiers like him. The ruling powers must be desperate to restore order and bring the wandering brigands and thieves under control. It would no doubt be his primary assignment.

As he watched, something made the three travellers pause. Jonah felt painfully isolated without a clear sense of sound. He leapt from vantage point to vantage point seeking the source of their consternation. The muted dance of firelight in the narrow streets guided him and, sure enough, a skirmish was breaking out not a block from where they were.

He let himself fall to the street and walked amongst the fresh melee. A large group of men, in similar garb to Lord Fauld, had engaged the rabble. The men they fought were dirty, their clothes ragged and wet. They fought bravely, however, standing their ground as the huge number of well-armed assailants cut them down in short order. Bullets tore through the air, swords and wielders alike passing through Jonah as he watched with interest. In moments it was over. The well-trained militia finished their gruesome work, obviously taking no prisoners.

Anxiety washed over him, like a fathom of crushing water. He was on the rooftops again in a heartbeat, looking down at Assara. More militia had appeared from somewhere and were attempting to separate the two girls from their guide. He rushed to her, mouth wide in a soundless scream at the men dragging her away. The older man managed to strike back once before being knocked unconscious by the butt of a short rifle. Jonah swung and punched, his ghostly arms and hands disappearing each time behind the faces of Assara's assailants.

Powerless.

Assara and her sister disappeared into a cart. Jonah punched again and again at the men around her. Suddenly his own screaming filled his ears.

"Pitt's, Jonah, wake up! WAKE UP!!"

Jonah's arms beat blindly into Rahim, who struggled to hold his shoulders against the bed.

"No! Rahim, I have to, I have to…"

"Calm down, Jonah! You'll have woken the whole ship by now!"

He regained his senses enough to stop struggling. He panted heavily, sweat from his chin making a puddle at the top of his chest.

"She… she is taken… captive…"

"Then there is nothing you can do – "

"No!" Jonah pushed Rahim aside before he could finish saying what he knew to be true. He paced twice across the small room then paused, hands against the wall, tense as a stone.

"Enough, cousin." Rahim began good-naturedly. "This has gone on long enough. It is a pointless fantasy that has almost gotten you killed once. Look at you. You're breaking apart."

Jonah barely heard. He longed to watch over her, to make sure she was alright, but he was too worked up to get to sleep again. For now, he would just have to wait, and hope.

"Cousin?"

He left the room without another word.

*   *   *

Assara felt very little of the cart's movements over the broken and debris-filled street. Tamra whimpered the separation from Sivvel against her chest, but even that was a distant thought. She was becoming numb. She wanted to sleep, to find solace in Jonah's presence, but it would not come. As the cart moved along, several others were added to the mobile jail cell, all female. Some cried, others sat in sullen silence. There was a fear somewhere, like a half-remembered warning, or a memory of a threat. It was buried, pushed to some far recess of her mind. In its place was only numbness.

As the night deepened, the smell of salt grew. Sounds from the working shipyard crept upon them, soon surrounding the forlorn cage and its inhabitants. Someone offered them reassurance. Assara wasn't interested.

The cart stopped. Immediately they were ushered out and herded into a larger group standing at the base of a gangplank leading up to a very dirty, white, single-hulled ship. A flag hung limply from the main mast bearing the same insignia as the shoulders of their captors; a single blue flame over a white diamond. Tamra kept her face hidden, clutching Assara's leg. A startling gunshot signalled them to climb. Up they went, accompanied by murmurs and tears. More uniformed men met them at the ship's deck and ordered them down a hallway. None argued.

They soon found themselves below decks, in a long room lined on either side with blankets. Questions began to rise from a few brave souls, which were quickly silenced with strikes and stern words. Assara sat, strangely glad to be stationary for a moment. She was so tired. Tired of moving, tired of not knowing what was around the next corner. The walls made her feel oddly safe. Even the presence of the armed guards gave her a backwards sense of security. Any thought of the well-being of Sivvel was quickly squashed. He would be fine. He was probably in a similar situation to them. He was old and tired too. Now he could rest a while. As the group settled into positions of forced rest and uneasy silence along the wall, Assara slipped into a trance of disconnected comfort, Tamra numb at her side.

Still, she could not sleep.

*   *   *

"Are you talking to me yet, cousin?"

Rahim's peace offering of bread and dried meat hung for a moment in mid-air. When it was clear it would not be accepted, Rahim shrugged and ate it himself.

Clear skies shone in stark contrast to the strong winds whipping the seas into a flurry of white foam. Jonah and Rahim watched in silence as the large ship rose and fell with each passing swell. Full sails strained at thick ropes, the powerful bow thumping through each monstrous wave it met.

Rahim broke the silence. "Did anything... strange... happen to you while you slept last night?"

Jonah looked at him incredulously.

"I know, I know, stupid question. I don't mean your little, ah, episode with your girlfriend." He continued semi-diplomatically.

"What then?" Jonah asked, his words barely audible over the pulsing gale.

Rahim paused while he searched for the words. "Last night, while I was going over my Bassk, there was this, thing…"

Jonah turned to gage the seriousness of his friend's words. "What thing?"

"I can't really explain. It was just beyond my vision, regardless of which way I turned. Something creeping and growing behind me, but every time I turned to see what it was it disappeared. Have you ever experienced anything like that?"

"I don't think so."

"Huh." Distant eyes turned again to the horizon, leaving Jonah genuinely intrigued. What was his cousin up to? Or had he actually seen something he couldn't make sense of?

A few moments passed before he spoke again. "Well, shall we study some more?" Rahim asked. The distant look was now gone. Jonah paused before replying.

"Okay."

*   *   *

Lord Fauld fell asleep, then rose immediately from his body. His spirit self could, of course, appear however he chose, but he chose his uniform. Despite the fact that no-one could see him, his uniform was everything he had strived for his whole life, every achievement he had ever gained. It was everything he was.

He turned west and built a picture in his mind of the King's offices. Everything blurred for a moment, before coalescing into the room he sought. On a table, held under a lion's head paperweight, was his next correspondence.

We have gained all we can from the Shareef. Return at your next opportunity. Lay plans to kill Shareef, but do not execute until we have disposed of the Banji rifleman en route. It may take weeks, so slaves have been taken and shipped. They will be bartered when prince Cul takes control of Banderat.

Fauld felt himself breathe a sigh of relief. His time in this backward country was almost at an end. He walked from the room, through the door to the balconies and appeared up on the ramparts. Below him stretched the fortified city of South Harbour, from which the nation drew its name. Smoke rose from sections of the slums, as it always did. The rebellious factions of the lower class had won a decisive victory at the Serventine Hold, but it would not last. When he returned, he would reclaim the country, one section at a time. Glory, honour and power would be his.

He turned from the balcony and walked back through the mostly empty room where he had found his orders. Once inside he veered left, heading straight for a large, ornate door. On the other side the King's guards watched their charge slumber in silence. Fauld shivered at the thought of never being alone. That would be the first thing he would change.

As he passed by the large bed in which the King rested alone, he hesitated a moment. Despite how lax the monarch had become in recent months he was still a wise and capable man, never to be taken for a fool. Fauld reminded himself of that fact lest his indifference cause his plots to be unveiled. His death would be a slow one indeed should that ever happen.

Two more guards waited at an adjacent door as he passed through to a sitting room identical to the one he had arrived in. The room was dark, unused and empty, as it always was. Fauld continued on.

The next door took him to the Queen's sleeping chambers. Her bed was empty of course. If everyone knew where the queen rested then any beggar or serf could observe her in her most private moments. There were no guards in this room. However, he was not alone.

The ghostly figure of The Seer, the King's own 'sleepwalker', regarded him from the far corner of the room. A slow nod affirmed Fauld's presence in the spirit, which Fauld returned. The King was indeed a fool, he thought to himself. Here stood one of the rarest gifts, the most powerful of allies, and in his arrogance the King had treated him as any other subject. Fauld had not been so naive. Now the King's oversight had become his opportunity.

A few paces took the sleeping Lord to the middle of the room. Immediately he began to sink through the floorboards to the secret bedchamber beneath.

The Queen was wearing her dark red shift, his favourite. She had known he would visit tonight. Her long blonde hair had fallen to cover half her face, which made her all the more alluring. Beneath a raven paperweight was a brief note which read:

Five Months. X.

Five months until he would return, and the final stage of their plot could begin. An 'x' to signal one solitary kiss. She could be coy when she wanted to be. His ghostly finger gave a near caress of her smooth cheek.

Reluctantly he rose from the Queen's bedside. With a long final look, he closed his eyes and returned once again to the distant land in which his body slumbered. He had other urgent matters to attend to this night.

*   *   *

The boat rocked, causing Assara's head to roll off her arm. Her chin bounced on the hard floor, jolting her awake. She blinked, trying to survey her surroundings to see if anything had changed over the last few hours. It had not. There was no daylight in the long room, so she could not discern what time it was. She knew it was nearly morning; she had been watching over Sivvel while she rested. He had been taken to another Hold, smaller than their previous and also dedicated to manufacturing the monstrous guns she was recently introduced to. He looked dreadfully tired, and sadder than she thought possible.

But he was alive.

She rolled over and saw Tamra playing with a stick as if it were a doll.

"Did you sleep?" She asked, groggily.

"No."

"Has anyone come to speak to us? To tell us where we're going?"

"Um… a man walked past before, but he didn't say anything. He just looked angry."

Commanding calls emanated from the corridor. The door to their room burst open.

"Up! All of you, now! Up on deck! Food, exercise. Come on, up! All of you!"

The dirty but authoritative man called constantly as he walked the length of the room, dragging people to their feet. In short order they were herded out, up stairs and into the sunlight.

Some crew formed them into a long pair of lines, filing them past a bucket of water and a single cup. Each prisoner was allowed one drink before the cup and water were passed along. Another deckhand passed out large chunks of thick, dark bread. Tamra and Assara ate hungrily.

Once the bread and water had been distributed the all-female group walked in a long procession around the main masts. Assara looked but could only see open water in every direction. She could have been heading straight towards Jonah and his ship. She could have been heading in the exact opposite direction as well.

Wait, the sun. She could gage their direction by looking at the sun. Probably. They did seem to be getting closer judging by the change in the time of day she found him in when she slept. Last night she had seen him wake, seen him wash, take his breakfast on deck while the sun rose. He had seemed haunted, distant. Something was troubling him.

Yes, she had watched the sun rise… over the back of the boat. Her eyes scanned the patchy cloud ahead. It was past midday, which would mean the sun would be falling, and if they were heading in the same direction…

Her heart skipped. It seemed, yes, she was almost certain they were sailing away from the setting sun, meaning her ship and Jonah's ship were headed toward each other!

Of course, that still left hundreds of miles of open sea in which to pass by one another. For some reason though that thought didn't dampen her excitement. Something had brought them this far.

Something would see them through this.

*   *   *

"What in the bleeding pits are you looking for out there?"

Jonah started. He hadn't even noticed Rahim approach; the wind speeding over the bow drowned out a lot of noise, and his absence of mind had done the rest.

"What? Nothing."

Rahim answered with a fierce but resigned stare.

"Tell me something, cousin. Have you noticed a change in the behaviour of our Western allies lately?"

"Actually, I have." Jonah turned to make sure they were alone, then leaned in closer.

"They were never very welcoming, I'll admit. But lately there has been an open hostility in how they regard us and our brothers."

"Yes, I have noticed it too - and we are not the only ones. Some are starting to speak of a confrontation. This situation will soon get out of hand."

"I better talk to the men, and have a word to the officer in charge of the Westerners. Perhaps I can shut this down before we all kill each other."

Clanging sounded from the crow's nest, high atop the ship's main mast.

"What's this now?" Rahim questioned.

"Incoming!" The call came from the sailor working the bell like he was trying to destroy it. "Incoming! Incoming!"

A pointed hand led their eyes to the starboard horizon revealing the cause of the alarm. Another ship was bearing down on them. Even at this distance, sunlight shining in flashes on the outrigger-style hulls marked the vessel as unusual. The flag flying high above picturing a black sword on red needed little further interpretation. Jonah and Rahim ran immediately for the rooms below decks, dodging the panicked crew along the way. Curses accompanied footfalls as swords and rifles were handed out.

Ninety-eight Banji riflemen waited patiently in their rooms for the arrival of their captains. Jonah burst in, calling as brief an order as there was:

"Brothers! To arms!"

Their fire ignited, they leapt into their light armour (vests and thigh plates of layered leather) and within moments were following Rahim and Jonah to the ship's armoury.

As they raced the few corridors between them and their objective the ominous boom of cannon fire began from the distant ship. At the armoury, a panicked storeman was handing out weapons as fast as his hands could manage.

Rahim spoke, his grasp of the language easily the best amongst them all. Despite his request, the storeman paused, obviously unsure as to whether he wanted to see the strange warriors fearfully armed. Rahim made his request into an order. The shaken storeman relented. Cannon fire made splashes close enough to be heard even below decks as they were.

"We have little ammunition here, and your targets will be difficult because both you, and they, will be moving. Take extra care. Rely on the explosive ammunition and aim for larger targets." Jonah spoke as he trotted for the deck and the battle above.

The enemy ship was close enough to see in detail. The captain of his own vessel had turned directly toward it, thereby making them a much smaller target. Cannons on the oncoming boat shot through gaps in a separate, outrigger-style hull made of metal; obviously in place to deflect return fire. Their own ship had no cannons, save for the ones he and his men wielded.

The bow was barely wide enough for a few men to shoot safely at a time, so Jonah began ordering them into firing ranks as soon as they were ready. With the first volley away in a loud series of snaps and cracks, he guided the second rank into place, his sword high above his head.

Most of the fire they offered in return popped and banged uselessly into the outrigger hull. A shot from the second volley found its target and one of the four enemy cannons fell silent. Moments later something ignited, perhaps shot stacked ready for the enemy cannons. Distant bodies flew into the water. The cries from the enemy men carried easily over the waves.

The approaching ship changed tack, veering to port to put them on a collision course. A cry went up from the sailors around Jonah. Swords emerged all around. Rahim reciprocated the order in his native tongue.

"Close combat! Close combat!"

With the large, three-hulled vessel bearing straight down on them, the distance closed quickly. They were a heartbeat from smashing into each other when Jonah's riflemen called his attention to long, sharp ramming rods between the main hull and the exterior of the oncoming ship. The rods would punch holes straight through them.

"Hard turn right!" Jonah called in his own language. Rahim heard, and immediately repeated the warning in the captain's language.

"Hard to starboard! Pitts of disgrace, starboard! STARBOARD!"

Finally, the helmsman deciphered the warning above the din of battle and madly spun the wheel. The great ship lurched, just bouncing off the oncoming vessel's port side. The impact threw everyone from their feet. Men from both ships were thrown overboard.

Shouts announced the arrival of the boarding party. Bright flashes and bangs came from small balls hurled at their feet. Jonah's rifleman covered their eyes and struggled to regain their footing.

He rallied his forces with a call. Small engagements had broken out everywhere. Ropes held the two ships alongside each other, their momentum having thrown them into a slowing spiral. Initially the boarders were falling quickly, due to them being greatly outnumbered, but more and more followed. Shots rang out at random, felling men indiscriminately.

Rahim fell in next to Jonah as he sheltered behind the guardrail.

"We have to get over there and take out the guns, or they'll cut us to pieces!" He yelled.

Jonah nodded. He called a familiar order; a defensive line around a rifle, and a specific target. Ten Banji soldiers formed a ring of swords around one of his artillery. Sword point verified one spoken word: "Cannon."

At the signal for fire he stood, and his artillery stood with him. At close range there was little room for error. Cannon and team alike exploded out of the adjacent ship's hull, leaving a nice sized hole.

"Cover fire!" He called again. As he and Rahim leapt over the side onto a beam connecting the outer, armoured hull to the inner, main hull of the enemy ship, every rifle at his back lay fire on the enemy deck. Debris from the gunfire erupted only metres in front of them, spraying him with wood and blood.

They dropped to a secondary beam below the fire line and climbed to the opening from where the cannon once protruded. A quick glance inside showed groups of men busy trying to reload those cannons still operational. He, Rahim and a few others got well inside before anyone even noticed.

Swords drew as the surprised men dropped what they were doing to meet this new threat. Jonah and Rahim formed a defensive line, giving their reinforcements time to climb inside. Each new arrival meant one more sword at their aid, and in short order their enemy began to fall.

When they had a moment's reprieve between engagements, Rahim called a question over the noise.

"Take it, or sink it?"

Jonah paused a second, calculating the probability of killing every man aboard, those he was aware of and those he wasn't. How many lives would it cost as the fighting drew on?

"Sink it."

With a brief nod Rahim set straight to ordering the men to gather all the cannon ammunition they could see close at hand while Jonah and others kept any newcomers from their backs. In a minute it was done.

"Go!" His old friend called as the Banji retreated back out the gaping hole in the hull. "Call the cover fire."

Jonah nodded. Above him the sounds of battle raged on, swords clanged, guns fired, men screamed. His own soldiers waited on the side of either hull, ready to reboard.

"Cover fire!"

Fewer guns lit up the enemy deck this time, but their devastating power at close range proved more than sufficient. The men under his command easily scaled the outrigger hull, joining the melee they found back on their own vessel.

No sooner had Jonah ducked once again below the guardrail than the cannon shot went up. A deafening roar smashed through the noise and confusion, shards of wood turned missiles spearing man and sail alike.

Everyone sat dumbfounded for a moment. Jonah's concern for his cousin got him to his feet first. Rahim sagged over a beam between the two ships, stunned.

Immediately he vaulted the side, landing heavily on the wavering length of wood. He grabbed Rahim's arm just as his friend began to slide into the water. The enemy ship was sinking fast, taking the hull they rode down with it.

His men were capable. A rope soon appeared at his side. He wound it around his arm, wincing against the pain as it drew taught. The effort of holding the semi-conscious Rahim on his shoulder forced a grunt through his clenched teeth. The enemy vessel slipped beneath the water as if being pulled. Men above began to draw the rope, and Jonah, back to the deck.

Their ship ruined, those assailants left behind were quickly overrun and dispatched. By the time he and Rahim were back on deck, it was over.

"What… did it…?"

"Rest, cousin. It is over."

Relieved cheers went up from the survivors, Westerner and Banji alike. A bloodied Captain approached Jonah where he sat, arm clutching a shallow sword wound at his flank.

"I'm not sure whether you can understand me or not, but… thank you."

Rather than respond Jonah offered a hand, which the Captain gladly shook.

*   *   *

"What do you think happened to him?"

She sat staring into space a moment before realising Tamra was talking to her.

"Sorry, sister, what was that again?"

"What do you think happened to Sivvel? We didn't see him after those men took us. Do you think he's on a boat too?"

Assara had wondered after the dear friend's ongoing safety several times since their parting. There had to be some reason why there were only female slaves aboard this ship. All the captured men must end up in other Holds.

"He is in a new Hold. I found him last night in my sleep."

"Another Hold? Like ours was?"

"Yes, Tamra, very much like ours was."

"Why didn't they take us to the new Hold with him?"

"I don't know."

"Can we ask? I want to stay with him. I don't like it here."

A brief moment of rejection burst into Assara before guilt overrode it. As much as she wanted to be everything for her sister, she desperately wanted to stay with Sivvel as well.

"Maybe there will be someone we can ask. Just wait a while longer, okay?"

Tamra didn't respond. Her fears for the moment allayed, she returned her head to Assara's lap.

More hushed conversation began further up the long room. Although no-one knew each other before boarding, small groups had quickly formed. Some discussed where they would eventually make landfall, others what sort of lives awaited them there. The weak, more panicked ones sought out the stronger, calmer among them. Fears of slave labour and prostitution were replaced by hopes of good work and fair living arrangements. Assara found herself somewhere in the middle. She dared not hope for anything even resembling a good life when their journey ended, but could not sustain a thought that resembled anything else.

"How old is she?"

The sudden intrusion on her bleak thoughts made her jump. Tamra somehow continued to rest. Assara hadn't noticed her fall asleep.

Across from her a girl watched them. She was maybe three or four years older than Assara herself, with an expression that spoke similar thoughts to those circling her own mind.

"She will be nine in a few weeks."

The girl let out a nonchalant harrumph. "She is fortunate. I hear the monarchs of the East like them young. She will at least live comfortably. Most of the time."

"What do you mean?"

She paused, regarding Assara directly before continuing. "Where are you from?"

"I, I mean we, we lived in a Hold, before…"

"Your whole life?" She interjected.

"For as long as I can remember. Why?"

"Lucky. Lucky to be off the streets, lucky to be protected. Although now, knowing what is coming… perhaps I am the lucky one."

"I don't understand…" Assara said, although she was beginning to.

"You will, girl. I have heard stories about the lands east of the oceans, but it matters not. Wherever you are, men are men, and slaves are slaves. We are slaves. And where we are going... there will be men." She threw a small pebble at the ground in front of her. It rattled quietly over to Tamra's sleeping form.

"It matters not."

She didn't speak after that. Assara began to feel uncomfortable.

"Where are you from?" She offered.

"It matters not." With that the woman turned and closed her eyes.

As the minutes drew on, the even swaying of the large vessel lulled Assara into a welcome sleep.

Again, she found Jonah cleaning up after a battle. She was glad she had missed it, she hated watching him fight. There was blood on the deck and holes in the hull. His friend was resting on the deck with a cloth over his forehead.

Jonah himself was organising his countrymen, sending them this way and that. He looked so strong, standing immovable amid the maelstrom all around him. Soldiers, obviously older than him, sought out his commands without a moment's hesitation. It calmed her, seeing him.

Familiar anxieties crept into her mind. If they were approaching each other, there was a chance they would meet. What would that be like? If she truly was a slave now, would she even be able to talk to him? Would she even be able to get to him if they were in the same place? Men of command such as he normally resided in large houses or compounds, which meant guards and gates.

Of course, all of this was secondary to her fear of meeting him and being rejected. Surely a man such as this would have a princess waiting for him somewhere. Surely, he would have no interest in a slave.

Her thoughts wandered as she watched him work. Something about the horizon became unusual. The pitch seemed to sway in the wrong direction to that of the boat. Sounds, already muted while you slept, disappeared altogether.

Assara took a few involuntary steps back, passing through a sailor working at a loose rope. Somehow, she was holding an unlit candle, but did not remember picking one up. In front of her the masts started bending to one side. She began to feel strangely heavy.

A crocodile had appeared on deck without her noticing. It wandered slowly between her and the man next to her, completely oblivious to the busy deck. The men on deck seemed not to notice either, telling her it couldn't be real. But if it wasn't real…

She startled awake, still leaning against the cool wall below the ship's deck.

What was that? She thought, rubbing her temples against her exhaustion. Did I imagine that?

Below her, still snuggled into her lap, Tamra twitched as she slept.

*   *   *

Sivvel woke to the familiar sounds of clanging and fire. It was a while before bells, but he rarely slept till they rang in the morning shift.

He had never been a big sleeper, and lately had trouble sleeping for more than a couple of hours at a time.

The Hold where he had spent his last twenty-three years was little more than rubble. Machinery from there had been salvaged and brought to this Hold, jammed into whatever spaces would accommodate them. None of the faces were familiar. The many young had been replaced by a few old. He could only guess as to what had happened to Assara and Tamra. Guess and feel the weight at having let them down.

Stupid man, he chided himself. You're old. What could you possibly have done? Powerlessness is no excuse, he argued in his mind. You should have found a way. Should have gotten them out of the city sooner. Should have been better, stronger.

A man further down the room awoke with a start, arms reaching for something unseen. The immediate confusion on his face showed the unusual nature of the occurrence. Poor fellow must be slipping.

Bells came, and Sivvel began the daily tasks as he had for half a lifetime. Slops, exercise, then to the assembly lines for the day's work. Another day assembling the weapons of war. Another day assembling guns.

He hoped the girls were okay.

*   *   *

As Fauld's ghostly figure slipped again into the Queen's hidden chamber he immediately knew something was wrong. He had found her staring blankly over a balcony while an attendant read news reports from a series of papers. She was wearing black, indicating her displeasure with him. What could she be upset about?

He moved immediately to her night stand where her latest communique would be waiting. Three simple words said it all:

No raven sings.

The attack on the ship freighting the Banji rifle men had failed, meaning they would be days out of reaching Safar and far harder to dispose of. He would have to wait until they reached South Harbour for another opportunity, which meant not only delaying the execution of the Shareef, but the much more difficult task of wiping out the remaining barbarians.

Fauld's transparent, filmy fingers gripped themselves painfully. There was no obvious way in which these supposed soldiers would impede his assassination of the King, but he didn't want loose ends. Any unpredictable element could at any moment ruin all of his carefully laid plans.

Immediately he moved himself back to the eastern continent, past the busy city of Bandarat, then further east still to a small town hidden high in a steep mountain range. Large men built like bricks of iron moved warily along narrow passages between huts of thatch and mud. Smoke rose from every dwelling. Inside, women worked ceaselessly despite the late hour.

Fauld flitted from a central clearing to a doorway guarded by two men with spears. He then appeared just inside, discovering the note he sought held against a wall by a dagger.

2 DAYS

The timing would have been perfect had the pirates done their damn job! Thank the throne he hadn't paid them yet.

He turned, jumping from the room to the central clearing and then again back to Bandarat. Although he didn't have a scheduled meeting with the boy, he would have to find him. He couldn't risk the attack on the Shareef going ahead just because he couldn't get a message to the Fallsten Prince in time. The last thing he needed was one hundred barbarians out for blood vengeance on his home soil, should they discover the death of their beloved leader.

The boy he sought wasn't in his small rooms, but then he never was. Even walking the muddy streets in his spirit was enough to turn Fauld's nose up. He hated this place. The rotting smell of the docks, the urine soaked streets… it was like walking through a giant refuse pit. That damned boy better be there when I –

Sure enough there he was, as always, watching the workers at the foundry assembling artillery.

"Marema-moie!"

The child, whose eyes were normally so large they seemed to be trying to escape his face, leaped and fell at the sudden noise. A long lock of white hair fell around his small nose. When he realised who was calling his name, he immediately prostrated himself.

Fauld, though proficient in the boy's native tongue, had taught the young sleepwalker some Engsam, more to satisfy his personal preferences than anything. This child was the only other sleepwalker Fauld knew of. He had to be claimed, groomed.

"Tell the Prince's assassin, wait! Wait until I say so!"

The child looked as if he wanted to argue, but fear kept him silent. Smart, Fauld thought. Without another word Fauld turned and disappeared, leaving the terrified, brown-eyed child to his task.

*   *   *

As the Queen entered her husband's chambers, a myriad of scents fought for her attention. Rich aromas of honey came from the roasted game hen the King seemed intent on suffocating himself with. Warm, spiced wine mingled with a plate of roast beetroot and carrot. There was also the distinct funk of body odour and perfume. She put it out of her mind.

For a while she just stood, allowing a sense of tension to build between them. Satisfied, she turned and made to leave.

"Well, what is it?" He yelled over a mouthful.

She paused but did not turn. "Elathern is dead."

The sounds of untamed chewing ceased. Heavy clinks punctuated the meeting of discarded cutlery and dinner plate.

"How?"

"Rebels attacked another train last night; the Milpine to Northpine run. Seventeen dead."

She still had not turned to face him, although she could feel his tension, hear his breathing increase.

His fists slammed onto the table, sending his goblet clanging to the floor.

"Gods of the dogs! He was my most trusted general! Slay these rebels!"

The Queen stiffened as the table crashed to the floor behind her, plates and food crashing loudly. She was not sure, but by the sounds he was making she guessed that he was stomping on the fallen crockery.

"Will that be all –?" She began.

"GET OUT!!"

It took some effort, but thankfully she kept the smile from appearing on her face before she had a chance to leave the room.

*   *   *

In a mountain village, some hours east of the city Bandarat, two men paused momentarily from their combat. A welcome breeze bearing all the chill of the mountains cut through the wide, open grounds. It wasn't just mountain chill in that breeze of course; autumn was well underway. Snow would soon follow. The young prince relaxed his grip on the practice sword just a little, allowing the dry air to remove some of the sweat on his palm.

He would welcome the cold this season. The oncoming winter would lull everyone into a near slumber, dimming their eyes to the snake in their bed.

His instructor raised his wooden weapon high, stepping aggressively forward in attack. The prince drew a deep breath, resetting his grip. In a flash he had lunged ahead, parrying the blow and stabbing his weapon painfully up into the flank of his assailant.

The bested instructor fell to a knee, clutching the point of the strike.

"Pitts! You move like the naked flame!"

"Seems there is little more you can teach me, war master." He replied a little arrogantly.

"Indeed, my prince. The only service I may offer is to keep your reflexes sharp, and give you something to stab!"

"High prince!" A call came from across the small village. A messenger was on his way.

"Approach!" The young prince commanded.

The man fell to his knees before he spoke again. "A pigeon arrived from Bandarat. Fauld has delayed the attack on the Shareef, high prince."

"What?" He roared, throwing his practise sword to the ground. "Delayed for how long?"

"Forgive me, high prince. He did not say."

For a moment he just stood there making the messenger fear more and more for his life.

"No! I will not wait! Send word to Bandarat. We will attack as planned. I will no longer take orders from the foreign shaver of rats!"

All within ear shot raised a cheer in the name of their prince. All except for the messenger of course, who had not yet been given leave to stand.

*   *   *

Jonah was surprised at the childlike excitement he felt as the call of 'land spotted' ignited a cheer from all the ship's crew. One more day and they would reach the fabled port of Safar, trading and resupply destination of any and every seafaring vessel this side of the world. He hadn't really stopped to consider the possibility that he might enjoy seeing far off, exotic places. Through his youth he hadn't felt he deserved possessions or rewards. Then the Shareef had given him both, along with a sense of value and undeserved favour. As Jonah grew, his underdeveloped sense of self-worth became an image of a man whose actions determined his value and, to a lesser extent, his life. That left no place or purpose for imagining exciting experiences like seeing far off lands or strange cultures.

"I'm going to find myself a fat wife to send home and raise my children!" The set of Rahim's smile spoke of his lack of sincerity. Jonah laughed. As Rahim joined him at the railing, he clapped him on the back.

"Be careful, my friend; the stranger the women, the stranger the ways. You may wake one morning to find yourself fat, surrounded by a brood of short-legged terrors."

"Then so be it!" His cousin boomed in a good-natured roar, arms outspread as if greeting his new fortunes. "I will grow lazy and cross-eyed as my offspring fill nation after nation!"

They both laughed then, lighter than they had in a very long time.

After a long pause, Jonah spoke again. "Did you ever think we would make it here? Our own commands, seeing new lands, power and influence?"

"To be honest, cousin, yes." Rahim replied, eyes still on the shrinking gap between the sun and the water. "Don't ask me how, but I knew my fate was more than that of a slave, or an orphan. Or... maybe I just wouldn't accept the life of a slave or an orphan. Maybe I would have done anything except resign myself to that fate."

Rahim's smile slipped just a little.

"Our fate was a fair one, though." Jonah replied. "How many from our beginnings can boast a life like ours?"

"We were lucky. Fate had nothing to do with us surviving the raids, or the fires, or the months living in the Silver Hills…"

"No, fate had nothing to do with that."

Behind them someone dropped a bucket of water. The second in charge of the ship's crew, a burly man with unnaturally hairy forearms, came charging up, yelling hoarsely.

"You know I think I'm starting to get a grip on the language." Jonah said as he returned his gaze to the horizon. "Thanks to these foul-mouthed sailors, I should be able to sufficiently insult every man, woman and child in Safar before the sun sets our first day."

"And considering how sociable you are, cousin, you will never need to know anything else." Rahim laughed again, still watching the exchange between the abashed sailor and his superior.

"Hey now, I can be friendly!" He said with mock surprise, casually backhanding a still chuckling shoulder.

"You are as outgoing as a blind mouse my friend, and as warm as a wet desert snake."

Jonah's mirth faded slightly. "I'm really that bad?" He found himself picturing Assara.

"Just ask the men. They fear you, Jonah."

"They respect me, you mean."

"No cousin, they fear you. Don't mistake me, they trust you. They will follow you into the Pitts themselves, but their bottoms tremble as naked babes when you approach them."

"Well…" Jonah began, a little flustered. His hands found his hips. "They should fear me. I am their Captain after all."

Rahim placed a hand on his cousin's shoulder. "Whatever you say. It is not for me to instruct you on how to lead your men. Fate's know you do a better job than I do."

A good leader was strong, he told himself. If his men feared him, fine. So long as they trusted him. So long as they were loyal.

He could not stop thinking about Assara.

*   *   *

Suddenly, in the wall facing him, he could see his own reflection. There was no mirror, and yet there he was, in an unnatural kind of clarity. He reached up to smear soot over his eyelids. The black lines made him look menacing, and yet also a little feminine. The reflection started to darken; not the whole picture, just himself. Soon it was completely black, as if only his shadow was reflected. It grew larger, and darker, reaching up to crawl out of the mirrored wall. On and on it grew, towering over the now petrified witness. He fell backwards, trying to retreat. His movements were slow and numb, as if he were crawling through thick mud. The sensation in his fingers began to change: at first there was nothing, then something soft like a blanket —

Rahim woke then. His hands were starting to ache, they clutched his bed clothes tightly. Only Jonah, still well and truly asleep, shared his room, thankfully.

He was panting.

It was getting worse.

The next morning the mood on the ship had changed. During the night one of the crew had thrown themselves overboard, and despite the night watch raising the alarm he was lost.

Though he wanted to tell of what he had seen while he slept, still he hesitated. Something held him back, forced a carefree smile to his face.

Soon, he reassured himself. Unless it goes away on its own, which it probably will.

The morning breeze cut like ice over his still sweating chest.

*   *   *

As exciting as it was to be nearing Jonah, it was also frustrating. They were both sleeping at similar times, so she was back to watching him at rest, even though in the past their relative times had not seemed to matter. It was how she had first watched him, but after watching him these last week's go about his day, she had begun to form a picture in her mind about his nature, his character, individuality, idiosyncrasies. Now her anxiety at approaching him was compounded by her no longer seeing him interact with his world, and already she felt like she was losing what little she knew about him.

To make matters worse, last night while visiting with Jonah, she had another unsettling vision. A cat had appeared suddenly upon his person, with similar colouring to her own hair. Under its paw was a spider, which she was certain had been dead, until it pulled itself free and walked casually away. Just as quickly as the cat and spider had appeared, they were, in the next instant, gone.

Thankfully, before she could convince herself she was losing her mind, Tamra shared a similar experience. Being far more innocent and trusting of the unknown, she had freely described also seeing strange things while she slept. Her visions were nothing like her own, however. Mostly Tamra seemed to be seeing things she wished were true, such as eating nice food or running in a verdant meadow. Perhaps the only unusual incident was a tooth falling out, but that was all. Assara was relieved, to a point.

And yet, the visions were unsettling.

Jasmine, the woman who had awkwardly enquired after Tamra, returned to her space between Assara and the still nameless middle-aged woman along their side of the long room. Despite frequent attempts at conversation, Assara did not know how to take this fellow prisoner. She would flit from nearly incoherent threats and curses to vital titbits of information regarding which guards to avoid and when to hide her face. She rarely responded to questions or comments, and seemed to sleep for just minutes at a time.

Jasmine turned her head just a fraction, indicating she was about to speak. She did not. A minute of uncomfortable silence passed.

When finally she spoke it was jumbled, words rushing from her mouth. "I heard them say we're close to Safar, and that we're not staying long. The sailors are complaining because they want to find themselves drink and women but aren't allowed off the ship."

Assara paused, wanting to engage with the unlikely friend but unsure of her intent.

"Oh." Was all she managed.

"I think we should…" The twitchy girl grabbed at her dress, clenched her teeth. "I think we should leave."

"What? We can do that?"

"No!! No it's not allowed, I mean…"

"Oh…" Assara whispered again, meaning becoming evident. She lowered her voice further.

"Escape?"

Jasmine gave her a look, fierce as a lion, fearful as a mouse. She moved off.

All Assara could do was sit, watch and wait.

The next morning at exercise Jasmine's haunted eyes seemed unable to resist seeking Assara. The conflict inside was painfully apparent in those darting glares. How much do I trust this girl? Dare I trust anyone?

Assara desperately wanted to communicate to the panicked woman, 'yes, please trust me', but she wasn't sure how to break through the barrier of fear built by what she guessed was years of neglect and abuse. For now, all she could do was attempt reassuring smiles every time their eyes met, which so far seemed only to cause further distance.

Jasmine started suddenly. It was an almost imperceptible pause in her already skittish meander. She then began working her way ahead in the ring of slaves one person at a time, much to the annoyance of those she passed. Assara stayed in the circle, moving in the now familiar path around the aft section of the deck. The sun was warm, but its ability to heat anything was severely compromised by the morning's chill. Tamra hummed absently behind her, a normally cheerful tune now completely devoid of mirth. A particularly burly sailor, missing one of his front teeth, leered at them as they passed by. A hushed complaint behind them marked Jasmine's steady approach.

The burly sailor reached out. Assara heard more than saw the arm extend and grab at Tamra. Before he could make purchase, however, Jasmine slipped between the two, interrupting the movement. From the corner of her eye Assara saw the awkward pause from the sailor who, with a grimace and a sheepish harrumph, returned to his guard duty.

Her head swam, heartbeat suddenly increased. An acute awareness of her powerlessness right now threatened to push her into unconsciousness. The only thing that kept her on her feet was the realisation that they had a friend; someone was with them, someone much more experienced in the ways of the wicked world than she.

She turned to look. As their eyes met, Jasmine gave one quick shake of her head. They were not out of danger yet.

Their circular path brought the sailor around once more. His focus was no longer on Tamra.

As Jasmine passed he grabbed at her arm, wrenching her from her place in line. She stumbled but remained standing till he struck her with the back of his hand, sending her to the deck.

"Keep your place in the line! No shoving! You want we should leave you for the many fangs of the murky deep?"

Jasmine said nothing, just cowered at his feet.

"Get back in line!" He yelled, words struggling to form through his gargling throat.

Jasmine wasted no time returning to the group, now more hushed and huddled than ever.

Tamra stopped her humming.

No-one spoke for the rest of the day, not even a whisper. Some of the sailors started to jest about how easily a woman's will was broken. Jasmine huddled further down the cabin, and Assara, wishing she could thank her for her bravery, found herself also frozen with fear.

A particularly quiet meal gave way to another dark night. The sliver of moon that rose struggled to make contact with the uneasy sea; fingers of moonlight severed by thin blades of mist and cloud.

In their usual fashion, the sailors were enjoying a loud meal in a room somewhere closer to the bow of the ship. Smells of food denied was torture, but this night the hungry slaves were spared some of their craving by their joy at being left alone. One by one they drifted off to sleep.

Assara's eyelids were getting heavy when a door at the rear of the room opened slowly. The sailor Assara now referred to internally as 'One Tooth', due to his one missing tooth, stepped slowly through. Jasmine's chosen position had him already near.

He paused in front of her, waiting for her eyes to meet his. Slowly she acquiesced. What was she doing? Assara thought. Please, just ignore him!

With a sick smile, One Tooth curled his finger upward in the unmistakable 'come with me' gesture. Jasmine shook her head. He sighed, then began cracking his knuckles. He stretched his head this way then that, smile widening with each movement. He paused then nodded.

A long minute passed with neither moving. Then, one jerky movement at a time, Jasmine stood.

Assara looked around as they slowly made their way from the room. All other prisoners were asleep or pretending to be. Tamra's breathing seemed convincing enough at least. Before she even had time to decide, Assara was crawling to the now closed door. No-one tried to stop her.

A short corridor led to a sharp stair. At the top was a very small section of deck at the very rear of the large vessel. Bitter cold slid down the now open passage, despite this part of the ship being very sheltered. At the top of the stair One Tooth, leading Jasmine by the hand, pushed the door closed but did not lock it. He was not expecting to be followed.

The stairs creaked as Assara climbed slowly, but so did the entire ship. Sounds of splashing waves above further masked her approach. At the top she reached toward the door but could not force herself to move it an inch. Some part of her knew what was waiting for her out there. One Tooth made an awful chuckling, laughing sound, sharp and bitter. Jasmine whimpered.

It pushed Assara over the edge. As slowly as she could manage she opened the door, just enough to peek around. All she could see was One Tooth's back, and Jasmine's feet behind. He was undressing her.

What do I do, she argued with herself? She looked but could not find a weapon, not that she trusted herself to win if she had one. The man was literally twice her size, and looked as though he was very familiar with brawls. A gust of wind whipped over the rail, flapping their clothes, sending his loose rope belt whipping like a protective snake.

His belt… it was very long. Hanging from the loops as it was, one end was dragging on the ground. Very near a spare anchor.

His head buried and his hands busy, Assara moved before thinking. She was only a few steps behind them and reached the loose rope quickly. A sharp intake of breath from Jasmine indicated she had noticed her approach.

One Tooth paused. He noticed too.

"Hello, what's this then? You got a friend, have you?"

He turned his leer and his focus on her. Assara dropped his belt.

"I like it when they're eager. I'm gentler that way. You'll have a good time, my little fish." He grabbed her shoulders then moved his hands down her arms. "I promise you that."

Assara fought through the terror, willing some semblance of cohesion into her fingers. She found the other end of his belt and looped it through his pants. One Tooth didn't struggle; he assumed she was obliging him in some way. A strange knock from over the rail caused him to turn.

"What was – "

Two words were all he managed before the slack on the anchor took. His body bent sickeningly as it hit the rail and went over. Jasmine was panting from the exertion of lifting it. She had cut her elbow on the rail, but already the blood was beginning to clot.

For a while the two girls just stared at the space where he had gone over. Jasmine recovered first, moving toward the door. There she paused.

Assara finally followed. In silence they made their way back to the space of wall which had become their own, then soon fell asleep shoulder to shoulder.

*   *   *

Rahim found Jonah at the bow watching the sun breach the horizon.

And he thought he was up early.

"You really are excited to see -" He began before he saw the set of his cousin's eyes. "Jonah? What is it? Did we lose another sailor last night? One of our own?"

Jonah waited a few moments before responding. "She's close, Rahim. I think that she's close."

"Huh? You haven't talked about 'her' for a while. Are you telling me you're still following this girl? Stalking her during your sleep?"

Jonah didn't even flinch at the slight insult. "I watched her. She is a captive, on a vessel somewhere west of us. The banner on the vessel is one I do not recognise, but the way of the captors is one I know all too well."

Rahim's mind took him to obvious conclusions. "Cousin... I... I am a fool – "

"She was nearly raped last night." He interrupted. "She went to the aid of another, and was nearly raped. She killed him though, with a little help from what I'm assuming is a friend."

The flood of information and its varied ramifications stilled Rahim's tongue. "What... ah, I mean... wow... I guess... Are you alright?"

Again Jonah paused before responding. "I do not know. I am relieved she is alright, furious that she is held captive, amazed at her bravery, petrified at what might happen to her before I see her next... I..."

With effort he took his eyes from the now blazing sun.

"I am lost. I have never felt this powerless."

"Be strong, my cousin." Rahim grabbed both his shoulders. "I have never seen you fail. You will beat this too."

"Beat it?" Jonah smiled in a way Rahim did not recognise. "I'm not sure I want to."

*   *   *

Assara and Tamra sat shoulder to shoulder in the section of corridor that had become their temporary home. Jasmine sat opposite, proudly watching over them both as all three nibbled on some rations.

"I have decided sailors are the smelliest thing in the whole world." Tamra spoke, breaking the silence. Where before they were afraid to make any noise, the slaves' confidence had grown along with their slaver's laziness. Having killed one certainly made Assara feel a little less timid.

"Sailors are bad, yes." Jasmine spoke without interrupting her surveillance. "But mercenaries? Mercenaries are worse."

"What's a mercy, a mermin," Tamra struggled, looking to her sister. Jasmine answered.

"A soldier who…" Jasmine filled the blanks with gesture. "For money, fights. For money, kills."

"Why do soldiers normally fight?" Tamra questioned again, innocently. The two older girls shared a lost look, and shrugged shoulders.

After a short pause, Assara asked the question she was certain she knew the answer to. "Have you known many mercenaries?" Her wording was unintentional, its double meaning occurring to her shortly after the words left her mouth.

Jasmine nodded, again without breaking her watch of the corridor and its inhabitants.

"I didn't mean –" She began in apology.

Jasmine interrupted. "I know what you mean."

Assara felt concern that she had made her only friend uncomfortable. Ask her something else, she thought.

"Do you, ah… Do you have a favourite food?"

Finally the surveillance stopped, followed by a brief giggle. "Favourite? Like if I could choose what to eat? Like a queen?"

"I, ah, I guess so. A queen would choose what to eat all the time, huh?" Assara smiled back.

"Sounds exhausting." Came the nonchalant reply.

More moments passed, and Jasmine giggled again. It made Assara jump.

"Queen Jasmine? What would you like to eat, Queen Jasmine?" She laughed. It was the most pleasing sound Assara had heard in months, foreign and rebellious in the dank space. It infected Assara, taking control of her cheeks. A laugh burst from her own mouth, loud enough to cause disapproving glares from half the prison group. She cupped her hands across her mouth in embarrassment, which made Jasmine laugh all the more.

The corridor filled with bright light as the door burst open. A sailor jeered at the crowd, and the girls' mirth vanished.

"Slops. Exercise."

Up on deck Assara was enjoying a sun that held genuine warmth. The sailors were unusually quiet, perhaps due to the sudden disappearance of the bully 'One Tooth'. Surely losing someone with a perceived strength as his would make the others feel vulnerable, she thought. Whatever the reason, it was adding to the shred of relief that lightened her heart. She was not alone. She had some power over her masters. As for what awaited her at the end of this journey… Well, that could be ignored for now. Squashing that thought was a small price to pay for a glimmer of hope.

One of the men in charge had joined the supervision, perhaps as a result of the crew growing smaller of late. He showed an obvious unease at the role, holding his hands across his front and shifting nervously from foot to foot, a motion exacerbated by the rolling swells.

A woman near him wobbled as the boat pitched, her arms windmilling slightly. The officer, as Jasmine had described them earlier, reached out a rough hand and grabbed her upper arm in what looked like a hard grip. Once the woman was steadied, she hurried back into place.

After the prisoners were locked back in the corridor, Assara paused from pulling some knots from Tamra's hair. Jasmine sat next to them pulling threads from her shirt.

"I think that officer might be alright, you know? The way he helped that woman today?" Assara suggested.

"Don't be fooled." Jasmine replied without looking up. "All men are the same. We are objects to them, like a fork, or a horse."

"I like horses." Tamra interjected innocently.

"You would care well for a horse, little peach." Jasmine offered kindly. "A man is cruel; to fork, horse, and woman. Officers are no different." Her fingers momentarily ceased their fruitless endeavour. "Trust me."

"Is it wrong to believe that there might be good men out there?" Assara asked, no longer thinking of the officer.

"Listen to me, Assara." Jasmine finally looked up. "Behind the clothes, the fancy uniforms, all men are the same. Don't be fooled by their station, or their disguise. When it comes off, they are all the same." She returned her attention to her threads.

"They are all the same."

They didn't talk much after that, and sleep came slowly.

She found Jonah also resting, still in his bunk on his own ship despite the ship having made port. Anxiety gripped her at seeing him close to land. Would he leave the ship and disappear into a foreign country? Stupid girl, she chided herself. Even if he remained on the boat what would you do? Wave, as his and yours sailed past each other? He seemed cold, wrapped in a blanket as he was, his arms around his chest. This place must be a far cry from the desert he was used to.

It certainly was for her.

She was curious about the city and the port he had arrived at, so she risked a quick glance, not wanting to move too far from Jonah's sleeping form. From the deck her ghostly figure peered out to the vista below. Many flames from many lamps cast an ethereal light over the hazy streets. People still worked busily everywhere, tending to fishing and cargo vessels that came and went ceaselessly.

I wonder if this is where I will meet my fate.

The thought brought a renewed influx of fear, so rather than face it she returned to Jonah's bedside to continue her lonely vigil.

*   *   *

Jonah was cold. Despite his spirit-self sitting facing Assara as she slept, he could sense his body clutching more at the blanket where it rested. He knew he should return and wake long enough to address the chill, but still he remained.

Daylight was approaching. He would be up soon anyway.

Her new friend was resting on her shoulder again. He was intensely glad for her support, and yet immensely jealous of her closeness to Assara. To be close enough to touch her, but not be able to touch her, was torture enough. To see someone be as close to her as he wished to be, made it all the more unbearable. Suddenly he could picture not just being close, but specific poses. Her head on his shoulder. His on hers. He would know how Assara smelt. Know how her voice sounded, really sounded, out of the spirit hours.

Jonah's pulse had quickened. He was making himself upset, which would wake him if he was not careful. In answer to his fears his cabin door opened and he opened his natural eyes.

His heart dropped, causing him to sigh audibly.

"Well good morning to you too, you sour grape!" Rahim slurred his words, and clanged a tall green bottle against the door frame.

"Mothers' milk, Rahim. How drunk are you?"

"Drunk enough, but not nearly drunk enough!" he replied, and promptly broke into hysterics.

"I take it you haven't slept?"

"No, old man, I haven't slept. Turns out sailors are the world's most respec-eted drinkers, and I have been being duly educated."

Jonah smiled as his cousin slurred. "That's making the most of your fancy language skills." He said wryly.

"Whatever, Jonah. We are in one of the world's most amazing places. I have seen more in one night than either of us have in half a lifetime, and you are chiding me? This is what we dreamed of, and you hide in your bed like a child from his father's backhand! Come! We finally have some freedom, come! Explore with me!"

Jonah stood and made to guide Rahim to the bed. "I have a meeting to attend, and you will be asleep in minutes."

Rahim made to fight, then looked down at his legs in genuine confusion when they did not respond.

"I will not, huh? I mean, we will, you and I, the places I have to show you cousin... all of the places...."

Rahim's head hit the pillow. It seemed like the loss of consciousness would be instantaneous, but a hastily grabbed arm turned Jonah as he made to leave.

"You were visiting her last night, weren't you? Arsa...?"

"Assara." Jonah replied, genuinely offended at the slip. "Yes, cousin. She is close, our nights are the same now."

"Cousin!" Rahim's tone changed slightly. "What is it like?"

"What is what like?"

"You know, cousin, I don't want to say it but you know?"

"Rahim, it is time you rested – "

"Love, Jonah. What is it like?"

Genuine surprise caused him to pause. In the space between question and answer, Rahim finally succumbed to the lack of sleep and considerable inebriation, and drifted off. Jonah chuckled. He had thought Rahim nearly immune to the forces that pulled one individual to another.

Seemed he had been wrong.

Dressed and clean he left Rahim to his sleep, and the headache that would follow. Up on deck the captain was overseeing cargo being loaded. He greeted Jonah warmly as he approached. Jonah's grasp of the language was still poor, so the meeting would be short.

"Good morning! Your men, are they well?" the captain said, stepping down from the rail to grasp Jonah's hand. "I saw Rahim come aboard just now with a few of my officers. He looked... tired!"

"Rahim, ah, sleep." Jonah replied, winks filling the gaps in his speech. A shared laugh described mutual understanding, and a wave led Jonah to a table, on which sat some maps under a wolf's head paperweight.

"Here, here." The Captain said, pointing first at the map then gesturing outwardly. His finger traced east across an expanse of water, stopping when it again met land. He looked up rather than spoke. Jonah nodded his understanding.

"When?"

"Tomorrow, first light. Sunrise."

"Okay. What, we do, for you?" Jonah asked, circling his fingers in a gesture he hoped meant his warriors. He had been asked to this meeting for more than a travel update, he was sure.

"Out there?" The captain began, pointing toward the docks and the city beyond. "Ah, bad. This?" He continued, pointing to the cargo being loaded. "Expensive. Men will come. Thieves, criminals; robbers. Bad men."

When Jonah caught on he nodded solemnly.

"Can you, protect? Guard? I lost many men to the pirates."

Jonah needed no more explanation. He had seen the losses caused by the attack at sea. He could also safely guess about these places and the people they would attract.

"We, make safe." Pointing at the cargo signified his understanding. The captain sighed in genuine relief. He must really be expecting trouble.

A polite nod signalled the meeting was done. As the captain returned to his supervision, Jonah retreated to the decks below to see to his own. His men, now numbering eighty-five after their skirmish with the pirates, had not even requested shore leave, although he was certain most of them would have wanted to. The young commander felt some guilt at his often-harsh command, but as always it was a smaller voice than that of his sense of responsibility. Or his need for control. Well, best not to dwell on that for too long.

His guilt swayed him. He issued sleeping shifts be put in place to prepare for the long night ahead, and gave those not resting permission to enjoy the port. The Banji soldiers could not hide their excitement.

A short while later the first group walked down the gangplank, talking and pointing like children. Despite the fact that many of his men were older than himself, Jonah always felt the senior.

Maybe I should take some time to explore myself? He thought. There was music on the late morning wind, grabbing at him. Still, he remained. Duty, or self-denial, sealed his boots firmly to the deck.

Duty, he chided himself. Duty above all.

Still he stood and listened, gleaning every discernible note before the wind carried them away.

*   *   *

"We are docking tonight."

The look in Jasmine's eyes made Assara nervous. Her bravery was the kind motivated by a greater fear. It did not inspire much confidence.

"Tonight? Are you sure?"

"Yes. I also found out this is not where we are being sold. We are only here for one night, to resupply, then moving on."

Not here then. The waiting would continue. Was she happy that her introduction to the life of slavery would wait? No, she wanted to know. Where was Jonah? Was he here, or was this some other port in some other land?

"Did you hear me?" Jasmine's voice dropped to a barely audible whisper. "We can leave, tonight."

Assara managed a nod.

"Many of the men are going ashore tonight. We will not get a better opportunity than this. Just follow my lead when the time comes."

Her mind was in turmoil. She felt safe here, on the boat headed for who knows where. The sailors weren't as mean as they had been, and they were protecting them, protecting her.

Tamra pulled at her sleeve.

"What are you two talking about?"

"Nothing Tamra. Play with your doll." Jasmine nodded, obviously assuming that keeping Tamra in the dark was a good idea. She didn't suspect that it was because Assara was too afraid to even speak the thought out loud.

That day was a long one. Unusual noises permeated the thick doors throughout, each one a fearful reminder of what was to come. The easy mood of the sailors up on deck only compounded Assara's fear. Generally speaking, the happier they were, the worse things got for the group below.

Finally, it happened. Although it was hard to tell, it felt like late afternoon when the boat finally met the docks. Despite all the noise from above and the shudder from the hull as it bounced against the wharf, the women were left alone. Hours later, the evening meal was brought to them in the corridor, instead of on decks. Assara began to relax. Surely there was no way they could get off the boat if they couldn't get out of the room.

More hours passed and, despite Jasmine's look of patient resolve, it seemed less and less likely their escape plan would become a reality. She longed to sleep and visit Jonah, but her anxiety was too great. Tamra, blissfully unaware, snored quietly beside her.

A sudden rumble rattled the boat, shaking the company of slaves awake. Any trace of Assara's sleepiness vanished. Panicked whispers arose. Assara checked Jasmine's reactions to see if this was somehow a part of her plan. Her look of confusion said that it wasn't.

"What was that?"

"I don't know…" Jasmine replied, not hiding her frustration.

The sound of the rear door's lock turning pulled every eye toward it. Heavy footfalls from the stair behind the front door preceded an unceremonious entrance from one of the few sailors still on-board.

"Look you lot!" He sounded a little panicked. "A monster blaze has broken out nearby, and maritime law states that no prisoner is to be locked in a room when there's a threat of fire to the ship. Make no mistake though, you are not free to leave this vessel. Besides which there are worse things out there than us and this room. Escape, and you'll find out what I mean." With that he turned and ran back up the stair, calling orders as he went.

Jasmine turned and gave her the nod. Assara's head swam. She nearly fainted. With a deep, ragged breath she turned to Tamra, now well and truly woken by the commotion. She could not speak for the thickness of her throat, so she simply helped her to stand.

They attracted some protests as they tiptoed along the crowded corridor. Jasmine resolutely ignored them, while Assara desperately wished for someone to take a hold of her leg. They passed through the front doorway, and soon found themselves peering out at the top side of the large boat, now bathed in the blood red reflection of the fire onshore. Four sailors were working pulleys, lining buckets of water along the railing. Before she could protest, Jasmine grabbed her hand and pulled her around the corner, headed toward the aft section of the ship where they had killed One Tooth. Tamra silently fell into their wake.

The occasional gawker ran by on the wharf, headed toward the commotion for a better look. She could see the fire now, only a few buildings away. No wonder the sailors were concerned, she thought; this whole place seems to be made of wood. At the rear railing Jasmine quickly found a rope and, after tying it off as best she could, began lowering it to the docks below. It would be a fair climb; they were at least two storeys high. When the rope met the wooden walkway below, Jasmine hopped lightly over the railing and began her descent.

"What is Jasmine doing, Assara?" Tamra's question was full of innocent concern, and uncomfortably loud.

Jasmine grunted and complained as she fought to lower herself down the rope. She slipped the last third of the length and landed with a tumble.

"You have got to be crazy!" Assara said quietly to no-one in particular.

"Come on!" Jasmine mouthed more than spoke.

"Tamra can't climb down like that!"

"She can. I can catch her if she falls." Jasmine extended her malnourished arms up in a feeble gesture. They wobbled, numb from the exertion at lowering herself.

"Jasmine, I…"

"Assara, this is your only chance!"

Behind the flames the sky began to lighten. A single ray of light added to the scene caused a golden orange hue to envelop the stricken city. As beautiful as it was, she felt exposed. They had lost the cover of night. It wouldn't work, couldn't work!

"Assara!" Jasmine called loudly this time. She looked, eyes apologetic. Jasmine paused only a moment before turning to disappear into the alleys.

"Where is she going? Is she allowed to leave? Won't she get in trouble?"

She couldn't answer. All she could do was stare at the space where her only friend had vanished.

Sailors appeared from the street, sailors from her vessel. They were pointing and laughing, clearly drunk, making light of the chaos as they piled back onto the vessel. A bell clanged loudly. Under her feet the whole vessel shuddered as the steam engines came to life. Assara didn't even bother to hide as the stern line was unhooked. Tamra, wonderfully naïve, turned and used the rear door to return to the corridor that was their prison, yawning loudly.

Alone again.

*   *   *

A dutiful knock at his cabin door startled Jonah. He should have gotten a few hours' sleep, but was wary of the situation; unfamiliar territory, terrain, enemy, it all made for a disastrous recipe. He wanted to be up if anything happened, and he wanted the last watch for himself. A glance out the porthole showed a deep black sky. It must be about an hour after midnight. If an attack was to come, it would come now.

The door opened, and a ragged Rahim peered in.

"I am awake, cousin." Jonah said, preempting the question.

"Thank the north winds that you are. Another hour and my eyes would have melted."

"Anything?" He asked, splashing water across his face.

"Some noise from further in. The occasional drunkard and some very enthusiastic whoring but nothing to excite you. I have changed the watch, fresh eyes await you." Rahim clapped him warmly on the shoulder. "Don't wake me 'til tomorrow."

"No promises." He replied wryly.

The air was cool on deck, which helped to wash the fatigue from his eyes. He had meant to check in on Assara but his lack of rest had meant no spirit hours. His men at least did seem fresh. Jonah paced the railing facing the port of Safar looking for the places he would launch an assault. Stacked crates created a shadowed alley with an obscured entrance. A nearby building also made good cover, although left a lot of open ground between there and the vessel. If it was him, he would set riflemen on the rooftops to bring down the guards. Either that or board from the ocean side, which he knew would be difficult with the lack of ladders and the water temperature. He set his few companions to watching the darker approaches, and set his instincts to the wind.

Somehow the smell on the breeze reminded him of her. He pulled his cloak about his shoulders, imagining it was her arms. The last time he had seen her she had been resting against a wall, crowded and dirty. A small part of him wished that they were close, but it was mostly squashed by his harsh, realistic nature. You can't help her, it said. But at least she is safe.

The thought carried little solace.

An hour or so passed, allowing him plenty of time to war with his thoughts. I want to see her. I will probably never see her. Surely there is a way. Your duty comes first. Our paths might cross? She might be taken by another.

At least the frustration kept him awake.

A familiar bird call, very out of place in the current surrounds, summoned him to one of his companions crouched low by the railing.

"Yes?"

"Movement. One, there."

It was the space between the piled crates. The most obvious, but most effective place to launch an assault. Jonah signalled the other men on guard, crouched low in preparation for gunfire, then moved off to find a higher vantage point.

In the distance, far off on the other side of the port, an explosion went up. One great fireball rose, drawing with it a column of flame that painted the city. The shadows between the vessel and the docks grew thick.

Gunfire followed immediately, taking chunks from the wooden rail. Six men burst from cover making straight for the gangway. Night vision compromised, Jonah and his men opened fire as best as they could.

Two attackers fell groaning to the wharf; a third on the gangway. Jonah felled a fourth as the remaining assailants met swords on two sides when they reached the deck. The fifth was felled so quickly the sixth turned and ran back toward the alley. Jonah didn't hesitate, he shouldered his rifle and pursued.

Let him go! A voice said as he bolted into the dark alley. Jonah raced on. Flimsy excuses affirmed his pursuit. If he lives he will know how to make a proper assault. If he dies the threat dies with him. They started to pass people, some sleeping, some drinking, some headed to the fire in curiosity. Jonah's target seemed to be running to the fire as well.

Every time he got closer, another quick turn down an alley added an arm's length or two between them. They burst into an open street then disappeared into another alley, narrower and strewn with garbage. Disgruntled homeless complained loudly as the pursuit went over legs and bodies, spilling bottles and spooking dogs. Still they approached the fire.

Across another street the chase went, this one crowded with people woken from their sleep by the threat of the burning building. Jonah's target veered right, skirting the stricken area. There were no more dark spaces, no more narrow walkways. Jonah shouldered his rifle and fired, but missed. The attacker slipped left and disappeared.

Still he pursued, running blindly down the narrow space his target had taken. A glimpse of a coat tail led him right, then heavy footfalls took him left. Crates appeared, similar to the ones opposite the vessel they had just left. Another right revealed another dock, and finally the chased made a fatal mistake. Running straight for the water ahead gave Jonah the shot he was waiting for. A heartbeat before his target could dive into the ocean behind a large boat, Jonah's shot took him between the shoulder blades.

Walking out into the open to ensure his man was down Jonah instantly felt exposed. His skin crawled like crazy. On the vessel a bell was clanging; it was making ready to leave. No, that wasn't it, he was definitely being watched. His eyes went immediately to a lone figure at the stern looking down at him. He froze, paralysed in the instant of recognition.

It was her.

*   *   *

Assara's hands flew to her mouth. Her initial shock at seeing a man shot in the back vanished, consumed by the immense wave of emotion when Jonah emerged from a space between crates.

He was looking right at her.

It couldn't be him! Yet it was, she knew his face intimately, his stature, his gait.

Lost in the surprise, confusion and elation she didn't notice the boat drifting away until a great shudder unbalanced her.

Jonah dropped his rifle in a sudden movement, as if embarrassed to be seen with it. Assara glanced over her shoulder toward the door she knew she should retreat to before a sailor discovered her on deck. Jonah took a step, then another towards the retreating vessel. Assara approached the railing.

"Hey!"

Her heart froze, desperation and panic gripping her chest. Involuntarily her hands went to her heart. One of Jonah's hands began to rise.

"Show's over little fish. Get back below decks." Calloused hands herded her to the back door, and he was lost from view.

She began to sob, conflicting emotions bursting forth from an exhausted mind.

"Someone's missing." Another voice from deeper in. "I count only ninety-nine."

The sailor still had a hard grip on Assara's arm. "Wait on, where's your angry friend?"

She spoke as best she could through the tears. "I tried to stop her, but I couldn't. I didn't want her to leave!"

"Went over the railing, did she? So that's what you was looking at out there."

"Damn!" the other sailor cursed, kicking whoever lay nearest him. "Lord Fauld will have our berries. Better tell him they was taken at port. Stuff always goes missing in Safar."

"Lucky you was there to see it happen." He released her to crumple into the section of floor that was hers. "Sure you didn't help her off?"

Assara didn't meet his gaze as she shook her head.

The men left then, discussing their cover story. Assara clutched her knees to her chest.

Jonah. He was right there, close enough to speak to. He even noticed her. His eyes seemed so kind, so familiar. She could have sworn he recognised her, but was probably just being chivalrous. Her heart would not stop pounding!

"Jasmine is gone, isn't she? She left us. Assara?"

"Yes. She left us. She wanted us to go with her, but… but we couldn't."

"What will she do here?"

"I don't know, Tamra. Just forget about Jasmine. Go to sleep."

Sleep, and let me think of him.

*   *   *

He stood, long enough for sunlight to meet the stern of the vessel spiriting Assara away. Had it been fear he had seen in her eyes? Her expression had been one of shock. Of all the times for their paths to cross… from the dock there was no chance to explain why he had killed a man in front of her, but he had sure tried in the moments their eyes met.

Assara. Here, in the flesh. He knew they were close, but here? On the same night? The odds at it being a coincidence were insane!

The wind brought a fleeting caress of heat and smoke. Voices, yelling as they fought to control the blaze, grew louder. Reluctantly he picked up his rifle, turned back toward the east port and, with one last look at the steadily shrinking vessel, returned to his own.

From on deck his men yelled at him, an element of panic in their speech. The gangway retracted as soon as he boarded. Rahim was there waiting, looking like murder itself.

"What? What has happened?"

"The Shareef. He is dead." His cousin's fists clenched audibly.

"Dead?" Someone took his rifle from his shoulder, he didn't turn to see who. "This cannot be! He was safe in Bandarat, the city was his! No, this cannot be, this…"

"Ven was visiting his family in the spirit hours this morning. They had moved into the city two days ago. The Honoured was found dead this morning in his bed. He was poisoned. They caught and killed the assassin as he tried to escape, but by then it was too late."

Jonah squeezed his jaw until it hurt. The pain helped to stop the tears from leaving his eyes. Rahim placed a hand on his shoulder.

"I am sorry, cousin, but there is more. The captain will not release us to return home. He says we are property, and will remain so until released by their King."

Jonah's shoulders rose and slumped as he drew breath. It was only then that he noticed the change in demeanour on-board. The tension between his, and the captain's men was thick. Though the words threatened to choke him, he forced them out in a croak.

"Stand down."

Rahim grimaced, looking over the seas toward his homeland. "Stand down." He repeated.

My father, Jonah thought to himself as his men returned to their cabins. My father is dead.

*   *   *

It had all taken place less than twenty-four hours ago. The assassin, already inside the walled city having been admitted under Lord Fauld's authority, had sat patiently waiting for the moment when the Shareef's tent was vulnerable. The previous evening had provided the perfect opportunity. The Shareef had stayed out late, leaving his residence lightly guarded. He had slipped in then and waited.

He waited for his target to return. He waited for him to avail himself of some company, to have a late drink, and to sleep for at least one hour. It was then that the assassin silently emerged from the shadows to drip the poison into his sleeping mouth. Again he returned to the shadows, waiting until all hope of revival was lost. He had tried, and failed, to escape.

East of the great city, high in the inhospitable mountains, the young Fallsten prince watched. In his spirit hours he watched his assassin do his bidding, die for his cause.

Finally, he had thought. The world would be his.

*   *   *

Fauld had seen it too, although he and the young prince had not seen each other. His fears at losing the ship transporting the Banji had then been revealed as unfounded. Who would have guessed that they would not go on a murderous rampage once word of their leader's death reached them? Perhaps he had underestimated these savages. But probably not.

Fauld's vessel was smaller and faster than the warship that was concerning him, and he was not stopping in Safar to resupply. As such he was days ahead of them on his way home to South Harbour.

In his hand rested a small glass vial, stopped with a cork. It was the payment for his betrayal; the very poison that had taken the Shareef's life. He had already written the note which his queen would read when she slept tonight. A note which meant, but did not say, that everything was going according to plan. Their enemies dwindled, and the instrument of the King's overthrow was now in their possession.

A poison fit for two Kings, he thought, and laughed. For a long while, he laughed.

*   *   *

A shudder, caused by the unnatural vibration of stone on steel, shot up the elderly man's arm and down his spine as he finished carving a name into the wall. Sivvel felt as if someone had not only walked on his grave but started piling on the dirt. At least it was done. If the girls managed to find him in their spirit hours, seeing their names on the wall would let them know they were not forgotten. Small consolation, seeing as they were probably days away by now. But it was something.

Work had finished early again. He had been making those enormous rifles non-stop for days, but resources had suddenly run dry. Now his work days only went for an hour or two, mostly making shells for the instruments of destruction, before he and his companions were herded back to their sleeping quarters.

He was glad for the respite, bored as he was. His knees ached from standing, his shoulders from lifting, his back from leaning. This was not an old man's game, he mused. But then, what was? Professional massage receiver? Full time ache-er? Opinion giver?

He hated being old.

The door to his shared room opened. One of the duty supervisors entered. He was alone, having no fear of a group of seniors making a break for it. Foolish man, Sivvel thought. Old men carry knives too.

The supervisor beckoned him with an upward cock of his chin. "You, Sivvel. Come with me."

Sivvel stood nonchalantly. He had no fear of the young man, knife or no. The one benefit of being older than you wanted to be.

Once outside, the door was closed and he was led a few paces away to ensure they would not be overheard. Good news or bad, it was the not knowing that created the greatest sense of fear in your slaves, and a slave who was afraid was easy to manage.

"Some say you know plants and garden care. Is this true?"

"Yes supervisor. In the Von Hold, before I was moved to Serventine, I tended to the gardens, growing fruit and vegetables for food, and herbs for healing."

"Very good. Pack your possessions, but speak to no one. You are being moved."

"May I ask where to, supervisor."

"You may. You are being moved to the palace. I hope you have remembered your manners, slave."

Indeed I have he thought, as he nodded his acquiescence.

*   *   *

Jasmine had seen slums before. The stink, the garbage, the people; it was more or less where she had grown up. But nothing had prepared her for Safar.

It was like the entire city had grown up without law or a moral code. There was certainly no law enforcement; it seemed anyone with money simply travelled with their own private army. Everyone was drunk as well. Those selling the liquor, and those buying the liquor. The only industry that seemed well regulated was prostitution, which made things all the more difficult for her. She had hoped to make some quick cash and get out of town but she couldn't attract a client without a representative, whatever that meant.

Within hours she was regretting her escape.

Turned out there was such a thing as the lesser of two evils. Surely anywhere would be better than this. She was mugged three times that first day, each attacker releasing her somewhat nonchalantly upon discovering how truly poor she was.

Then the guilt started. Assara was being dragged into a world very foreign to her. She had been a guide, a lifeline, before she abandoned Assara and her sister to whatever was waiting for them at the end of their journey. She had felt a real sense of pride in being able to care for someone.

She had also enjoyed having a friend.

The brief moment of relief at not having responsibility had been instantly squashed when she left them. This place seemed a perfect punishment for her treachery.

"Whooo-hellooo!"

Another group of drunks interrupted her self-flagellation.

"Do you have representation, crumpet?"

"Yes." She lied.

"It's not The Heron, is it? I am a little on the light having seen to other, ah, business already."

"It is." She lied again.

"Another time then." He kicked dust at her, then jogged to catch his group, their combined mass somehow collectively supporting each other down the dusty street.

About another hour later a tall, semi-clean man with four guards appeared. Jasmine stood, striking her most alluring pose.

He noticed, and approached. For a moment he simply stood, then in a halting manner asked the question. "Do you have representation?"

"The Heron."

"Of course…" He remarked with a hint of disappointment. "Very well, we in accord be thus?" His hand extended toward her, palm up.

"Just you, not the guards."

His hand twitched, retracting just slightly. She had offended him. "I have engaged The Heron's women before. Who do you think I am?"

Quickly she grabbed his hand. "Just, making sure."

Apparently the handshake was something very binding, judging by the look of resignation it brought to his face.

Strange place indeed.

Once he had her hand he held it tightly, heading for the nearest inn with lodgings. It was late afternoon and already bustling. The party cast menacing glares in every direction as they moved between the tables, headed towards the bar. Once there Jasmine's client spoke perfunctorily.

"A room. The Heron."

A handful of money crossed the bar. In despair Jasmine realised that probably included her fee. About half an hour later her suspicions were confirmed.

Curse this place! She thought as she returned to the street. Curse me for my stupid ideas, curse this stupid world and curse everyone in it!

Well nearly everyone. A single tear marked the hour as she followed the sinking sun north.

*   *   *

The young prince did not set a standard as he entered Bandarat. He did not follow a fanfare, or set a parade of horses, despite the fact that before long he would be recognised as ruler. In many ways the assassination was the easy part. Actually controlling this largest of cities would take patience, and a delicate touch. The Shareef of the north had been a strong and wise ruler. His followers were loyal, mostly. A mourning period would give their anger time to die, and with it their ability to resist.

If he was honest with himself, he would turn his nose up at this place. It was a far cry from his villages in the mountains to the east. There were a hard people. Land like that brooked no waste, no laziness. All who remained after a winter in the highlands were those who were worthy. The rest fell under the snow and were swallowed, devoured by the hungry earth.

His caravan passed a man sleeping on the street. The way the man snored reminded him of rock falls and rams bucking horns. In a strange way it made him homesick.

He would just have to make this place into something he could be proud of. In answer to his thought a group of tall men nodded solemnly to him as he rounded a corner. Many more groups would enter the city over the next week, placing themselves on more corners, in every Inn and meeting place. They would spread tales of the prince and his deeds. They would speak of his heart for a leaderless people, and his plans to bring security and prosperity to them.

They would also kill those still loyal to the dead Shareef.

Finally they arrived at their destination, the modest lodgings the previous ruler had been using. One of the Shareef's captains, a horse master named Falan, had taken over in a feeble attempt to take the position for himself. His doorway was lightly guarded.

A decision had already been made regarding Falan. Now it was time for the northerner to decide what kind of a day it was. A day to live for his new prince, or die for his dead Shareef.

Seven men suddenly converged on the two guards, killing them with knives before screams could leave their lungs. The prince did not break stride.

"Who dares!" Falan began, before the sword point at his throat ceased any following outbursts.

"My name is Prince Cul and I have claimed this city. You may join with me or you may die. Choose."

Cul was not surprised by Falan's response.

*   *   *

Assara sat, in the spirit hours, watching Jonah stare at the wall. It was very late, well after midnight, but still he didn't sleep. She was torn at having reached a new level of closeness, having seen him in the flesh, but also feeling pushed aside by this sudden tragedy.

Something should have changed! She saw him! He saw her! This man she had been pulled towards for what seemed like a lifetime had appeared literally under her nose, and then, nothing! It was like fate had a sick sense of humour, and a talent for torturing her. Oppression pressed in now, squeezed by the corridor that was her cell and the bleakness of her situation. She hadn't realised how much she had been relying on Jonah to lift her spirits. With Jasmine gone, and Jonah sealed in a pit of grief, she was feeling the same fear that had gripped her when Sivvel was taken. If she didn't have Tamra to care for, to lean on...

The world blurred, shifting in a motion of breathtaking speed. Had she moved her spirit-self somewhere else? No, Jonah was still there, frozen in place.

Wait... no it couldn't be...

She was back in the Hold, but it was no longer in ruin. Or was it the Hold? Walls were in different places. A cage separated her from Tamra, now glowing and sitting cross-legged. A window appeared behind. Outside, on the street, a bear prowled. She had only ever seen them in pictures, drawings which had described them as terrifying, dangerous creatures. This one... she desperately wanted to reach it, or have it reach her...

She turned to Jonah, feeling a sudden need to be away from him. A black cat hissed; the sound was terrifying. Her heart began to pound.

She woke then, her agitated state breaking her slumber. Tamra opened her eyes; she must have been dozing.

"What is it?"

"I... saw strange things in my sleep again." Guilt washed over her at sharing her burden with one so young, but she no longer had the strength to bear it alone.

"Really? What did you see?" Tamra questioned excitedly. "Once, I saw this field, bigger than anything! The grass was soft like a pillow, and I could even eat it!'

"What? Why would you eat grass?"

"Um, I don't know why. I just did. What did you see?"

Assara quickly decided which elements of the vision she was comfortable sharing. "I saw the Hold, sort of, it was a bit different. I saw a bear, not a scary one, though. I saw you too, my little peach. You were glowing."

"Really? Was I magic?"

"I don't know. I didn't see you cast any spells, if that's what you mean. You looked very happy, though."

"Does it mean something?"

"I wish I could tell you." Assara pulled her sister close, drawing comfort from her blissful ignorance.

That morning the sun was warm on deck, the air fresh. As always her thoughts stayed on Jonah, and Jasmine, and poor Sivvel, wherever they all were. Perhaps it was the visions. Perhaps it was her run in with Jonah at the docks. Something inside gave her hope; hope for her friends, hope for her sister. Things would work out in the end. They had to.

They just had to.

Her arms curled just a little tighter around her chest.

*   *   *

"Did you sleep at all?"

"No." Jonah stared at the water in his wash basin, cryptic messages rippling from side to side with the hum of the ship's engines. It offered no solace.

"The men mourned as well as they could last night. They are in a bit of a state, they didn't sleep much either. I am expecting they will want to rest today to visit the funeral procession in the spirit. They are not happy that we are still sailing west, but that is no surprise."

"Tell them they are free to rest today as they will."

"I will." Rahim waited a moment, but the words of consolation would not come. He turned to leave.

"I saw her."

"Huh? Oh, Assara? I thought you said you didn't sleep last night."

"In Safar. She was there, on another ship. I saw her."

Rahim turned, then moved over to the bed. "She was in Safar? How is that even possible? When did you see her?"

"I chased that man through the port after their failed raid. I followed him across the city to the docks on the western side. I shot him, moments before he could leap into the water. She was on deck, right there, right then. She watched me kill him."

"Is she still there, now?"

"Her ship was pulling away. Men moved her back below decks."

Rahim's hand moved though his hair. "I don't believe it. I thought she was on the other side of the world. But you did say she was getting closer, didn't you? Do you where she is going now?"

"East."

"East? But the only thing east of here is… she is going to Bandarat?"

Jonah looked up at his cousin, his face a thousand emotions. "Did I miss her, Rahim? Was this my chance?"

"Jonah…"

"I should have given the order. We could have taken the ship. My Shareef is dead, we offer no allegiance to the foreign lords anymore…"

"No allegiance but our honour. I would not have had the strength to do what you did. I do not like it, but it was the right thing to do. We swore we would serve, and thanks to your leadership we will hold to that oath."

"Strength? If this is strength, I am not sure I want it anymore. The men mourn their leader. We mourn our father. I mourn…"

Jonah gripped the wash stand in defiance of approaching tears.

"I will give you time, cousin. Spend some time with the men when you are ready."

"They will not want me."

"They will when they see you, you will see."

Rahim left then, closing the door softly as he went. Jonah returned to the space on the floor, still warm from his night-long vigil.

*   *   *

It didn't take long for Sivvel to reach the palace. As he had expected, the Holds that had fallen were the ones further out from the seat of power. Guards who escorted the carriage and patrolled the grounds carried the large rifles he had spent weeks assembling. Despite his revulsion at war and all aspects of it, he felt safer than he had in years. If the uprising from the slums really was as bad as he suspected, there was no safer place than this right now.

The servant's quarters were modest, but a huge improvement over the crowded conditions he was used to. He had said some polite greetings to his fellow workers and gone straight to work, eager to earn his place. The grounds he would tend were extensive. Two water features adorned three complete gardens, all in need of a green thumb. He had no assistants either.

Times must indeed be tough.

In the afternoon he was called to the master of affairs for an initial report. At first, he had assumed his superior to be simply a thorough man. Turned out there was more to it than that.

As he had given his report, another fellow had watched the exchange from the shadows. His presence made Sivvel very uneasy. The master of affairs outlined some of the restrictions he would be placed under, such as minimum work hours and restricted areas. Then came the giveaway.

Sivvel's sleep would be watched to ensure he did not explore parts of the palace in the spirit hours. No wonder the veiled individual made him uncomfortable.

Sleep walker.

He knew they patrolled places like the castle to ensure people did not snoop while they slept. He did not know how the sleep walkers kept intruders out, but he did know they were the only ones who saw others in the spirit.

The next day he met the King. While clearing the gardens closest to the smaller of two fountains, a tap on the shoulder announced the arrival.

It was a guard who, without looking at the kneeling gardener, announced the imminent arrival.

"The King approaches."

Sivvel dropped his implements, turned to face the fountain and took a knee. A small procession appeared, ringed the area and stood to attention. He heard, but did not see, the King sit on a nearby bench.

"You there!"

A boot to his leg signalled he should respond.

"Yes, my King?"

"You are my new gardener then?"

"Yes, my King."

"Approach."

Two well-armed men flanked him as he walked. A sword left a sheath, pressing flat against his chest when he came close. He returned to his knee once more.

"The roses have become choked here. I spend some time in this garden, and I would see it full of roses once more. Can it be done?"

"It shall be as you wish, my King."

He couldn't see, but he knew he was being approved of. Royalty were like that, he thought. They weren't interested in training, and less interested in waiting. They wanted everything just so, right now. The King was pleased that Sivvel held his station well.

"What is your name, gardener?"

"Sivvel Black, my King."

"Sivvel Black, serve me well and I will make your days here pleasant. You may return to your duties."

"Thank you, my King."

Though his thoughts that afternoon still centred on his girls lost in the world, as he tended the King's roses he was happier than he had been in a very long time.

*   *   *

Jasmine raced across the ocean swell, rising and falling rhythmically. She leapt off the crest of a particularly big wave, willing her spirit form to stay aloft.

Where were they?

An ocean was a big place in which to find one ship, but at night the lights should be visible for miles. No sooner had her ghostly figure sank to the ocean surface she leapt again, looking this way and that for the ship she had abandoned.

She had never been very good at this. She knew some people could 'spirit' themselves from place to place just by thinking it. She had never been able to figure that out, always having to 'run' from place to place. She even heard one person say they could stand on clouds while they slept.

That would sure come in handy now.

She checked the stars to make sure she was still heading east. At least she could move fast. Years of running in the spirit had made her good at that.

Finally, it appeared: a bobbing twinkle, winking and waving in the distance.

Please let that be them!

Her legs stretched, increasing every bound. The sense of speed was vague; like hearing, but not feeling, the wind rush past. It was definitely them. Familiar letters on the hull emerged from the veiled darkness a moment before she reached the vessel and slid through the corridor's rear entrance.

A huge sense of relief washed over her when she saw Assara and her sister huddled together in sleep. She was not sure what she would feel when she caught them, but she had not expected that. Guilt, certainly. Sorrow, possibly.

Above Assara, scratched into the wall was the letter J. It was the only letter Assara knew how to write, thanks to her instruction. Despite her leaving, Assara had left it as a message, a way to reach out to her despite the distance.

Hence her relief.

Jasmine's sobs woke her, snapping her back to her body in Safar. She purposed then in her heart, a promise to herself:

I will come for you, sister.

*   *   *

Jonah spent the day in a haze. After another hour or two alone in his room he finally made his way above decks, not yet ready to face his men.

The sailors were surprisingly compassionate, perhaps more so for the gratitude at not having to fight the intimidating group of warriors. In the afternoon the captain had approached with an offer of rum. He did his best to be polite when he declined.

As the sun sank and the wind turned chill his men began to wake and speak of the funeral procession Jonah hadn't been able to face. They were taking their evening meal on deck, slowly allowing their grief to become a fond remembrance. Rahim waved him over. Reluctantly he approached.

The chatter slowed as he approached, then stopped altogether. He felt he should say something, but had no words for this. He was hurting more than his men, yet they were the ones who wished to rush home and complete their mourning. For a moment or two he just stood, facing his men, they in turn regarding him.

One stood, approached and placed a hand on his shoulder. "Peace." The warrior said, then returned to his seat. Another repeated the gesture, then another. Before long a swarm of warriors surrounded him, each uttering the traditional commiseration when one has lost family. Rahim waited until all had had a chance to pay their respects.

"Peace, cousin. Did you see the procession at all?"

"I did not. I could not sleep."

"His honour was great. He will be remembered." Rahim paused before continuing. "He loved you like a son."

"Both of us."

Jonah finally began to relax. He managed to get some food down and retired soon after, lack of sleep finally overpowering him. As soon as his spirit rose, he was with her.

Immediately he saw it; the letter scratched above her head. His Engsam was still terrible, but he was nearly certain he recognised the character.

It was a 'J', the first letter of his name.

His pulse quickened so much he woke himself up. How could this be? She couldn't possibly know his name, she wouldn't know he existed before the docks...

But then, he knew her name...

He needed to walk off some anxiety so he headed on deck again. The world was becoming a strange place. He tried not to believe that she could be as aware of him as he was of her. He tried all kinds of rationalisations to stem the tide of desperate hope that threatened to overtake him. It even occurred to him that the message might be for someone else.

His heart would not listen.

Faith overcame him. Faith in some guiding force that had tied them together. Though his head continued to offer protest, he was now open to the possibility in a way he had not thought possible.

Wait, a test. Yes, he thought. I can leave a similar message for her, and if she responds...

He turned from the bow railing to find someone on watch. At the wheel, in the bridge room of the vessel, two sailors watched over the night.

"Hello!" He said, fumbling over the language. The sailors jumped, startled. "Ah, Assara, how you, how I, how..."

The sailors looked at each other, lost.

Jonah rushed to the desk, grabbing a paper and pencil. He scrawled a line, mocking the action of writing.

"Assara?"

"What is Assara?" One asked, finally engaging. "Hang on." He said, gingerly taking hold of the pencil. He began to write. "Is this what you are saying? Aa-ss-aa-rr-aa?" Letters appeared. That was it.

Jonah grabbed the paper, hugged the sailor, and ran from the room.

Now if he could only get to sleep…

*   *   *

Assara saw it all. She saw Jonah wake with a start, then head up to the bow of the ship. She had watched in frustration as emotion after emotion had played across his face. She had followed him to the bridge, and watched him speak to the sailors there. Though the words were muffled and vague, watching mouths form what seemed to be her name had nearly woken her.

Watching them write her name had woken her.

He knew her name! How could he possibly know her name? Hands rushing to her mouth could not hide her smile. Suddenly the fact that they had crossed paths only to be separated once more seemed insignificant.

He knew her. At least, he knew of her.

Her mind raced, trying to make sense of the revelation. How? He was a captain in a distant army, a world away from her own. How?

But then, how had she found him?

Could Jasmine have told him? No, even if their paths crossed, he wouldn't know Jasmine. Assara had never even spoken about Jonah with her.

Then how?

Again, she asked herself, how had she found him? The question had seemed unimportant before, as she had thought her feelings for Jonah to be inconsequential, something that would amount to nothing.

But if he also saw her, knew her…

Did she dare imagine a world in which he saw her as she saw him? A fantasy was one thing, but if this was the case, if he was watching her too…

She turned to the wall behind her intent on writing a 'J'. It suddenly occurred to her that she had already done so.

A small wash of guilt rose, as she thought of betraying her message to Jasmine, but through it laughter broke. Someone shushed her.

Was this the catalyst? Had he seen the message intended for Jasmine and mistaken it as being for him?

She desperately hoped so.

A long hour later she managed to fall asleep. Her spirit woke by his bedside. Crudely scratched into the wall, and misspelt, was her name.

Hope returned to her heart.

*   *   *

By the time Jonah managed to get back to sleep Assara was in full slumber. Would she get his message? He hoped he had written it okay. He still feared this whole situation to be a gross misunderstanding, that he was just a silly dreamer lost in a fantasy. Perhaps it was a message to someone else. Only time, and maybe another night's rest, would tell.

"She wrote your name on the wall?"

Rahim was less confident.

"Not my name, just the first letter."

A cool breeze eased the sweat from his men as they drilled on deck.

"So it might not be you she is sending messages to. Could be someone else."

"Could be, yes. Which is why I wrote her name on my wall. I had one of the sailors show me how last night."

"Wrote her name on the wall?"

"Yes."

Rahim placed a hand on his shoulder. He grinned, then laughed. "Who are you?"

"This is serious!"

"Okay, cousin, I'm sorry. Have you thought this through, though? She is headed to Bandarat, and will be sold. You are headed to South Harbour, to fulfil your oath of service. Even if she is reaching out to you, you will be many weeks away from each other. You're not suggesting we turn our backs on honour and kill all these nice men, are you?"

Despite the sailors not understanding the language, a few looked over nervously.

"No."

"Watching her live as a slave will not be easy. The Shareef was hard enough, and Bandarat will be in chaos now that he is gone."

"I know, I know, you're right. But I can't give up hope. Something is at work here, something I don't understand. I don't know how, but I have to believe we can find a way to reach each other."

Rahim sighed, his expression suddenly serious. "I can see there is no reasoning with you. The very definition of love, if ever there was one. This will be hard on you cousin, so I will do what I can to support you."

"Thank you."

"In the meantime?" Rahim questioned, gesturing to the ship and the mix of men on board.

"In the meantime? I really need to practise my Engsam."

*   *   *

Sivvel's back complained as he slowly transferred the gravel from the wheelbarrow to the garden bed surrounding the white rose. He could not manage a shovel, so he used a trowel instead. It was slow work, but it would mean being able to work again tomorrow.

He hadn't gotten much further than this garden. He was only one man, and an older man at that. If he weeded all if the grounds before he planted, he feared he would never stop weeding. Thankfully his encounter with the King had given him guidance into ensuring his efforts were satisfactory.

The sun was high but carried less warmth than the previous day. Autumn was in full swing. He was not sure how the roses would fare over winter, but he did have a trick or two up his sleeves. He had begun transporting the hardier plants to more spaces in the garden, which had cost him a variety of roses whose colour bordered on pink, but would mean a better overall harvest when spring arrived.

Shortly after noon a soldier appeared, repeating the request of the previous day. Once Sivvel was prostrate, the King entered the garden.

As the dignitary sat, he regarded Sivvel warmly. "Please, continue."

"Yes, my King."

A few minutes passed this way, Sivvel clearing the ground around his transplanted roses, the King sitting in silence. Finally, the only one who could speak, did so.

"Mr Black, I see you are favouring the darker varieties?"

"Yes, my King. If it please you, they seem hardier, and darker colours generally survive the winter better as they can bleed more heat from the sun."

"I see."

Another pause.

"The Queen, she prefers the pink."

"Apologies, my King." Sivvel replied innocently. "Shall I save some?"

"No."

The next few days followed in the same way. The King would visit and sit for a while, exchange some pleasantries about plants or the weather, then leave. The old slave-turned-gardener found himself quite enjoying the company.

On the fourth day it rained, delaying Sivvel's labour and the King's visit to the garden. It was four or five in the afternoon before, once again, the two began their daily ritual.

"Mr Black?"

"Yes, my King?"

"Join me a moment."

Sivvel carefully placed his trowel in the wheelbarrow, dusted off his grass stained trousers and slowly approached. A disdainful gesture from the monarch caused his retinue to retreat a little, affording them a measure of privacy.

"I tire of it, you know." He began, suddenly sounding less like a king and more like a man. "I can't remember the last time I was alone." He chuckled, a gurgling sound that came more from his belly than his lungs. "Believe it or not, this is as far away as they will go. It doesn't matter how I order them, or how I curse at them or even what I throw at them." He laughed then, and despite Sivvel trying to remain respectful he snorted a little himself.

"I am certain the burdens of ruling are many, my King."

"You are wise, Mr Black."

"I wish that were so."

"Yes!" The sudden change in tone made Sivvel jump a little. "Such is the burden of age, is it not? Suddenly, no matter how much you learn, somehow you feel... a little foolish..."

"I know how you feel, my King. Getting to the end of one's life makes one look back, and looking back inevitably leads to dwelling on mistakes, missed opportunities, the loss of loved ones. It is hard to feel anything but foolish then."

"Indeed, my good fellow. Indeed."

Another moment passed. Sivvel was a little unsure of himself, so he thought it best to wait patiently for his superior to lead.

"The Queen is plotting to kill me."

Mothers embrace! He thought. "Ah, surely not, my King!"

"Yes, yes, I am quite certain. There has been little love between us for many years, and I am much older than she. I think this may have been her plan for a very long time, perhaps as long as we have been together."

"But, how can you be sure?"

"She tells me herself when she looks at me. She thinks she hides it when she smiles, but I see the hate, the murderous intent. You know what the strangest part is?"

Sivvel shook his head.

"I think I am ready to die. I think of slipping away quietly and the thought brings me peace. Oh, don't look at me like that!"

"Apologies, my King..."

"Oh enough already. Just once I would like to speak with someone as a friend."

Sivvel thought of spewing clichéd commiseration and protests, but decided against it. "Are you really that unhappy?"

Through a sigh the King's confession began. "I no longer know the man I see in the mirror. I am angry, so angry, much of the time. And I am tired. Tired of watching people starve, and fight, and being powerless to do anything about it. It is too much. Too much to put on the shoulders of one man."

"I am - aware - you fathered no children." He began cautiously. "Who will rule in your stead? The Queen?"

Moments passed without an answer. The monarch stood.

"Keep up the good work, Mr Black."

"Thank you, my King."

He did not visit again.

*　　*　　*

"Do you, ah, are you represented?"

"Wouldn't you like to know...?" Jasmine replied, squeezing every ounce of seduction she could manage from the words.

She was not beaten yet. There were other ways to manipulate men, she just had to find the right method for the right man. Today had been spent in the inn, the same inn the name 'Heron' had brought her to the previous day. Though she could not make coin that way, she could at least get some food. And get drunk.

Most men had lost interest in the game after one or two drinks. This latest target was far more gullible. Dangling the carrot in front of him had resulted in a decent meal and some fortified wine. Maybe there was one man in this forsaken place who still thought getting a girl drunk was the only prerequisite for sex.

"Just tell me! Then we can get out of here." His hand caressed her thigh. She did not push it away.

"I'm not sure you can afford me, and I would hate to paint a frown on that beautiful face."

"I'm quite sure I could afford you! Who is it? The Dean? The Marksman?"

Jasmine bit her lip in feigned consternation.

"The Heron? It's The Heron isn't it?"

Jasmine leaned in close to his ear, bringing the lobe into her mouth with her tongue. "I want to tell you, I really do…"

The man giggled, then stopped abruptly. "Wait… I know what's going on here." He stood suddenly, grabbed her waist and threw her over his shoulder. A beer mug clanged to the floor but did not break. He turned for the door. No one turned for their tables.

"Wait!" Jasmine yelled. "Where are you taking me? Hey!" Her hands drummed on his back without effect.

Once outside he turned immediately down an alley and all but threw her onto the ground. Her head thumped painfully against the wall.

"You have no representation, do you?" He said, unbuckling his trousers.

"I – "Was all she managed before the man facing her was clapped across the back of the head with a cudgel. As he fell, behind him was revealed a large fellow in a long black overcoat, despite the heat.

"Always someone thinking they can sneak a freebie. Well, who are you then?" The newcomer asked.

Confused, sore and afraid Jasmine chiselled a familiar lie. "I have representation. The Heron."

"This is new!" He smirked, as gloved hands formed fists atop his hips. His head cocked curiously to one side. "I can assure you miss, you are not one of the Heron's."

She began to protest. He interrupted.

"Allow me to introduce myself. I am The Heron." He removed his hat, revealing a youthful face displaying the familiar signs of age; greying temples and crow's feet. It was a conflict of imagery he wore well. Shoulder length hair hung in a loose pony tail down his back.

She had no idea what this would mean. Lost in-between the urge to run from him and hug him, she sat in the dirt forlornly.

"Now, perhaps you would like to tell me why you have decided to work for me for free?"

He helped her up. As she stood, she saw three other men waiting in the street in similar garb. They followed her and the Heron back into the inn, sitting with them around a table sectioned off from the rest. Not a one among them would have been less than six feet tall, with shoulders to match.

Water and whiskey appeared with some dried fruit and nuts. The Heron gestured, and Jasmine took some water. She was still very drunk.

"So, is this your way of requesting to join my staff?"

She was quickly deciding on whether there would be any advantage to lying. Most ideas quickly turned to mud.

Man, she was drunk.

"I escaped from a slaver." She drawled. "It was taking myself, and maybe a hundred other woman kidnapped from South Harbour east."

The Heron leaned forward, his demeanour changing noticeably. "This slaver. Is it still heading east?"

"Yes." She slurred through some pitted dates.

"A hundred slaves… Your captors, how were they dressed?"

"Sailors, officers. Military men."

"King's men?"

"Yes."

"The King selling slaves in Bandarat… how odd…"

One of his men chimed in. "Bandarat is leaderless. Those slaves will be as good as lost."

"The King will send word to have the slaves returned." Another spoke.

"The King does not advocate slavery, at least not publicly. He is having a hard enough time maintaining loyalty among his people as it is. I am surprised by this barter. Perhaps things in South Harbour are more fragile than we thought." The Heron mused aloud. "What is your name?"

"Jasmine."

"Jasmine? I want that ship, and I want those slaves."

Her heart dropped.

"What was the name of the ship?"

Suddenly the lie came easily. "I don't know. I didn't see it."

"Would you recognise it if you saw it?"

"Yes. Yes, I am certain I would."

"Good girl."

It wasn't ideal, but somehow it seemed she had found a way back to her friends.

The next day on the ship was the closest to 'nice' as Assara had ever known. Every day seemed a little warmer. Their captors were relaxed for some reason, and the captives had settled into a comfortable routine of eating and exercise that had everyone at ease. Tamra played with one of the officers, running out from the line as it passed him. The fear of whatever awaited them had been bled away by the many days at sea. How strange, she thought.

She had searched Safar for Jasmine last night, but had not found her. Truth was she had spent so much time with Jonah that she hadn't left much time for a search. Jasmine was clever, and strong. She would be alright.

Jonah. She beamed when she thought of him. Despite her night ending earlier than his, due to her eastern travel, he was still up before she was. He had run a hand along the name that he had carved into the wall. Her name.

Her heart yearned, clenching at the thought that he was moving away from her. However, nothing, not even watching him sail away from her as fast as she sailed from him, could shake her faith now.

They would be together.

Tamra appeared at her ankle, grabbing her legs in a mock tackle.

"Sailors are smelly!" The words were loud, even with the wind and breaking waves.

"Tamra! You mustn't say such things!" She chided. Thankfully those sailors close enough to hear laughed it off, accusing each other of being the perpetrator of said foul aromas.

"It's okay, we're friends now."

Oh, for that innocence, she thought to herself.

"How much longer are we going to be on the boat?" Tamra asked her.

"I don't know."

"Another week or so." The officer chimed in. "Depending on the winds."

Tamra trotted innocently over to him. "Then what?"

He paused. "Then, you start your new life."

"Doing what?"

The officer looked at Assara, a hint of apology in his eyes. "You will go with a new family, and work for them. I am not sure what work you will do. Maybe cooking, maybe cleaning."

Maybe something else, Assara thought.

"We will stay together though, right Assara?"

"Of course we will." The lie came easily, as it was one she was so desperate to believe.

As their time on deck came to its scheduled end, she had a quick check of her reflection in a window. At least she had been able to wash, not that Jonah could smell her in the spirit. Still, her face was clean, although her hair was becoming increasingly matted. Her clothes were also in a terrible state, as she had been living in them for some time now, and there was only so much a rinse could do.

She hoped he liked what he saw. He must, right? Why else would he be writing her name on the wall?

How long had he even 'known' her for? She had been following him for what seemed like months now. Had he been doing the same? She had only just noticed a change in him since Safar. Perhaps their closeness or their crossing paths had somehow revealed her to him. Or had he been following her even longer than she had been following him, and when they saw each other it sparked the change she noticed?

She longed to speak to him. Silly, she thought, he doesn't even speak my language.

But he was learning it.

She laughed aloud, and Tamra hopped excitedly as they approached the section of wall that was theirs.

"What? What's funny?"

"Nothing. Everything." Assara hugged her sister close, the conversation with the officer still fresh in her mind.

"I saw Sivvel last night."

"What?" Assara balked as she sat. "Why didn't you tell me?"

"I only just thought of it."

"How did you find him?"

"I was just looking for him, and I thought to look in the castle, and I found him."

"Tamra!" Assara grabbed her sisters arm and pulled her from the line. "I have told you the castle is forbidden. You mustn't spirit there!"

"But that's where he was and I wanted to see him."

"How did you know?"

"I just did. I looked for Jasmine too, but I couldn't find her anywhere. Have you seen her?"

"No. Tell me about Sivvel, is he okay?"

"He is a gardener. He didn't talk to even one person, but he looked alright."

Sivvel is in the castle, Assara thought. That is good. Surely he will be safe there.

"Why can't I visit him?"

"Well, I'm not really sure how it works, but... do you remember the last night we spent in the Hold?"

Tamra's face dropped. "A little."

"That day, before the explosion, some men came looking for you. You had seen a train get attacked while you slept, do you remember?"

"Yes?"

"Somehow, they know, when we go places we're not supposed to, in our sleep. Somehow they know."

"Who knows?"

"The people in charge. They came for you that day, and I don't know why or what they would have done. That's why you must be more careful."

"I don't understand…"

"I'm not sure I do either." Assara hugged her sister again. It was still before midday, which meant the longest part of the day, waiting until it was time to rest, yet lay ahead.

* * *

It was slow going: the officers describing South Harbour and what they could expect, Rahim translating and Jonah instructing the men. The environment would be completely different from home, which meant their entire approach to engagement would have to change. The large rifles they brought with the explosive ammunition would not be anywhere near as effective in narrow streets or village alleys. New methods of maximising their destructive force would have to be devised.

Jonah schooled himself time and again to concentrate, to invest in what he was doing. Constantly his thoughts returned to her, headed as she was to his homeland. It almost felt like betrayal, investing all this time in a venture so far away. Honour, he reminded himself. Fulfil your obligations, and you will bring honour to the Shareef.

At least he was motivated during the language class. He was picking it up slower than Rahim, but still faster than many of his men. They were less motivated than he, and it showed.

There was talk of a new power in Bandarat. Though it was hard to be sure, some were speaking of groups of Fallsten men moving about; men from the mountainous region east of the city. It wasn't that there had been a battle, or victory parade. One thing in particular though was fuelling the rumours.

Someone had seen Captain Falan with a group of the foreigners, seeming to take orders from one in particular. Authority had been observed, despite the absence of a crown.

It was to be expected, Jonah thought. Well, someone taking control of the city was to be expected. A leader from the east moving in soon after the Shareef's assassination? That was suspicious.

That evening the two captains discussed the ramifications of the power struggle back home.

"The men are fearful that their families will be killed." Rahim was saying. "It makes them nervous that there hasn't been any fighting yet. I have heard talk of Prince Cul. They say he is ruthless, and an expert swordsman."

"Perhaps he is taking control more subtly. If he has recruited Falan, it is likely there will be others." Jonah thought aloud. "Which means he knew the captains beforehand, singled them out. Once the captains follow him, the rest of the warriors would most likely fall into line."

"He killed the Shareef, didn't he?"

"It seems likely. He was very well prepared for Bandarat to be leaderless. He had people in the city, and a plan for a fast grab at control. It fits. Damn it!" Jonah's fist bounced off the small table fixed into the wall. "If only we hadn't been sent on this fool's errand!"

"Don't do that to yourself, cousin. If you had stayed you would be in the middle of another war right now. Yes, you would have had to kill Falan and personally, I would have had to hold my belly while I laughed over his corpse, but after that all of the Shareef's men would have rallied to you, and then Cul would have come for the city anyway. At least this way there will be little bloodshed."

"But we bought that city with blood!"

"We strolled into that city. It was laid out for us on a carpet, as it has been again for Cul."

"Don't you care about protecting the empire of the Shareef?" Jonah said, just a hint of hostility creeping into his voice.

"Cousin, I served him well, you know this. He was family to us. But he is gone now, and his empire will be swallowed by the dunes like so many others. It cannot be changed."

Jonah punched the wall, hard.

"You know I'm right."

"It's not that." Jonah sighed. "I'm just not used to you being the wise one, and I being irrational and hot-headed. Mother's milk, cousin. Am I losing my mind?"

"Insanity runs from you as a lion from a drunk elephant. It knows better. No cousin, you are just being tested. You carry the burden of many, and more."

"I still don't like the thought of letting Bandarat be taken over, just like that."

"The city sees many summers, many storms, and many sultans. How does she even note their passing?"

"Okay, now I know I am crazy, because there is no way cousin Rahim could speak words so profound!"

"You do me honour, cousin!" Rahim grabbed Jonah by the shoulders, throwing him into a bear hug.

"I am still concerned for Assara. What do we know about Cul? How will he treat his slaves?"

"I wish I could say."

With a look of patient support Rahim left. JJonah prepared for rest.

She was asleep, as he had expected to find her. So many nights spent sleeping sitting up, her sister resting on her legs. He was in awe of her strength. If it were him trapped in that room, the fate of a slave smothering him… well, he was certain he would not cope as well as she.

She seemed so peaceful. He looked again to the 'J' above her head and smiled. Had she gotten his message? He needed to find another way to reach out to her. He had learned some basic phrases in her native tongue, but nothing he cared to use in pursuit of her heart. 'Which way to the lavatory' was hardly pillow talk.

What to say? Find some common ground, he thought. We have no common ground, he promptly realised. Tell her it will be okay? No, it would sound hollow considering her circumstances. What then? That I will come for her? That sounded presumptuous, and a little intimidating. I see you? That sounded downright creepy.

Someone down the corridor coughed loudly, waking Assara with a start. Her expression went from startled, to annoyed, to stretching. She must get sore always sleeping in a sitting position, he mused with no shortage of concern.

Something occurred to Assara. A look of realisation leapt across her delicate features. She glanced about, then began straightening her clothes.

Jonah's pulse quickened. She knows I'm here. At least, she suspects I'm here.

She seemed so nervous! Her hands fidgeted, smoothed, brushed. He longed to console her, to relax her somehow. He was, of course, completely powerless to do so.

Then again, maybe he wasn't completely powerless.

He closed his spirit eyes, focusing on his body many miles west. In a silent swoosh he woke, immediately rushing from his bed to the door, down the narrow hall and up to the bridge.

Two sailors, slightly less startled by his visit this time, acknowledged him from the wheel of the large vessel.

"Hello." Jonah said.

"Hello." The sailors repeated.

Jonah gestured for a pencil and paper. The sailor not currently steering the vessel obliged. "What would you like this time?" He asked politely.

"You, are…" Jonah began, then became stuck. "Ah…. nice… nice to…. be looked at…"

The sailors shared a nervous glance.

"What word?" Jonah queried, and made a gesture with his hands that simulated a woman's curves.

"Oh!" The man at the wheel exclaimed in genuine relief. "Our man here is looking for some local tail in South Harbour." His hands left the wheel long enough to repeat the gesture of running hands down a prominent set of hips. A raised eyebrow filled in the gaps. "Eh? Looking for some action, my man?"

"Right, now I'm with you." His counterpart replied. "You are, um, pretty? Nice looking?"

"Come on, man!" The sailor said, hands back on the wheel. "Send him in with some calibre! Write, you are a real looker or, you are curvier than a stormy sea through rum-addled eyes!"

"How is that better? Let's just stick with, you are b, e, a, u…"

"Sounds cheesy."

"Better than your salty pick-up lines. Here." Finally the note was presented to a very confused Jonah. "You are beautiful. Keep it simple."

Jonah bowed his head in thanks, then returned to his room. Maybe he should wait till Rahim could properly translate before he left the note where Assara could see it.

*   *   *

Come on, Assara, relax! You'll never get any sleep at this rate!

What if he is here? She thought. Again and again, the words filtered through her mind. It was the strangest thing! Her whole life she had known that at any time some stranger may have passed by in the spirit while she slept. It was as common a thought as standing outside in the rain invariably made you wet. But now…

She was so self-conscious. She both loved and hated the thought that he could be there, at any moment, watching. She wanted him to know her, to visit her, to yearn for her. And yet the powerlessness of not knowing when he was near!

Well, needless to say it was costing her some sleep.

Relax, Assara. Take a few deep breaths. Let your mind wander. Tamra rolled on her lap, and Assara stretched out underneath her. Relax. Relax.

Like sinking a single inch into the floor, finally she found sleep. She wiggled her fingers to be sure, and sure enough white digits flickered out from her sleeping hand.

Jonah, she thought. The world blurred soundlessly. There he was, in bed, handsome and peaceful.

He had taken to wearing a shirt while he slept. Drifting south on his way to South Harbour was starting to tell in the temperature. He was going to really feel it when he arrived, she mused.

On the cabin's only table, Assara spied a note. The writing was good, it can't have been his. It sat, held in place by a bracelet he wore most every day, a piece from his homeland.

Assara had never been taught how to read, not properly anyway. She could recognise a few letters and words, but one here was long and complicated.

Are, was the second word. The first had 'a' 'y', she was fairly certain. Wyuuooo? Oh, you. Of course. You, are…

B… be…. Boooot…. Damn it! In the second half she spied the 'f'. Ful, that made it. Boot ful…. Wait…

Beautiful? You are, beautiful?

She wanted to cry. His first words to her were 'Assara, you are beautiful'. Despite her living in a corridor, with no way to properly wash, no brush for her hair, no clean clothes… She had to get a message back to him!

*   *   *

Though the dock was misty and cool having not yet felt the warm caress of morning, Fauld was elated at seeing his homeland birthed from the grey. Finally, he could execute the last phase of his coup. Finally, he would take the throne.

The king's sleepwalker met him at the base of the gangway, hooded as always. Trying to seem like a magician or a soothsayer, Fauld thought. Whatever, as long as he knew what he really was.

"Welcome back, Lord Fauld." The sleepwalker said, forcing an element of mystery into his voice, as always. Fauld dismissed it easily. He was in a good mood.

"Is the King expecting to see me?"

"Yes, my Lord. Are we… introducing our policy suggestions immediately then?" The sleepwalker asked suggestively.

"Not yet. One more thing remains. A minor matter."

The carriage door 'thunked' wetly, despite the rain having stopped.

"What reports do you have?"

"Assaults on the rail network have all but ceased. We lost only one shipment of Banji rifles, but have made many more. We have re-taken the contested regions south and south-west of the palace. Two Holds are now being rebuilt."

"What of the King?"

"He takes his meals in his study and visits the gardens most days. He is disinterested in reports of war. He also has not spoken to the Queen in days."

Fauld's pace quickened at the thought of her. She was exquisite, perfection in both woman and ruler. "Has she asked to see me?"

"No, my Lord."

As much as it galled him that she did not pursue him, he had to admit it was smart. The king could have him killed for less.

"What of the people? How do they sleep?"

"The people are afraid, my Lord. They stay close to home, watching the borders of their properties as they rest. Some even sleep in shifts."

"Good. They will welcome my changes." His gaze revealed his coded message. The sleepwalker nodded his understanding.

A little over an hour later Fauld snapped his legs together in as sincere an attention as he could muster, considering he was saluting the man he would be killing in a few days.

"You have returned." The king said, nonchalantly chewing minted roast lamb.

"My mission was a success. We are repelling the rebellion using the Banji rifles bartered from the late Shareef. The new ruler in Bandarat, Prince Cul, has already drafted trade agreements, which I will peruse and approve, once you grant me extended trading powers…"

The king's chewing paused, his knife suspended an inch from the table. Had he overstepped his bounds?

"Extended trading powers?"

"Yes, my King." Fauld opened his palms. "Similar to those drafted for trade in Safar. New ruler, new district, new challenges, I'm afraid. A solid contract now will dissuade further conflict."

Many emotions played across the king's face then. Fauld tensed despite himself. *He knows something…*

"Bring me the contract." With that, the meal resumed. Fauld exhaled slowly. He bowed quickly, leaving with a barely contained haste.

*　　*　　*

The Heron's ship was fast. Sleek, and lean, she made full use of the two masts and the leading sail; a spinnaker that dragged them east along the swell as a child pulls a kite. Though Assara had two days lead on them, it seemed that at any minute the slaver would emerge from the horizon.

Jasmine stood at the bow, letting the salt spray matt her hair. It was safer than associating with the crew. For once she could not predict how any of them would behave. They were men, for certain – they swore, they smelled, and they jibed at one another. Yet despite their origins, they seemed to have a more defined code of honour than the officers of the king from back home. It was the last thing she had expected to find in such a lawless land.

She heard the Heron approach, and tried her best to nod respectfully. For a moment he stood, leaning on the bow railing, ignoring the spray. Without turning he spoke, projecting his voice over the squall.

"You looked for the slaver last night." It was a statement, not a question. He was used to obedience.

"Yes."

"And?"

"I could not find it." The truth was she had found it. She had visited the girls last night, seeking the comfort of their closeness. She feared, however, that losing her usefulness would cost her her life.

"No matter. My scouts have spied a ship with a group of slaves on board. It is called the 'Alexia'. Ring any bells?"

"Ah, I am not certain."

He turned to face her. "I know I seem ruthless. In truth that is because that is what I am. I am not an evil man, though. You fear me, because you think I will mistreat you, or kill you. What you should have realised by now is that I do not throw away something of value. This is how I have risen to such power. It is how I inspire such loyalty. Ruthless I may be, but I protect what I value." He stepped in closer. "You, my dear, have value. You need not fear me, only fear disappointing me. I reward the faithful, you see."

He smiled at her, a strange expression that almost showed genuine concern but also revealed something to be feared, despite his assurances. Full of purpose and self-confidence, he turned and strode away.

She feared him now more than ever.

Last night had brought her some hope. They were indeed close to the Alexia, and Assara and Tamra seemed to be doing alright. They both rested well under the watchful 'J' carved above them, a physical reminder of Jasmine's ephemeral presence.

A bell clanged loudly from the crow's nest. Crew scrambled this way and that, taking to the masts and railings. Jasmine felt the vessel shift slightly underneath her, its bow fighting the waves to match the pointed finger of the crewman above the deck.

Was it them? Her eyes clawed the horizon. From tiptoes and the crest of a wave miles and miles of sea came into view, but no ship. She checked the crow's nest: yes, the sailor there was still pointing over the bow. Something was out there.

Another tug from the ocean breeze brought them again atop a wave's crest. Something glittered. It was too far away to distinguish, but it was definitely a ship.

"Jasmine!" His voice was terrifyingly authoritative.

"Yes, ah, Heron?"

"Yes, my Lord Heron." He corrected. "Stay right there until you can tell me whether or not that is the ship from South Harbour that bore you hence." He smiled that unsettling smile again. Her spine shuddered. He spoke to a man beside him, quieter though she could still hear. "Be wary. If it is a pirate slaver we will need to get away, fast."

So the mighty Heron feared someone.

Jasmine was where she wanted to be, regardless of the order. Over the next hour or two every crested wave was a confirmation of what she knew in her heart to be true. That was the Alexia, and she would soon see Assara again.

Which meant it was time to decide what to do when she finally caught her friend. This depended largely on what The Heron had planned, and so far, Jasmine was completely stumped there. He was a most unusual fellow from a most unusual place. Would he try to take the slaver by force? It didn't seem his style, although he had proved when they had met that he was capable of violence. She was certain that he had another move planned, one that wouldn't risk the slaves and cost him the lives of any of his men. Not because he cared for them, mind, but because they were a commodity, and he was frugal.

There was nothing for it. All she could do was consider some contingency plans if things went one way or the other, and then wait to see how it all played out.

*   *   *

Jonah was sleeping, he was certain. Something was pulling at him though, a shapeless hand beyond form but with a determined will. Though he had moved immediately to Assara he was having trouble staying there, his spirit not only being pulled away but pulled somewhere unfamiliar.

Or not… he was back in his room on the ship. His bed was too big, it had become a double. To his alarm the upper deck of the vessel shimmered and faded. Looking down at him was a man-shaped figure, but there the resemblance ended. Enormous black eyes stared at him from atop a gaping mouth, frozen in a silent scream. Its skin was slick, limbs gangly and reaching. Jonah wanted to fall to the ground in shock, but found himself instead floating. A rifle appeared in his hand. He immediately began firing. The creature showed no reaction, bullets passing harmlessly through.

A great beast slammed into the wall above him, scaled like a lizard but a hundred times as big. Wings as broad as the ship stretched wide, as a breath of fire engulfed the creature. Instantly it was gone.

The great lizard regarded Jonah. Despite the enormity of the thing he felt little fear. It became a horse, elegant and strong. It floated down, curled up at his feet, then seemed to sleep. On its back, draped across in great bunches, were red berries resembling cherries...

He woke then, not due to fear or alarm but in genuine confusion. The visions were getting worse.

The next day he watched over his men as they drilled. Sweat warred against the sea breeze which bore a chill fiercer than anything Jonah had felt before.

"Mine are also becoming stranger." Rahim said between breaths. "Last night, while I rode a donkey into battle, one of my teeth fell out. Then I began pulling up grass and stuffing it into my shirt. I tell you cousin, I have never felt closer to lunacy than I do right now."

"Perhaps if it was only affecting you there would be cause for concern. As relieved as I am to know these visions are not isolated to my own weakening mind, I would still like to know what is causing them."

"I had wondered," Rahim continued, "if it was something to do with the water out here. Or maybe the ship has caught some wild disease. Some of the men have seen letters from their families in

Bandarat. The visions are there too and, like us, it is only while people sleep. Something is happening to the spirit hours."

"I fear you're right, Rahim. But that thought terrifies me most of all."

Rahim looked over at him as he finished his exercises. He knew what Jonah's concerns were before he voiced them.

"If I lose the spirit hours, I lose her."

"Peace, cousin. If I have learned anything about your luck, you will fall out of this boat tomorrow and into her lap, or my eyes be turned backward."

The ship captain approached then, nodding politely to the Banji warriors as they donned warmer clothing, having finished the morning's drill.

"Good morning to you both."

"Good morning." They repeated, the words a little over-enunciated.

"My communications officer received some updates regarding you and your men last night. I thought you would like to know." Rahim filled in some blanks for Jonah. He nodded when he was up to speed. "Your men will be working to reclaim large sections of land north of the city which have been lost to fighting over the last six months. I imagine this will suit you boys best seeing as you're more accustomed to the open spaces. There is also news from Bandarat." Jonah stiffened at the familiar word. "Someone named Prince Cul has taken control. I thought you would want to know that Lord Fauld has already signed trade agreements with him, so there will be no further conflict there for your families."

Jonah and Rahim shared a knowing glance. "Thank you, Captain." Jonah replied sincerely. "The men, happy, their families, happy."

"You're welcome. We should make port in South Harbour in a few more days." With that he nodded, and left.

"You are thinking as I am, right?" Rahim questioned. "How can Fauld have trade agreements with Prince Cul already? How did Fauld even know Prince Cul?"

"If Fauld knew the prince before the Shareef was murdered, how much did he know about what was going to happen…? Fauld was the reason we took Bandarat in the first place. He was the one who organised the sabotage of the city's defences from inside the night we attacked."

"Why kill the Shareef, though? He went to all that trouble to get him into Bandarat? For what?"

"I don't know. I know it had something to do with the Shareef's mighty rifles but… There must be more." Jonah replied, mind racing.

"Come. Your Engsam still needs some work."

"Yes, cousin." Even to his own ears, he sounded more determined than ever.

*   *   *

Jasmine's heart dropped. Something was off about the ship, what was it?

It looked the same, at least she thought it did. It was shaped the same, the colours fit, the masts, the hull… what was it?

From the bow of The Heron's sleek vessel she could just make out the name on the stern; 'Alexia'. It was the ship they had been chasing, the one The Heron's men had said it was carrying a load of slaves. Everything seemed to fit.

Jasmine had a sudden bad feeling, though. Her previous confidence at finding Assara had gone, dropped to the sea and washed away in a breath of breaking spray.

"This is the ship, yes?" The Heron questioned this time. He was sensing her uncertainty.

"My lord Heron, I - I don't know…"

"It is a ship from South Harbour, one hundred slaves on board, bound obviously for Bandarat. This must be the ship."

"I apologise, my lord Heron, but I won't know until I sleep again."

"There is no time." He barked, dismissing her. "My men have seen the slaves. Your departed ship or not, I am taking them."

He didn't order her below deck so she remained, willing her instinct about the vessel to be wrong. Twenty men armed with rifle and sabre filled the deck. Their quarry came close, seeming to balloon in front of her in a heartbeat. She could make out soldiers on board, more rifles, more sabres. Her heart pounded, warning her about the precariousness of her position. Still her legs refused to take her below.

The two ships came alongside each other. Mooring ropes with small anchors flew from vessel to vessel. A large group of armed men faced The Heron and his raiding party. How could he be so confident?

"State your business!" An older man with roped shoulders yelled as he walked to the opposite railing.

"You are a slaver headed for Bandarat. You carry the King's merchandise: one hundred slaves destined for the Shareef of Bandarat."

"What of it?"

"Let me rephrase." The Heron continued. "Your distant monarch, an elderly man who has long since lost the desire to rule, has sent you on a mission to barter with a foreign dignitary who has since died. I assume you are aware of this, and as such I have come to offer a trade."

"What trade?" The Captain yelled back, obviously losing patience.

"Your slaves for your lives."

So that was it, Jasmine thought. The Heron was banking on there being no value in the trade anymore. He was hoping the crew would not consider their cargo worth any bloodshed.

The vessels thumped against one another, scraping flecks of paint which fell into the merciless deep. After a long pause, the Captain of the slaver finally retorted.

"You know nothing, Safar'lian dog!" His hand flew skyward, thumb folded against his palm. A shot rang out from the crow's nest above him.

Slivers of wood assaulted Jasmine's face. Screams penetrated her ears a moment before she could make sense of what had happened. The deck had exploded under The Heron's feet. He and half his men were simply gone. A few feeble shots rang out as one or two attempted to return fire. They were quickly dispatched.

Just like that it was over. Soldiers swarmed the deck, yelling, pointing rifles and swords at her. Jasmine cowered, letting them stand her, walk her off the Heron's ship onto the slaver. She looked around for him; for the self-appointed, self-made success of Safar. He was nowhere to be seen.

*　　*　　*

Assara had pondered and fretted all day about what to write to Jonah. Tamra kept pestering her, telling her she looked funny, like she had eaten bad cheese. She had an alright relationship with the other slaves, and knew of one or two who could write. She was not the only one who had written a message in the wall to someone missed. She had so little space though, and so little time. Plus everything she thought to write sounded foolish.

'You're handsome'? Sounded silly, and too alike to what he had written.

'I saw you'? Bit obvious, and at the same time too vague.

'I want to see you, in person'? Also obvious, and not especially romantic. She may want to see him to say I don't want to see you. She had no idea how he would take it!

What she really wanted to ask was, 'how did you find me?' She hesitated though, because she was already convinced she knew the answer. He found her the same way she found him. And how was that?

She had absolutely no idea.

In the end she had resigned to simply writing his name in full, or at least having someone else write it for her. She also wrote Jasmine's name, in case her friend visited and felt replaced.

The new message brought on an uncomfortable conversation with her sister.

"What does it say, Assara?" She asked, as innocently as a babe.

"It says 'Jasmine' and 'Jonah'."

"Jasmine, in case she visits in the spirit?"

"That's right. I want her to know we're not angry with her, and that we miss her."

"Oh."

The pause was long enough to give Assara false hope. Then the question she had been avoiding was asked.

"Who is the other one for? Jo, ah…"

Assara sighed. "Jonah."

"Jonah." Tamra repeated a little awkwardly. "Who is that?"

"Jonah is a boy. He is... a boy on another ship."

"Why do you know a boy?"

The question barely made sense, and yet as soon as she heard it, she desperately wanted the answer.

"I - saw him a while ago, in the spirit. It has been interesting watching him. He is going to South Harbour."

"Where was he before?"

"Well, he was in Safar when we were, and he is from the place we are going to."

Tamra gave her a strange look, then lost interest. "Whatever. Boys are yuck."

Assara sighed, knowing the conversation to be over.

"I saw Jasmine last night."

"You did?" Assara started. "Why didn't you tell me? Where is she? Is she alright?"

"She was in another boat, different to this one. She is coming this way too, like we are. Why did she go away, if she is still going to the same place? Doesn't she like us anymore?"

It was a fair question. Why leave them if only to follow in their wake? Maybe Jasmine had just wanted to be away from them.

Don't be silly, she chided herself. After everything she had done for you? But maybe that had been the problem. Maybe Jasmine had decided they were too much work. She had been very independent.

Assara turned and looked at the name engraved above her head. It was too late to do anything about that now.

That night she looked for Jasmine in the spirit but could not find her. She did find Jonah however, in his cabin, studying her native tongue.

*   *   *

A knock on Sivvel's door roused him. He was not yet asleep but certainly close to it. It was one of the runners, younger servants who carried out the more menial tasks of the palace.

"Sivvel?"

"That's me, young man. What's the fuss about?"

"Your presence is requested."

Odd, he thought with more than a hint of anxiety. Quick as he could he donned a clean shirt, already laid out for tomorrow, then followed the youth into the common area.

Though it was his back that Sivvel first saw, he immediately recognised the king. It was the strangest thing: to see this feared, imposing individual in nearly simple clothing, sitting at a very modest table, in a very plain kitchen. The runner left immediately. They were alone.

"Sivvel." The king said as he turned. Hiding behind him was a bottle of liquor and two glasses. "Will you join me?"

"Of course, my King."

"Please, no 'my King' tonight." As Sivvel sat, the liquor began to pour. "My name is Dowd, and I have not heard another man speak it in over fifty years. Do me the honour."

"Of course, Dowd." Though he was uncomfortable, Sivvel wanted to be congenial at least. "So, what, may I ask, will be gracing our tongues and addling our minds this evening?"

"This, my dear man, is a sixty-three-year-old scotch gifted to me when I first brokered peace with the northern tribes. It has been sitting in a cellar since then, nearly three decades." The King, Dowd, drank then. Sivvel reciprocated.

"God above, that is remarkable!"

Dowd laughed, hearty and warm. "Indeed! Perhaps the only benefit to being king!"

"A drink this fine deserves a toast, Dowd. To what do I owe this rare and prestigious honour?"

The smile waned from the old King's face just for a second. With some effort he forced it back. "Not yet, Sivvel. Not yet. For now, let us drink and, as the songs all say, be merry!"

"As you wish, my, ah, Dowd!"

As the drink flowed the two men discussed women and wine, politics both near and far, the changing world and the one left behind. In a few short hours, the bottle ran dry.

"I hope you're not expecting me to do any work tomorrow!" Sivvel jested.

"Ah, I already gave the grounds staff an extra day off. Figured you would need it."

"I'll be lucky to be able to stand by Saturday!" Sivvel laughed at his own joke, inviting a roar from his drinking companion.

When the laughter died, Sivvel probed anew. "So, come now, why have we raided the kingdom's cellars this evening? Is there something I should know?"

"Well, I suppose I should divulge." Dowd slurred. "We are out of whiskey after all." A gruff hand clamped heavily to Sivvel's shoulder. "The time has come, my friend. The plans are in place. I am to be assassinated tomorrow."

Sivvel balked. "What? What do you mean?"

"You remember our talk in the garden?"

"Well, yes but, forgive me as I wasn't sure how serious a threat you were under! How do you know all this? Is there something we can do? The guard must be informed!"

"Sit man, sit, and forego your panic. I am at ease. I have made my peace with it."

Sivvel's mind raced. "Then… why? Why tell me?"

"You know, I have not really figured that part out." Dowd scratched at the back of his neck. "Perhaps I just wanted one person to know the truth."

"What truth is that?"

Dowd's face went a shade darker. "That Lord Fauld is not as clever as he thinks he is."

"Fauld… so he is behind it…"

"Oh yes, it has been his plan for many a year, power hungry sewer rat that he is. I think I am perhaps not too angry with him, as I believe the crown will be a fitting punishment for him, when the time comes."

Sivvel's jaw hung open.

"I wish you to know everything. I am not sure why, or whether it will make any difference in the general scheme of things, but I just…"

"Please." Sivvel said earnestly. "Go on."

A brief look of relief showed on a tired man's eyes. "Thank you. Are you familiar with my sleep walker?"

"In reputation primarily, but yes."

"Fauld got to him, turned him against me. Sold him this story about how important he was, made promises about how high he would raise him should Fauld ever take the throne. The irony is, had Fauld waited long enough I would have gladly given him the throne, as I have no children. He was too short sighted. Well, first he recruited the sleep walker. Then…"

"Yes?" Sivvel promoted, quite literally on the edge of his seat.

"Then he turned my wife. Oh, I know it was never a marriage borne of love, but when times got tough, she began to look for a way out. Fauld has made her many promises, half of which he will be able to keep."

"Dowd, how is it that you know all this?"

A cheeky smile glanced one corner of the king's mouth. "What I have never told a soul is this: I too am a sleep walker."

"You…"

"Yes, ever since I was a child. This is why I never paid other sleep walkers much attention, I simply didn't need them. I just preferred to have them close at hand rather than leaving them to barter their services to other parties."

"Of course."

"Which brings me to... recent events. Fauld struck a deal to gain weapons for the crown. The foreign ruler he bartered with, he double-crossed and had killed. He also has plans to kill the person he used to kill the last ruler. There is barely a soul he has not double-crossed. His first deal gained him the weapons for war. His second gained him the poison for me. He will put it in my meal tomorrow night."

For a moment Sivvel sat stunned. "This is a lot to take in. It certainly explains the scotch though." They laughed then, despite everything. "What do I do with all this?"

"I don't know, my friend. Something, nothing... I'm not sure it matters. Please understand though that telling you, knowing you know... It brings me great peace."

"Then I am happy to have helped."

Dowd, King of South Harbour, said his goodbyes and retired soon after. Sivvel, despite his head swimming, had trouble finding sleep.

* * *

Through a grisly morning mist, a tortured coastline came into view. So this was Assara's homeland, Jonah thought. He was surprised. He had kind of assumed that where he came from was the hardest place on earth. However, something about the weather-worn cliffs and rocky hills gave a whole new impression of hard earth.

Rahim pulled his cloak tight around his neck. "I'm not sure I realised this before, but I don't much like the cold."

Jonah chuckled despite himself. "Something tells me we're going to have to get used to it."

"Remind me again why we're here? Oh right, to chase a girl who ended up, ah, right where we were when we started."

"Don't forget, you would most likely be dead had you stayed. You should be grateful."

"Grateful?"

"And you always said you wanted adventure, excitement, to see strange foreign lands. Well," Jonah yelled, arms sudden outstretched, "there you go!"

Rahim gave him a sideways smirk. "I'm going below where it's warmer."

For a while Jonah admired the strange coastline as the ship meandered south in search of port. Cliffs gave way to beaches, then the first signs of civilisation appeared. Small fishing outposts quickly became cramped towns. Buildings rose from a storey high, to three, to four. Smaller vessels passed by on their right, manned by men with dark eyes. This place had a pall over it, like it had lost the sun. No wonder the ruling powers were searching the other side of the world for help, he thought.

The captain appeared at his shoulder for what would likely be a brief conversation, considering all the progress he hadn't made in his Engsam.

"Home at last."

The tone of the man's voice, and manner in which he exhaled the words, filled the blanks in Jonah's understanding.

"Ah, away, big?"

"Big time?" The captain laughed. "Big enough. I have a wife." Hands ran down the side of his face, mimicking the flow of long hair. "A daughter." Flat palm at waist height demonstrated the smallest member of the family. "I have not seen them in months."

"Family." Jonah affirmed.

"Yes, family. How about you? Family?"

Jonah nodded, but not in a sad way. "Rahim, family." He reinforced the point with a palm against his chest.

"Rahim? Well, that explains a lot!"

Jonah didn't follow the words, but he could guess at the source of the captain's laughter. He grinned and shook his head.

"He is a good man." The captain continued. "As are you. I will not likely see you again once we make port, but I would like to thank you. I am aware that this journey could have gone very differently."

Jonah smiled politely.

"Thank you." The captain repeated, offering a hand.

Jonah shook it warmly. Left once again to himself, his thoughts as always returned to Assara. They were close to Bandarat now, and whatever fate awaited them there. The thought brought him no small amount of anxiety, and despite him being aware of the fruitlessness of his worry, he could not help returning to it. If only there was a way he could help!

He knew very little of Prince Cul. He could be a fair ruler, or a ruthless one. He was clever, that much was certain. He had taken Bandarat with little to no bloodshed. The city ran on, prosperous as ever, only now that prosperity was the princes.

What would a man like that do with female slaves? Keep them in brothels? Kitchens? Sell them to clans outside the city? It was impossible to tell.

If only there was a way to help. To be close enough to watch, but unable to affect the world...

It did not suit him at all.

*   *   *

Assara had been both desperate to see, and dreading seeing, land again. As tired as she was of life on the boat, the uncertainty of what lay ahead was an even more distressing notion. Her eyes had been opened to the world outside the Hold in a flood and once again she found herself at the mercy of the waters.

That morning the call of 'land' had been made. The slaves had been permitted a break in their exercise to survey the brown land mass peering at them from between each swell. For now, it was just a distant thing, featureless and vague. Soon though...

Escapism brought her thoughts of Jonah, which she delved into with relief. He had not posted another message, but had left the previous one where she could still see it. Perhaps he was waiting for her to say something. It was a little embarrassing to ask one of the few literates to write sappy messages, even if she could decide on what to say. More and more the question which she most wanted answered returned to her mind:

How did he find me?

The answer to that may also help to explain how she found him, she thought, if it could be explained. Seemed there were still some aspects of the spirit hours that were not fully understood.

Clean water and a brush appeared on deck. Seemed they were to be made more presentable before they were traded off like cattle. Still, Assara enjoyed the opportunity to wash. It had been more than a week. Even Tamra did not complain. Fresh clothes appeared as well, and before long the ninety-nine women were as aesthetically pleasing as they could be.

A steadily growing shoreline soon revealed the city beyond. Small wooden ships were all of a sudden everywhere. The slave group remained on deck, grouped in the centre of the vessel. Foreign sailors on small boats spoke loudly, and often. Their speech was so strange, garbled and confusing. People everywhere worked shirtless.

Ahead on a dock more men waited with long poles to guide the boat to its destination. It all seemed a bit primitive; like Safar but more rudimentary. No sooner had a gangway hit than a local rushed on-board firing words about like a broken hose. The captain presented him with a piece of paper, then gestured at Assara and the others. They both approached.

Assara became suddenly terrified. Tamra grabbed her leg as all the women recoiled. The foreigner nodded, then turned and left. Down the gangway he went, his hands waving and his tongue flapping.

Moments later he returned, a small retinue in pursuit. Manacles dragged on the ground, the rasping of metal on wood singing hopelessness with every clang. No-one struggled as they were chained. After more than a month living as a slave, and now facing a land as far from home as possible, there was simply no resistance left.

She may have felt relief when her feet finally met the earth had she not been so anxious. The city smelled, the sun was uncomfortably warm and all her eyes found seemed foreign. Before long the slaves were arranged in a courtyard and appraised. A newcomer, obviously a man of authority, despite wearing the same rags as everyone else, began sorting the women into groups. Assara understood nothing, of course. She pulled Tamra close when the man's gaze found her. There was a moment of cold understanding before, much to Assara's relief, he sent them both the same way.

Again the herding began. Assara and her sister, along with most of the younger women, were moved off first. A pathway led them to a dusty street, filled with people and noise. Animals bayed, chickens squawked. It was all so overwhelming.

A boy was staring at her, with eyes as wide as dinner plates. Staring right at her…

She recognised him… so long ago, when she had first found Jonah, she had been investigating a town here in the spirit, and that boy… that boy had seen her. Could he be a sleepwalker, like the ones Sivvel spoke of back home?

The crowd swallowed him moments before they reached their destination: a bunkhouse, filled with maybe thirty beds. A woman waited inside.

"Come, a bed, choose." She yelled in broken Engsam. The manacles were being released. Assara took her sister's hand and led her to the nearest corner. After a few minutes the now small group of women all stood by a place to rest. The local lady yelled loud enough to frighten everyone.

More local women rushed in carrying food and clothing. It was all laid out on tables in the centre of the bunkhouse.

"Come. Take."

Naturally the slaves were a little shy. When no one moved, the mistress suddenly made straight for Tamra.

Tamra whimpered as the forceful women pulled her from Assara toward the table. Without speaking she quickly selected a pair of tops and dresses, pressing them into Tamra's tiny hands. She then grabbed what seemed to be a sweetened bread roll, and sat that on top. Grabbed shoulders spun Tamra, and a pat on her bottom started her walking back to her sister.

A gesture prompted Assara to follow suit, then the flood started. In moments the table was ravaged.

Five claps sounded from the mistress at end of the bunkroom. She then motioned everyone to their knees. Immediately a youth strode into the room, very assertive in his movements. He couldn't have been much older than Assara, but the way people followed him indicated his station. Another captain perhaps?

"My name is Prince Cul." He spoke, his near perfect grasp of Engsam making Assara gasp. "You are now the property of my reign. You mustn't fear, I will treat you better than your previous slave masters ever did. I will work you, but I will provide for you also. You will find me to be a hard, but a fair master."

It occurred to her that he was assuming they had been slaves their whole lives, but then she realised she was the one who had been wrong. She had been a slave her whole life.

"You have been set aside for duties in the palace related to clothing and linen." The young prince continued, dazzling the group with his eloquence. "Consider this a favour. There are less desirable duties a slave may perform. Serve me well."

His eyes met hers. Suddenly she realised she was the only one looking at him. Was she supposed to not do that? Uh oh...

"You." He said as he approached. "Do you show such disrespect to your rulers where you come from?"

"No, I just, I'm sorry Prince! Really! I am just, very, surprised... I didn't mean..."

"Surprised?"

"You're just so young!" She blurted. "And you speak Engsam better than I do, I just... well, I wasn't expecting..."

The prince smiled, and the surprises kept coming. "Seems you have not yet met a ruler worthy of the position."

Assara instantly thought of Jonah. Her lips, however, had finally figured out how to stay shut.

"My name's Tamra. She's my sister."

"Tamra! You mustn't!" Assara admonished.

"Listen to your sister, little one. Only speak to one above you if spoken to."

He seemed so wise! Maybe things here wouldn't be so bad, she thought.

The mistress strode up, speaking something harsh on the foreign tongue. The prince nodded, turned and left.

"Today, rest. Tomorrow, work."

*   *   *

Jonah and his men disembarked to tolling bells and chaos. The King was dead.

He had been found not breathing in his bed that morning, and pronounced deceased shortly after. By the time the boat had moored late morning, the city of South Harbour was a mess. Some mourned, others cheered, and everyone drank. He, Rahim and the remnants of their detachment were shuffled into a storehouse like cargo and abandoned.

"So Lord Fauld has taken power?" Jonah questioned Rahim who had been gleaning information from locals where he could.

"Yes. First the betrayal in Bandarat, now this. It can't be coincidence." His cousin replied through clenched teeth.

"You're right. Doesn't leave us in a good position, though. We are still technically his soldiers. Without him we have no food, shelter or transport."

"So what then? We help him further his rule? Align ourselves with this snake?"

"Damn it Rahim, I don't know. I have seventy odd men to feed, no money, no clue how to find a bed in this place…"

"Pitts! Damn this place! Damn Fauld and damn Cul! I should be fat and drunk in Bandarat right now, not freezing my soldier off in some pit half a world away! I say forget Fauld. I don't care what awaits us, we should go home, Jonah."

He was thinking the same thing. His decision to honour the agreement of service seemed a little moot now.

"Jonah!"

"Pitts, Rahim, just give me a minute!"

A troop rounded the corner, approaching when they discovered the Banji warriors. Their leader, marked by a ridiculous looking tall hat and feather, stepped forward.

"Who speaks Engsam?"

"I do." Rahim spat more than spoke.

"You and your men will follow me."

Rahim looked at Jonah, who nodded sternly. Reluctantly the group allowed themselves to be led into the streets.

They walked for a good couple of hours at least, trailed by two caravans hauling the thirty-odd high-explosive rifles they had brought from home. It rained the whole time, a miserable mist that clouded the vision and soaked through their clothing. They all had been given oiled cloaks before arrival, but even they offered little comfort against the cold. Crowds ebbed and flowed, congested then parted, each time imparting suspicious glares to the foreigners.

Eventually they arrived at some barracks, cramped bunkhouses ringed by a high fence. They stank of bad food and mud. With little more than a sideways glance, they were left to fill a pair of houses. The rifles were wheeled away.

"We need a plan. This is not what we were shipped halfway around the world for." Rahim began as soon as they were out of the weather.

"What were we traded for? Exactly this. Service to a foreign lord. I don't know what you expected, but it is what it is."

"Things have changed, Jonah, and you know it! We were part of a snake's bargain! I will not hold to it, and neither should you!"

"So, what then, huh? What would you have me do?"

"Get us out of here!"

"Wake up, Rahim! We can't just wander onto a ship and commandeer it! Even if we had the rifles, we are unimaginably outnumbered!"

"I don't care!" Rahim yelled as he stalked. "We wait till night, slaughter the crew – "

"And who pilots the vessel then? You?"

"At least I'm trying!"

"No, you're panicking." Jonah admonished.

"And you are afraid! So frozen in fear you won't even consider fighting back. Where is the brave champion of the Shareef now? Huh?"

Jonah held his tongue.

Rahim waved a dismissive hand then stormed out leaving the men, and Jonah, to their sullen silence.

*   *   *

Jasmine stood on deck, watching Bandarat take shape before her. She had slept well, being afforded a bed for the last few nights. Being back with her own people had meant being able to call on some old tricks to guarantee her some simple pleasures, such as food and a place to sleep.

Being the only actual slave on board had seemed to work in her favour as well.

The hundred 'slaves' the Heron's spies had surveyed on board were not spies at all, and this was certainly not the boat that Jasmine had originally been on. They were, in fact, soldiers masquerading as slaves. Jasmine could only guess as to why soldiers were being smuggled into Bandarat. Considering all she had been through, she was feeling safer than she had in weeks.

She would be traded off once they made port, however. That much hadn't changed. Seemed that was as much a part of her life as the nose on her face.

Searching the city in the spirit last night had not revealed the fate of Assara and Tamra. It was a big place after all. With relief she, at the very least, had not found them at the few brothels she had stumbled across.

Ahead, finer details of her destination became clear. Bandarat seemed more closely related to Safar than her home of South Harbour. Similar streets, similar looking people. Same warm climate, maybe even warmer. It was nearing winter after all. This place had to be better, she reminded herself. It had a ruler, so there would at least be some structure.

She had never imagined she would be glad to see more structure.

Before long the ship met the dock, and her heart met her mouth. The ruse of passing soldiers off as slaves was obviously due to continue as they were gathered on deck for local inspection. A short, wary man ran on deck looking like he was chewing rocks.

"What?" He uttered weirdly to the captain. "What, men? You say, slave, woman."

"Must have been some error." The captain replied.

"We take. Men better. We take."

You're gonna regret that, Jasmine thought.

She was singled out immediately as the men were led away. Suddenly she was alone. People tapped her arms and legs, speaking in a language that seemed devoid of sentences. Someone grabbed her arm and yanked her away.

The city was alive. The street was wall to wall markets and stalls, with barely a door between them. Had she not been battling crippling anxiety it might have been exciting. They were headed towards a two-storey residence, surrounded by well-tended courtyards, at what seemed the centre of town. Jasmine had seen it last night. It appeared to be what passed for a palace here.

It was bigger than it appeared. Inside, the corridors stretched out of sight, as did the courtyard walls. Lush bushes with bright green flowers adorned pools of water. It was quite beautiful.

Presently they turned into a doorway leading to a room adjacent a kitchen. It was a flurry of activity, sounds and smells of food being prepared warred with clinks and clangs of cutlery coming and going. Her escort barked a name.

A heavyset man approached, speaking as he did so. Some garbled words were exchanged. Her escort bowed and left.

The heavyset man grabbed her wrist and again they were off, down corridors that twisted left and right. Outside a large set of doors the man spoke to a guard who disappeared for a moment through them, then reappeared with a nod. Jasmine was led through.

It was a throne room, and the throne was occupied. Her escort bowed so she followed suit, dropping to both knees and finding the floor with her eyes. More words were exchanged.

"You may stand." Came a surprisingly youthful voice from the ornate seat ahead.

She stood.

"My name is Prince Cul. Tell me, are you indeed the only female slave to be brought from South Harbour?"

"Yes, my Lord."

He paused, then continued. "You will work here in the palace, bring in food and drink and take out plates and glasses. Do you understand?"

"Yes, my Lord."

"You may leave." The prince said curtly, turning to some men to his left. She and her escort did so immediately.

Shortly they arrived at a room with four beds and a washbasin. The heavyset man who had been leading her around grunted and left.

Okay, she thought, what now?

Each bed had clean clothes at its end, so Jasmine washed and changed, before seriously considering doing some exploring. Before her feet found the courage, a woman entered.

"What name?" She spoke in an authoritative manner.

"Jasmine."

"I am Utha. I am in charge. Come with me."

Utha led them back to the kitchens and adjoining room she had first been brought to, doing her best as they went to describe how the kitchens ran. Seemed all Jasmine had to do was carry things and not speak. Utha was very clear about the latter part.

Finally, Jasmine was once again in the room, alone. No female slaves meant more would have to be sourced to fill the room, and the other positions. It wouldn't be long, though.

At least she had made it here. Assara was here, somewhere. All that remained was the search.

*   *   *

It had been a strange experience watching Jonah in her home country. He and his men were not doing well. They seemed cold, tired and very lost. The one called Rahim, who was normally so jovial, had turned cold and distant. Jonah himself had lost something; his fire, his spark. She had watched him training local soldiers in how to use the foreign rifles she had been assembling so long ago, drilling them in use, maintenance, posture. She had never seen him look so detached.

Word of the king's death had reached them, of course. At first there was talk about whether they would be safe, now that the one who had sold them was gone. Some talked of leaving before realising it was probably hopeless. Whatever had brought them to this place was done. Nothing could change that now.

There were no language classes, only work. The mistress, a woman named Utha, gave them a crash course in where to go and what to do, then left them to their work. Assara and Tamra would each morning walk to the palace and collect a cart full of dirty laundry, then bring it to a section of the city close to the river for washing. They would then collect the dried laundry from the previous day, fold it and return that and the trolley to the palace. That was it. The clothing they were given had a specific mark on it, which Assara guessed marked them as property and maybe described the job they had been given. At any rate, they were not bothered as they went about their duties.

On their second day Assara spied a group of men from South Harbour. They were working as well, on wood and steel. They looked at her in a strange fashion, not like men who had resigned themselves to slavery. They looked dangerous somehow. She tried to avoid them when she could.

She also saw the strange boy she had encountered in the spirit. He seemed to stare at her when she went past and, though he seemed harmless, his gaze made her uncomfortable. She tried to avoid him as well.

She desperately wanted to leave a message for Jonah but had no paper or pencil, nothing sharp enough to carve into a wall even if she was brave enough to do it. It was probably just the change in his demeanor, but she couldn't shake the feeling that he was forgetting about her.

If she lost him, she thought… well, then she would be no worse off than she ever was. Fated to live and die a slave.

*   *   *

"You haven't talked about Assara for a while?"

"I did not think you were interested."

"Well, we're stuck here for a while it seems. No one in this accursed army gambles, or dices. I am bored." Rahim punctuated his statement by throwing a pair of rolled socks at his cousin. They smelled terrible.

Jonah paused, unsure about how much to divulge. "She and her sister are in Bandarat. Cul has her running laundry."

"That's it?"

"That's it."

When it became clear that Jonah would not go on, Rahim stood from his bed dramatically.

"So all that talk about 'her', all your wild imaginings about some love fated in the stars, crossing oceans to find each other… where did that go?"

"It's not that I have given up on finding her."

"Seems to me that it is exactly that."

"You are full of criticism, cousin. Would that you would be full of suggestion."

"I am, and have always been, the one who says it like it is. You are the one who has changed, cousin."

"Changed? Changed how?"

"You have become weak. Like a babe newly weaned, still hungry for his mother's breast."

Some of the men looked over in surprise. They expected a fight.

"Chide me all you want, Rahim. I am doing what I can."

"You are doing nothing." Rahim dropped heavily back to his bed.

The bunkroom door swung open, letting in a wet gale. One of the officers entered, dripping.

"New orders. You and your men are moving north tomorrow at day break." With that, he left.

Rahim's hands flew skyward. "Sun and stars, what next?"

"You heard him." Jonah called, addressing the room. "Prepare your things and get some rest. Tomorrow at daybreak, be ready to march."

Jonah's eyes met Rahim's. He didn't speak.

In his sleep Jonah watched Assara and her sister work. Tamra complained a lot, it seemed. She was young, it would take her time to adjust.

That afternoon after running the cart back to the palace she passed another group of slaves from South Harbour. They were all men, returning from some errand or another. They looked at her in a strange way. He could tell it made Assara nervous.

It was strange that a boat-load of male slaves had arrived, they had not been bartered for. It seemed unusually generous, unless people here did not value male slaves as much as female. With the prostitution trade what it was here, that may have been the case, however Jonah still sensed something amiss. The men did not move like slaves, or even craftsmen.

They moved like soldiers.

If Fauld had changed the agreement to include soldiers, why were they working as slaves? Something didn't add up.

Early the next morning the march began. Jonah and his seventy-odd countrymen, with thirty of the rifles they brought, headed out into mist and mystery with only a few officers to guide them.

Despite the situation Jonah was curious about the country. It was so dense, nothing like home. Three and four storey buildings stood so close together they seemed to lean over the narrow streets. He didn't think he would ever be comfortable up there.

Soon though, the buildings shrank, then separated. A large wall, with a rather serious gate, marked the perimeter of South Harbour, and the reason the buildings went up rather than out. Grass appeared, thick and dark green. Hills began to rise all around, peppered with sections of rock. Those farms not set aside for grazing were well toiled, revealing rich soil. A cold land, but a fertile one.

The hills quickly grew large but could not hide the huge stone structure that emerged from the weakening mist. Jonah's men, even Rahim, gasped audibly.

Leading out from the massive building, which must have been ten storeys high in places, were houses made of a mixture of wood and stone. It was a beautiful village, rising up from the earth in defiance of things naturally formed.

The officers led them into the town proper. Close to an inn was another bunkhouse similar to that in the city. With barely a word they were dismissed, so Jonah ordered the men to settle in.

"I'm going to look around." Rahim said.

Jonah was expecting as much. "No."

"With respect, my Captain," Rahim intoned, words drenched in sarcasm, "I wasn't asking permission. You dragged me out here, I am going to at least look around. Come with me if you don't trust me."

"I don't trust you. Malden, you have the lead."

The truth was Jonah wanted to look around as well, but he wasn't about to let Rahim know.

The people were the first thing he noticed. The way they moved reminded him of slaves, so hurried and humble. Their clothing was simple and functional, but then he realised so was his. Walking past a blacksmith at a forge was a familiar experience. He felt relaxed for it.

"I wonder if the sun ever shines here." Rahim complained over his huddled cloak.

"I like it. It is a lush place."

"Lush, huh?"

"Yes. Fertile, healthy."

"Seems sad to me. Choked." Rahim sounded serious.

"What do you mean?"

Rahim stopped in the street, thn turned to Jonah but kept his eyes on the street. "The feel of this place, of the people. It is oppression. That's what I mean."

"Things are very different here to home. I have yet to fully understand."

"You have yet to agree, you mean. You already understand, as I do. This place has been under a heavy rule for a long time, and something tells me it is about to get worse."

"Fauld." Jonah spoke, despite disliking the feel of the name on his tongue.

"Yes. A man who will do what he has done to take power, well it doesn't exactly speak of peace and prosperity to come, does it?"

Jonah resumed his stroll. "This I have also thought on."

"We need to know more about him, about what we can expect over the coming weeks, and I know just the place to find the answers we seek." Rahim tapped his shoulder, nodding in the direction of a tavern. Jonah nodded and followed.

The mood inside was light, the space warm from the large open fire. That all changed the instant Jonah and Rahim were noticed. It wasn't hostility they saw in the eyes around them.

It was fear.

Jonah smiled as good naturedly as he could as he moved towards the bar. The man standing there eyed him a full ten seconds before finally speaking.

"What do you need?"

Jonah surveyed the crowd, picked out a drink that seemed more or less harmless, and pointed. The man behind the glass turned pale.

"That one, ah, please?"

The man at the table began to rise slowly, knees trembling.

"No, no!" Jonah stammered. "Drink." He cupped a hand over a palm in imitation of a glass.

"Oh!" the barman exclaimed, profoundly relieved. "He wants an ale! You wants an ale!" The man with trembling knees sat slowly, trying to smile. "Here! And for your friend." Rahim began taking coins from his pouch. "No, this one is free, keep your coin, please!"

"Many thanks." Jonah smiled, with some confusion, before turning to find a table. In his native tongue he said "Talking to these people may be harder than I thought."

Rahim nodded, then gestured to a table at the back where three larger men were seated.

Every eye followed them as they crossed the room. "May we join you?" Rahim asked.

Chairs moved aside, but the men did not speak.

"My name is Rahim. This is Jonah."

Still the men did not speak. After a shared glance, Jonah attempted to break the ice.

"What, your names?"

The fellow opposite him raised a hand. "Jehan, Jard, Bayern."

A long pause followed allowing the two cousins to sample their 'ale'.

"That's not bad." Rahim said in Engsam, slapping Jonah on the back. "Think I finally found something about this place I like."

"You wear the cloaks of the King's guard." Bayern spoke cautiously. "Are you?"

"That is a matter of some debate." Rahim began before realising he was speaking too fast for Jonah to follow. "Yes."

"You are, um, I mean no offence mind... you are not from around here?" Bayern continued.

"We come from the East." Jonah joined. "About four weeks' sail."

Though the three locals looked confused, they did not press.

"Not to worry, my friends, I don't know what we're doing here either." Rahim said with a wink.

"We're here to help." Jonah said, trying his best to look genuine.

Bayern, Jehan and Jard shared a look. "Ah, again, my - sirs, I mean no offence but… help who? The king, or the Four Families? "

Jonah had the word on his lips but something stayed it. Rahim voiced the question in its way.

"Tell us about the four families."

"Pardon, sirs. It would not be well for us to know much of the Four Families."

"Speak plainly, gentleman. Fear no reproach from us." Rahim's tone had changed. He knew he had found the information he sought.

Though one shook his head and the other shrugged, Bayern began. "The Four Families are clans from north of here." He paused to see if his words triggered anything. When he saw that they hadn't, he continued. "Two years ago, they rebelled against the crown. They felt abandoned, in defending their own lands against bandits, policing their own roads, feeding their own people. Some said the more they took control, the better things got. People began leaving the city because the north was safer. When the crown emissaries asked for an increase in taxes, the four families together refused. That's when the fighting began."

"Go on." Jonah encouraged.

"It started at the border of Jenn, a village not far from here, which is also the namesake of one of the four families. Tax collectors returned with armed men, demanding payment. When they were refused, they tried to take the town by force. They failed."

Jonah and Rahim shared a knowing glance.

"The Families massed soldiers there. When more men came, the local militia pushed them back. Entire towns turned to the Four, allowing their army to get closer and closer to South Harbour. The Four might have taken the entire nation, had it not been for the king's artillery."

"Large rifles, big cylinders at their centre, with shot that explodes?" Rahim questioned Bayern, but looked at Jonah.

"Yes. This village was reclaimed but a week ago, willingly surrendered. For fear of these weapons, the Four Families are retreating."

"Gentleman, thank you for your time. We must go." Jonah dropped a few local coins on the table and stood. Rahim also nodded his appreciation and followed.

"Well, now we know." Jonah spoke in Banji once clear of the Inn. "Fauld wants to put an end to this uprising once and for all."

"And he wants us to do the dirty work." Rahim spat. "Where do we stand on this, cousin?"

"I am unsure."

"You can't seriously be considering supporting Fauld?" Rahim stopped dead.

"Mind your words! People here obviously fear Fauld's men, and they will mark those who speak it, and how. No, I do not wish to support Fauld and his cause. But were it our King, and northern tribes refusing their taxes, would we act differently? Whatever ills the previous king was guilty of, Fauld is in charge now. We may just be stuck with him for the time being."

"Jonah! Do not order me to follow the man who assassinated our Shareef."

"We still do not know for sure! And if we defect? What then? Will these 'four families' welcome us?" It was Jonah's turn to stop. "Have you considered that if we defect, we will be facing the rifles with which we have wrought such destruction? And how will we get home without Fauld?"

"That's it, isn't it? You're worried about being stuck here. If we fight for Fauld, once his land is reclaimed, he may release us."

Jonah said nothing.

"The man I grew up with knew no fear, only honour. Where is that honour now?"

With that Rahim walked off, leaving Jonah to his thoughts.

*   *   *

"You there."

Sivvel dropped his trowel.

"Pack your things. You are being sent to Hamtel."

"I don't understand, I am the only groundskeeper."

"King Fauld is removing these gardens and changing the palace staff. Pack your things."

The messenger's tone was curt. Sivvel knew better than to press his luck in these circumstances. He abandoned his equipment and, with a polite bow just in case, made quickly for his room.

In the common area more servants were being herded. Their one defining trait was not lost on him; they were all older. Seemed Fauld wanted a new staff to go with his new crown.

He was not entirely disappointed. His and Fauld's paths had not crossed yet, and he was not certain he could hide his hatred if they did. He would miss the lodgings here, but something told him he would live longer if he left.

"Does anyone know where they're sending us?" A lady asked as they walked to a carriage. Sivvel recognised her as one of the chefs.

"Hamtel, they told me." He replied.

"Isn't that close to the fighting?"

"It was, but I understand the line has moved further north lately. We should be safe." In truth Sivvel was wary of how the people in Hamtel would feel about the crown, as they had welcomed the rule and protection of the Four Families not six months past. Now, to have to bow to not only the crown but a new king? Tensions would be high.

"Why are they making us leave?" A baker named Olf asked no-one in particular.

"It may be best that we have." Sivvel replied.

"What have you heard? Something about the new king?"

"I will not say, friend." Sivvel spoke in hissed tone as the carriage got underway. "For all our sakes, I will not speak ill of our new king."

His words said little, but created much doubt. Doubt enough to create fear. Yes, the more Sivvel thought on it, the happier he was to be moving away from wherever 'King' Fauld was.

A few bumpy hours later the carriage arrived in Hamtel. A slightly overweight official met them at what appeared to be a barracks.

"The King has brought you here to care for his soldiers at this station. You are to cook, clean, and keep the grounds. Your lodgings are this way."

Could be worse, Sivvel mused, as he carried his bag across the courtyard. Soldiers could be hard men, but they could be fair as well. The village was nice, fairly affluent by the looks of things.

Stars above, thought Sivvel! Across the yard he spied a large group of dark-skinned men running drills. It had been many years since he had seen or read anything about the east, but he would swear they were from lands a few seas away. What on earth were they doing here?

*   *   *

An assault of words was all she was aware of. She had done something wrong; stood wrong, bowed wrong, she had no idea. The other server was giving her a thorough telling off.

Shame she didn't understand a word that was being said.

Hands flew skyward signalling the end of the tirade. Jasmine fell in behind the departing woman.

It had been a lonely few days. Three other servers, local women, had joined Jasmine in her room, filling all the beds. At night they would talk and laugh. Jasmine would listen, but could not join the conversation. The women were not rude, they just had nothing to say to her. Nothing they could say to her.

Work had been simple so far. Following literally in the footsteps of her counterparts had been a solid strategy so far. That was until today when some lord or other had asked her a question which naturally she couldn't understand. He had been quite upset when she hadn't done or said whatever she had been expected to. Her throat clenched. This was a strange place. Did they kill slaves who didn't behave?

The mistress entered the room where she and the other servers were resting. Silence fell immediately.

"Jasmine." Surely even the pompous lord would flinch under that tone.

"Yes mistress?"

"Learn this: 'patra'." A rolling of the mistress's tongue made the word sound alluring. "It means server, slave. You. You hear this, you answer. Say it: patra."

"Patra." Jasmine replied, without the rolling 'r'.

"Patrrrra."

"Patarrrrr."

The other women giggled.

"It will have to do." The mistress said through a sigh. "Clean yourself. You are serving Prince Cul tonight."

Once the order was repeated in the squawking language of the locals, the mistress left. Jasmine's roommates seemed a little shocked as they washed. Cul must be someone important. Very important. They were all quite pale. Good, Jasmine thought. This was the man to seduce if she was to have any kind of life here.

Short minutes later the four women were laden with sweet wines and cakes and sent to the dining hall. Jasmine fell into last place as usual, which she was fine with. She should create a better impression that way.

She had been in this room once before, but quickly she noticed how much it had been altered for the prince. Many cushions had been added, drapes hung, and flowers brought in. The scent was amazing. The prince, or at least the young man at the head of the room being addressed by arrogant fellows in flowing robes, reclined comfortably on several pillows. The chairs and tables which had been forefront were gone.

One by one the servers approached him, offered their trays, then moved on to the others in the room. Jasmine tried to note the order; it had turned out to be quite important. Mostly though she was watching the behaviour of her fellow slaves for a clue as to how to approach her seduction.

"Alla Baraket." The first said, before being dismissed.

"Alla Baraket." The next followed suit. When the third repeated Jasmine decided to gamble.

"My Prince."

A tall man next to her choked on his drink. Angrily he garbled something which sounded more like a drowning man speaking backwards. The prince retorted, silencing him immediately.

"You are from South Harbour?" He addressed her in perfect Engsam.

Her gamble was paying off.

"Yes, my Prince." She breathed more than said, dipping her eyes above a half smile.

"*Alla Baraket* means with respect, not '*my Prince*'."

"Apologies, great one. Have I offended you?" Her eyes dripped with feigned sorrow. A youth standing behind the prince snorted in derision. Jasmine flicked him a glance. He was dressed like a server, but in far nicer apparel. Jealousy flared behind his eyes.

"Your flattery is appreciated, but not as much as your adherence to our ways will be. *Alla Baraket*. Remember it."

"Yes, my Prince." Genuine panic washed over her. That hadn't gone well. The prince turned back to his conversation, leaving Jasmine to awkwardly finish her duties.

It turned out to be a long night.

*   *   *

Oceans away, in the secret bedchamber of the palace of the king, Fauld and his new queen recovered from their first lovemaking. Hair still damp with sweat framed a slender cheek, which the new king of South Harbour caressed between breaths.

"You are beautiful, my Queen."

She harrumphed, and turned from him. Though the wine was on the bed stand, she donned a gown and stood before topping her glass.

So the games would continue then? Fauld thought with a smirk. Very well.

"My army moved on the lands to the north as we speak." Fauld intoned grandly, dressing in red flowing silks. "With Hamtel as a staging ground, I will easily reclaim the lands lost in the uprising."

"You kings and your land." Came the nonchalant reply. "Why do you care so much?"

"Principle. Respect. Power." He barked, turning on her. "Not to mention the very farms that bring food to your table and wine to your cup."

"And when will you rebuild the city on our doorstep? South Harbour has fallen into filth! That is where you should be directing your attention."

"You are beautiful, my queen, but your gaze is narrow." Her eyes flared at the slight. He suppressed a smile. "When my conquest of the northern farms and the eastern port countries is complete, when I control all trade across these two oceans, then I will build you a city so beautiful it will live on into eternity."

"Safar? Bandarat? Squalor! How you can have dealings with those people is beyond me." She spat between sips.

"One need not respect a man to profit from him. In fact, one should not." He rounded the foot of the bed. Her eyes watched him as a beggar watches a stray dog. "You will see, my queen. When all the world is bowing to King Fauld, you will see."

He kissed her, but only because she allowed him to.

*   *   *

"I have to send her a message. It's been days since we spoke."

"Spoke?"

"Well, communicated."

The morning was cool, cooler than the deepest winter back home. Jonah exalted in the exercise though. It cleared his mind, renewed his senses. It also helped keep his unit strong, not just physically, but mentally and emotionally as well.

"What would you like me to write?" Rahim grunted between push-ups.

"I am thinking 'are you alright'. What do you think?"

"Not terribly romantic."

Jonah switched to a leg thrust. His men followed suit. "I know, but I also need to know that she is. It's hard to tell how she is coping. All I know is she isn't smiling anymore."

"Very well, cousin, leave it to me."

"Actually, I want you to show me, that I may write it myself."

Rahim rolled his eyes. "Very well, cousin."

The two stood, forming the first of the stretches that rounded out the exercise cycle. Jonah surveyed the camp, watching the new slaves scurry this way and that on their various appointments.

As he dismissed the men to breakfast, he became aware of one set of eyes quite intent on his. An older man was working at seeding some muddy earth. Those eyes had followed him a lot during training. Jonah sensed no malice, but sensed something.

The day was long, and dull. He and Rahim ventured into town with a few men for another visit. The townspeople dutifully avoided them. Night fell and again Jonah wondered what on earth they had been brought all this way for.

Penning his message to Assara lifted his spirits some and, despite his shaky attempt at her language, he was feeling quite satisfied as he drifted off to sleep.

All candles had burned out when the call of 'intruder' came. Despite it not being requested or required, Jonah had insisted on having a two-man patrol of the camp each night. The call was in Banji, so he and Rahim responded first.

They were out the door before speaking, hastily donning cloaks against the bitter cold of the deep night. The call was coming from the armoury.

"The rifles." Rahim called. Jonah nodded his understanding.

"This way!" His man on guard called. "Two intruders have broken in. They have stolen one rifle."

"Lead the way!" Jonah called, taking a weapon of his own.

The camp was quickly roaring into life behind them as they raced for the break in the fence which had allowed the thieves access.

"They'll be too far gone by now!" Rahim called.

"Give me hot arrows, an even spread over the field."

Jonah figured if this is where the intruders had chosen to enter, they must have thought that the meadows on this side would create a good escape. His guardsman began lighting and firing burning arrows from left to right, creating a small but effective beacon at each point it found earth.

The third arrow landed and, as it did, two silhouettes were birthed suddenly from the dark. Two men, sharing the weight of the weapon between them, turned in surprise.

"I know that man!" Rahim yelled. "Bayern, from the tavern!"

Another arrow was notched, but as the bow string met the archer's cheek Jonah signalled the stand down.

"You're letting them go?"

"They don't have the shot for these weapons. Plus, they have rifles of their own. If they are risking two lives for one more, they are desperate."

"Aren't you worried they will pull them apart and figure out how to make more?"

"I have already considered that. They mustn't possess the recipe for the metal yet. If they did, they would not still be stealing them. And that formula can't be discerned from the finished product."

"You hope."

"This will work in our favour. If they are still trying to replicate the rifles, they will be causing themselves far more havoc than we are."

Rahim turned, regarding his cousin with surprise. "You mean when the rifles they make explode when they try to use them?"

"Yes."

He was quite certain that thought should have brought him some feeling of victory. It did not.

Looking for Assara in the spirit later that evening had brought only visions. He entered Bandarat from a ship, but was not alone. Before he crossed the gangway, he allowed an adder to slither past him. The snake slithered oddly, as had become the norm in these visions. Stranger still was his recognition of the adder, like they had been introduced. The city itself was covered with locusts, long dead; an image which would normally be pleasing but instead brought him feelings of frustration. Vaguely he remembered wandering the streets looking for her, but the memory of it was faint. The only other image that came to mind was that of a small boy, cowering but clear amid the confusion.

When he woke, he found he was not the only one rattled by what he had experienced during the night. Nearly all of his men, Rahim included, had their spirit hours interrupted by the bizarre imagery.

"It is getting worse." His cousin spoke as he returned from a quick meet with the others. "Many tried to reach Bandarat last night while they slept. None succeeded. Some are saying it is a bad omen, that our home is about to fall prey to some terrible calamity."

"What do you think?"

Rahim drew a breath before continuing. "I have overheard some of the Westerners. There is something called a 'dream' which they keep speaking of. Apparently it was thought of as a sickness, only it has caused the sufferer little real harm other than missing out on the spirit hours. Now that this so-called 'dreaming' has spread though, more attention is being paid to those who have been living with this malady already."

"And?"

"So far as I can gather, there is nothing to fear. Those who dream do not become ill, their bodies rest as ours do, and the images they see so far have amounted to nothing."

"What is it for then? And why now?"

"Questions that are plaguing many minds this morning." Rahim placed a reassuring hand on his shoulder before rousing the men to breakfast.

Was Assara suffering this 'dream' as they were, he thought? And if so, would she get his message? Or would she slip from his grasp forever?

*   *   *

Sivvel was pruning small trees behind the mess that morning when the Banji approached for breakfast. They were fascinating to behold! The way they moved, their actions socially and as a military unit, their speech and language, everything was unique. He simply had to meet them. He just had to figure out how they treated slaves. He didn't want to lose a hand for speaking out of turn.

Those two were the leaders, he was certain of that. They were the first out of the bunkroom and the last into the mess hall. Always their eyes were surveying, assessing. What was truly amazing was how young they were. Not children of course, but younger than the majority of the men they led. Unique indeed.

As always, the man who seemed to call the shots gave the camp one last survey before turning to the mess hall entrance. His eyes met Sivvel's. A polite smile came easily to his face, then he was gone.

And the strangeness kept coming! Men in command here would never smile at a slave.

He had heard some talk about a break-in during the night. Some were saying the Banji had not only been the first to discover the intruders but had also let them escape. Loyalties were being questioned.

Sivvel resolved himself to getting closer to the foreign captains. He felt quite compelled to deliver a warning, as he could smell the conflict ahead.

That afternoon there was some argument as to who should be changing the linens in the Banji bunkhouse. Trust toward the foreign detachment had suffered since the break-in. Sivvel seized the opportunity, claiming an old man had little to fear as his enemy had little to gain from killing him. There was little protest to a loss of chores, and as such the job became his.

Delaying the task until evening would ensure the men had returned. Sivvel took his time working the garden. When dinner was nearing its end, he collected a trolley with fresh sheets and entered the bunkhouse.

He was seven or eight beds in when the Banji troop arrived. His pulse raced as they discovered him amid their few belongings. However, to his relief, the soldiers did not react to his presence. Sivvel worked on, making his way as quickly as he could to the leaders' beds at the end of the room. When finally he reached the captain's beds he bowed low and averted his gaze.

"Forgive me, lords." He said slowly. "I'm a little behind schedule today."

A hand clutched at his upper arm, gently pulling him erect. It was the troop's main leader. From the bed across from them his counterpart spoke in surprisingly good Engsam.

"Save your bows, friend. We are no lords. Just simple soldiers a long way from home."

"Indeed, ah, sirs? I have read of the lands to the east but my knowledge is sparse."

"My name is Rahim." He spoke proudly. "This is Jonah."

Jonah smiled politely. "Hello." He said, his grasp of the language yet fractured.

"We sailed from Bandarat over two months ago. Your country is pretty. And cold."

"Thank you, Rahim. My name is Sivvel." He inclined his head. "A pleasure to make your acquaintance."

"Forgiveness…" Jonah interjected. "You look, ah…" Some garbled words flew between himself and Rahim.

"Familiar." Rahim translated.

"Familiar?" Sivvel replied, surprised. "I can't imagine where our paths would have crossed, unless you have spent some time in South Harbour in the spirit?"

An uncomfortable look passed across the young man's face. Perhaps the spirit was not discussed in their culture. He resolved to change the subject.

"If I may ask, what has brought you here?"

"We were bartered to the king of South Harbour by Lord Fauld. Now Fauld is the king of South Harbour so we are serving him." A look passed between the Banji captains that spoke volumes.

"He brought you here to fight the Four Families?"

"Yes, although we only just heard of them two days past. What can you tell us about them?"

"Little, I'm afraid. It is not prudent, you understand?"

"I think so." Rahim spoke leaning forward. "And Fauld? What can you tell us about him?"

He is a murderer and a cheat, Sivvel thought. "I would not speak of Fauld, Rahim."

"You need not fear your words here, friend. We do not kill people for being honest."

Sivvel glanced at Jonah who seemed a little lost, but smiled reassuringly anyway.

Could he trust these men? Would they be likely to turn him over to the crown for treason? They had spared the thieves last night but that didn't mean they wouldn't arrest him. Still, there was something about these two that swayed him toward trust despite his fears…

"Fauld assassinated the king. Poisoned him."

Rahim and Jonah shared a look. It was not surprise.

"How do you know this?" Jonah spoke.

"The king told me. He was a sleep walker, though he told no one. He watched, in the spirit, Fauld's schemes. He watched Fauld recruit the queen and other members of his council. He saw Fauld procure the poison and even told me of the day when he would be killed."

"And he did nothing? You did nothing?" Rahim said, incredulous.

"I have never seen a man so ready to die. Burdened by rule, despised by the people he tried to help, betrayed by his closest advisors, betrayed by his wife… his heart was too broken."

Rahim spoke something in Banji. Jonah stood, walking to the window. "The king had no heir?" Rahim questioned.

"No. Fauld took power immediately."

Rahim spoke in Banji again. His words were hate.

Genuine sorrow overtook Sivvel's eyes. "I am sorry that you have been brought so far to serve such a one as this."

"It is worse than that." Rahim explained. "We had suspicions that Fauld organised an assassination in Bandarat, our home, after we left. Our king was also assassinated. Poisoned."

"How can this be?" Sivvel said, stunned. "Can his reach really have grown so far?"

"What do we do, Jonah?" Rahim spoke in Engsam for Sivvel's benefit.

Jonah's fist clenched, but he did not speak.

"We cannot serve this snake brother any longer! Jonah?"

The youth took a deep breath then turned slowly. "Sivvel. Will you, about the Four Families, tell us?"

An explosion close to the bunkhouse blew the door open. All around Sivvel men exploded into life. Leather chest plates appeared on breasts and swords emerged from nowhere.

"Stay here!" Jonah yelled before disappearing out the door.

*   *   *

At the armoury the man on guard was already laying rifles on the ground. Jonah and Rahim were there in a heartbeat, their well-trained men falling into firing groups without direction.

A section of wall went up, showering wood splinters like ocean spray.

"Explosive rounds. Jonah, they're using the Shareef's rifles."

"I know!"

"We can't go head-to-head over the open ground. It will be a slaughter!"

"I know!"

Pierced air overhead shrieked a second before a building to their left erupted. A section of wall vanished.

"What do we do? Are we actually going to fight this war for Fauld?"

"No, not anymore."

"A fine time for you to make up your mind!"

Smaller shot rang out, as soldiers from the local guard ran past, headed for the gaps in the wall. Swords left sheaths everywhere.

"So, shall you tell the nice men shooting at us that we're on their side, or shall I?"

"Rifle teams! Split! We will flank them in the field. Non-lethal shots only! Fire and move, use the night for cover."

Stray bullets brought two men down before they could escape the camp. Once they made the fence line, though, the flames behind hid them from the eyes of their assailants. The meadow grass was long and the night dark. Jonah signalled for Rahim to follow him, staying low.

The rifles gave a bright flash and loud pop with each shot, giving the two captains something to make for. As powerful as the weapons were, everything had a weakness. Ground erupted nearby as Jonah's own men returned fire, halting any advance. Rahim pulled a small round piece of mirror and flashed it back toward their men to avoid friendly fire.

Jonah huddled low over a rise, plotting the advance of the enemy with each flash of light. Engagements like this ruined night vision, but even that was an advantage to the right person. Every time the camp lit up with fire, they moved ahead for a second. Men with rifles passed close by, eyes focused far ahead, searching for the targets, which were constantly appearing somewhere new. A firing team ahead became more and more isolated. Jonah crept well past, then approached silently from behind.

Together he and Rahim dragged two at the rear into the field, their arms closing off the main arteries to the brain on each side of the soldiers' necks. Once the men were unconscious, they approached the last three operating the devastating rifle.

As they burst from cover the surprised soldiers tried in futility to react. Jonah rammed the butt of his sword into the base of a skull, causing the man to drop heavily into the swaying grass. As Rahim wrestled his target unconscious, Jonah levelled his sword tip at the last man, the rifle operator. Rahim repeated the disabling. They grabbed the stolen rifle and searched for their next targets.

All advance had now ceased. Jonah's men were everywhere, turning the ground between them and the barracks into a mine field. Rahim and he managed to take down another fire team before their attackers began to retreat. Clutching two rifles, they lay on the lee side of a crest while the attacking force disappeared into the night, now completely routed. Some soldiers from the barracks gave chase, but Jonah knew they wouldn't find much in the dark countryside.

Due to Jonah and Rahim leaving men unconscious rather than dead, seven captives were taken. Bayern was among them. Looks of recognition passed between them, but no words were spoken.

In the camp slaves ran this way and that dousing fires and tending wounded. Sivvel approached, face sooted and hands dirty.

"How bad is it?" Jonah asked slowly.

"Three dead, seven wounded. Those things…" Sivvel gestured at the rifles as soldiers came to take them to the armoury for assessment. "They don't wound do they?"

"No." Rahim replied. "They kill."

The Banji soldiers reported in. No deaths, but some scoring from near misses.

"That was a good idea, to keep the men moving between shots." Rahim said as he dismissed their own.

"It was. Now they know it, too. If we meet them in the field again, they won't go down so easy."

"About that. Are we going to meet them in the field again?" Rahim questioned, turning to face his cousin. "Will we stay here and hold the line for Fauld?"

Jonah looked about the camp. Bayern and six others knelt in the centre of the compound. Again, their eyes locked.

"No." Jonah spoke with finality.

*   *   *

"You look happy."

Assara took a second to look up from the cart. Tamra rode on top of the clean linen, legs folded.

"I do?"

"Yes, you do. You're smiling. You weren't smiling yesterday."

"Oh." The road angled up, causing Assara to groan with the strain of pushing. "Jonah wrote me a note. I saw it last night."

"What did it say?" Tamra asked, jumping off the cart to ease the load.

"It said, 'are you okay?'"

"Oh. That's nice. What is he doing at that camp?"

"I'm not sure. When I tried to look around the visions made everything blurry. I ended up back here before I knew what was going on."

"Last night I saw a swing on the inside, and a scary lion chased me under a chair. I wish they would go away."

"Yeah, me too."

Her legs ached and her feet burned under her, but somehow today wasn't as bad as the day before. They would be allowed a day of rest soon; she had been assured. She just wasn't sure how soon.

"Hey!" Someone called from a side street. Several men, pale enough to be slaves from South Harbour like herself, waved at her. She did not stop.

Two men emerged and began walking alongside the cart. "You are from South Harbour, right?"

"Yes." She answered cautiously.

"Something is coming. King Fauld has not forgotten his subjects, even as far away as we are. When the time comes, stay close to us, or anyone else from home. That will be safest."

With that the men peeled off and disappeared.

"Who were they?" Tamra questioned.

"I don't know."

"What were they talking about? Who is King Fold?"

"Fauld." She corrected. She was certain that was the name of one of the king's closest advisors. So that was what the other women in the room had been talking about.

Over the last two nights Assara had overheard some hushed talk about the king having died. She had no love for him herself, so had thought little of it. Now there was a new king and he was planning some kind of rescue? Would he take back the slaves and build new Holds for them? And if so, would she and Tamra be better off there, or here?

Seemed to her to make little difference either way. Except… Jonah was in South Harbour. If the new king rescued all the slaves here, they may at least end up on the same continent.

The mood in the palace when they arrived was slightly tenser than normal. Prince Cul was about, walking the halls and surveying the work. Assara tried her best to smile, suddenly realising she was in possession of very dangerous information.

"You." He spoke to her. She nearly fainted.

"Yes, my Prince?"

"Hello Prince Cul." Tamra said smiling. Assara balked, but the prince smiled back.

"Hello Tamra. Hello Assara. How are you both?"

"Fine, thank you, my Prince." Assara replied without meeting his eyes.

"My feet hurt." Tamra said, grabbing one to rub.

"You will have a day of rest soon, little one. The day after next, I believe."

"Can I have some paper and coal?"

"It will be done, Tamra. Assara?"

"Yes, my Prince?"

"How is the mood with the other slaves?"

Her tongue swelled. "Fine, I think - My Prince…." She almost forgot the honorific.

"I heard your King has passed. How have they received the news?"

"Um, alright, I think… the last king was not very well liked, so people don't seem to be very upset, my Prince."

Tamra began rubbing the silk on the hem of his coat.

"What of the new king, Fauld? What do they say of him?"

"Ah, I am not sure, my Prince." Please let it end, she thought.

"If they speak of him, for good or ill, you will tell me." He stepped in close. There was definite malice in his tone. "I see the men, the slaves I did not barter for. I see menace in their eyes. I see them huddle and whisper. They think I do not see, but I do. Do you understand, Assara?"

Her fingers began to tremble. "Yes, my Prince."

He dismissed them then. The very next day they were given rest, and paper and a pencil were delivered for Tamra.

*　　*　　*

Had Jasmine's services been needed that day, her's and Assara's paths would finally have crossed. As it was, she was given rest as the previous evening had seen her attending to a gathering of generals. The upside to such a raucous affair was the palace would be quiet the following night, allowing her some time for herself. Though she had no money, she was allowed a brief reprieve from the palace. A chance to explore the city at last.

In the streets the atmosphere was tangible. A collection of sounds and aromas swamped and swelled the mind. Under cloth awnings people cooked, sewed and sang. Though the cacophony at first suggested otherwise, spending time in the streets proved how together this place really was. There was much less filth than at home, fewer beggars, plenty of armed men patrolling the streets. It was not at all what she had expected. She felt safer here than she had in longer than she could remember.

Hawkers called sales to her in their strange fashion as she passed, which naturally she understood none of. Despite the isolation of not speaking the language, it brought her a strange sense of relief. Normally she had to work to keep people at a distance. Now she had no choice.

Two girls ran around her legs, laughing. A man approached, chiding them gently. He offered some seemingly apologetic words before herding the children off. Jasmine smiled despite herself. This place was strangely inviting.

It was then that she noticed a group of pale-faced men working at washboards. Their look was different. They stared at her as she approached.

"Hey." One called in Engsam. "You're not from here, are you?"

"What gave me away?" Came her sarcastic reply.

"Are you from South Harbour?" When she nodded, he continued. "Have you heard? Fauld has taken the throne. He is making plans, plans for us."

"What do you mean, plans?"

"Just be ready." He replied cryptically. "Fauld has not forgotten about us."

"Okay…" The men returned to their labour so she walked on.

King Fauld? In her experience it hadn't mattered much who was king. Slave was slave. Now that she had seen other countries, she was more convinced of that than ever. So, what was this new king planning? To take his slaves back? It had taken her all of three days to realise this was the best life she had ever had.

She was never going back to South Harbour.

*   *   *

"What did he say?"

"He's moving us north to another, smaller village. Apparently it's our job to push the front line. What should I tell him?"

Despite Jonah's men single-handedly routing the attack the previous evening, their local counterparts were being far from friendly. The commanding officer of the barracks sat somewhat contemptuously behind an oak desk. It was obvious he had expected the order to be received instantly, not discussed dubiously.

"He looks like a man smelling arse and parsley." Rahim jibed. "Better tell him something."

"Just tell him okay. We have some decisions to make, and this is not the place to do it."

It was mid-morning. Jonah was tired. The clean-up from the assault had started immediately, which meant clearing debris, putting out fires, tending wounded. Even after he had found his bed the noise outside had prevented any real rest. Now he had to decide whether or not to defect. He was not in the right state of mind to be making decisions, but they could not wait.

"Sivvel!" Jonah called as they passed near the elderly gardener. "Will you come to us?"

"With us. Please." Rahim added for clarification. Sivvel dutifully obliged. The three entered the bunkhouse and closed the door.

"We are leaving." Jonah spoke slowly in Engsam. "I need - more about the Four Families to know, before, -kill them. Understand?"

"I believe I do." Sivvel replied, nodding.

"We could use a guide." Rahim continued. "Someone who knows local custom, townships, someone who can help us make contact with a representative from the Four Families."

"I can help. Light knows I want nothing to do with Fauld. He is a traitor to the crown, and I would see him pay for his crimes if I could."

"Good." Jonah continued. "My men and I will rest now. We leave after dark. Be ready."

"Very good, captain." Sivvel said as he bowed. He then took a handful of linens to cover the reason for his presence in the bunkhouse and left.

"Order all the men, including those on patrol and clean-up, to their beds." Jonah said once Sivvel had left. "We will need the rest."

He was no stranger to resting during the day. Many times, whilst serving under the Shareef his detachment would sleep during the day in preparation for attacks during the night. He began by slowing his breathing, which slowed his heart rate. He tied a black strap about his eyes, and focused on relaxing his muscles. The fog in his mind began to thicken…

Instantly he was by her side. She was sleeping with one arm up over her head, on her back with her face tilted toward her sister's bed. A thick lock of hair covered one eye, running down the side of her nose to fall beneath her chin. He could tell it itched, her cheek trembled every now and then. His spirit knelt, extending a ghostly finger to pass in futility through the strands.

His hand blurred as a vision threatened to take him away. What had Rahim called it? A dream? Jonah focused on her closed eyes, willing the dream away. He needed to be here with her. Shadows crept and receded to his left and right. Her body shrank from him, then returned. Still he focused on her eyes, picturing the colour as he remembered it from the night in Safar. Focus! He thought. I must stay…

Her sleeping form shimmered, then snapped abruptly into place. Had it passed? His hand remained cradled alongside her cheek. One of her eyes opened, then the other.

She squinted, then focused. It seemed as if she were staring right at him… perplexed, his head tilted without thought, his mouth formed the beginning of a word.

Ever so slowly her hand left her pillow, creeping toward his face. Her eyes were a mix of confusion and amazement… what was she seeing?

Her hand, slightly cupped, crept closer and closer to his cheek. It was as if he was there, finally within arm's reach. Her hand reached his cheek, pausing at the threshold of passing through. The bed fell away beneath her, replaced instead by a violent wind cradling her beneath his embrace. An ocean swept over them. Though they were submerged, they needed no breath.

He gasped as he woke. It seemed he had actually stopped breathing. His heart was pounding madly, his hand was still cupped. He wiped sweat from his brow.

"Are you okay?" Rahim asked groggily. "Did you dream?"

"I… yes, I suppose I did."

"Assara?"

Jonah nodded.

*   *   *

Assara had stayed up late fretting about her message to Jonah. She had resigned herself to a simple 'yes, thank you' in response to his question. It just seemed very, well, not romantic. She had to say something, though, and despite her best efforts, any flowery words or poetic suggestion just wouldn't come.

Frustrated, she had resigned herself to sleep, deciding her next message would have to be the one with the carefully crafted expression of feeling. If she could decide on one. If Jonah actually saw it. Was he as affected by the visions as she was?

Every morning the sleeping area was dominated by talk of visions in the night. The more examples Assara heard of these nocturnal events, the more confused she was as to their purpose. They seemed so nonsensical, and yet they left people with a feeling that there was something profound contained within them, if only they could be deciphered. All she knew was they were getting in the way of her connection to Jonah. She hoped they were not affecting him as badly.

This was where she found herself as she drifted off that night. As always, her spirit woke in her body, ready to begin the night's journey.

She thought of Jonah, expecting to flit from her bed to his camp somewhere north of South Harbour. Instead she became fixed in her body, as if it and her spirit were attempting to re-join. A feeling of intense warmth rushed through her, ending in her head and causing it to swim madly. Not an unpleasant feeling by any estimation, but what was going on?

As she lay her body went increasingly limp. Her cheek began to twitch, and though her hair rested there it did not feel like hair agitating the skin. Something above her took shape in the dark. Was this another vision?

Dark eyes, soft and caring, emerged from nowhere. She would know those eyes anywhere. Focusing on them brought more features to light: cheeks, dark and strong under high bone. Hair that had grown long of late. Though she didn't want to move, she felt quite compelled to reach out and touch those cheeks. Her hand moved sluggishly. She did not care. She felt close to him, closer than she ever had been before.

The room blurred and became noisy. Wheeled machines spouting steam, baying horses and fire came in a bizarre combination of movement and mayhem. It woke her abruptly.

The room was dark and still, her breathing the only noise. Her chest was still full of the emotion of being so close to him. Nothing, not even seeing him in the flesh had come close to that.

Whatever that was…

*   *   *

As Marema-moie wandered the streets of Bandarat, as usual he saw many people in the spirit with his waking eye. His large eyes darted this way and that, doing their best to not follow the ghostly figures as they passed by. Too many people knew of his strange talent already, and all seemed intent on using it. On using him.

Though he was tired he hadn't yet eaten so he walked to the restaurant district, where he knew food would be available soon. There was always food being discarded there, and no-one complained if he sifted through the garbage. It meant fewer rats.

It had been a strange few months for the small homeless boy. Normally at this time of night the streets would be crowded with spirits, walking this way and that, never seeing each other but blending into indistinguishable blobs. Lately there had been fewer and fewer people about, at least in the spirit. Something about the way people slept was changing. Now they appeared and disappeared, talked to things that weren't there or simply never appeared at all. A girl from that other country whom he had seen in the spirit, suddenly arrived in the flesh.

Plus, there were all the other changes. First the fat king from the north had taken over, then the young prince from the west, now the mean king from the other country said he was going to take over. It was enough to make a small boy's head hurt.

The mean king, Fauld, had visited him that day. Fauld was having trouble getting messages to his men here in his sleep because people were seeing visions. That meant Fauld was talking to him again. For some reason Marema-moie could still be found. Sometimes he hated his talent.

He had been delaying passing on the message all afternoon. Now it was late evening. If he waited too long Fauld would seek him out again and yell at him. He hated that.

Some bells rang out from the street. Someone important must be coming. Without much thought the boy climbed atop some crates, then up the side of an awning to gain a glimpse at the people who deserved bells.

No carriages? That was strange… several guards on horseback ringed one man in a brilliant red cloak. He seemed young….

Oh, it was the prince. Marema-moie climbed a little higher to get a clear look at his face.

As the prince passed their eyes locked. The boy's heart clenched a little. The prince, however, smiled at him, dispelling the panic.

"Prince! Prince Cul!" He yelled, climbing down the rail as quickly as possible. The guards stopped to hold him back, but the prince dismounted.

"What is it, boy?"

"There is something I have to tell you. I'm not supposed to tell you, but you can keep me safe from Fauld, can't you?"

"Fauld?" Cul straightened. "How do you know this name? Speak boy!"

"I'm sorry, he, sometimes he gets me to send messages. He yells at me, in the spirit."

"Wait… are you telling me you are a Seer, boy?"

"Yes."

"Bring him! Return us to the palace immediately!"

Shortly thereafter, in the safety of the palace, the child did his best to relay what he knew.

"He does not speak very well." Little Moie said between mouthfuls. "He is hard to understand. But I am pretty sure he said more soldiers were coming."

"You were right to come to me, boy. I thank you for your loyalty." Cul turned to his generals. "So Fauld means to betray us. We were right to suspect his so-called 'slaves'. He is massing an army inside the walls and means to catch us in our sleep."

"Give us your permission, my Prince." One of his generals began. "Let us slaughter them now."

"Patience. They are waiting on one more ship with reinforcements. That gives us three days to turn this situation to our favour. They cannot take the city without weapons, let us start there. We will find out where they have been procuring weapons and where they are storing them. Once they are disarmed, they will pose no threat."

"Then, my Prince?"

"Then they will truly be my slaves."

*   *   *

In less than an hour Cul and fifty men surrounded the bunkhouse where Fauld's sleeping army rested. Assara woke to the sound of armoured men running through the streets. She had not yet found the spirit, affected as she was by her vision of Jonah.

Other women, disturbed from their sleep, began to murmur.

"What's going on?" Tamra asked groggily.

"I'm not sure. Try to sleep, Tamra." Her sister ignored her request, now focused on the hushed speech all around her. Tamra's bed was close to a window. Innocently she pulled the thin curtain back to survey the street.

"Tamra, I don't think that is a good idea!" Assara whispered, rushing over.

"Look at all the soldiers!" Tamra's small finger pressed against the cool glass. Assara saw that they were grouped outside the men's slave house.

The door furthest from them burst open. Men from South Harbour poured in. Some women gasped and screamed.

"Quiet, all of you!" The lead man whispered. Where did he get a sword?

More poured in behind him, maybe ten in total. They moved immediately for the storage lockers where clean sheets were kept. Landry began flying everywhere.

More swords emerged! They were keeping those here? They were risking the lives of every woman in the room! Their prize claimed, they ran for the door at the end of the room, next to her bed.

Moments before they reached it the door flew open revealing Prince Cul's men. Before Assara knew what was happening the lead slave grabbed her from the bed, placing a cold blade against her throat.

"What are you doing?" She demanded as they slowly backpedalled into the room. Cul himself raced in, sliding to a halt when he saw her.

"Release my property, slave, and I will make your death quick." He spoke calmly, raising the tip of his sword.

"More men will come!" Came the defiant reply. "We are not your slaves!"

He took another step back. The steel pressed harder into Assara's neck. She was afraid to breathe.

Cul watched unblinking, holding the man's gaze. Assara's attacker turned his head, surveying his escape route. The action sparked Cul and before Assara could gasp, the prince's blade was inside the slave's head. She looked down at the sword against her throat; Cul's fingers lightly gripped the blade. As the body fell away behind her, he drew the sword slowly from her now bleeding neck. Tamra screamed.

Someone launched at Cul and his delicate fingers became an iron thrust which propelled her onto a bed. She grabbed Tamra, wrapped her arms around her sister's head and hid from the noise and death in a tight ball. In a moment the pleas began. Swords dropped heavily to the wooden floor. Hands grabbed at her shoulder, pulling her from Tamra. She had bled onto her sister's fair hair. It would need a wash.

"Assara!"

A numbness came then, the after-effect of shock wearing off. Her fingers trembled lightly as she was carried outside and up the street. The air was cool, but she was aware of it more than felt it. The palace loomed ahead, a menacing vision in the dark night. Thoughts of a harsh interrogation danced threateningly at the edge of her consciousness. She resolutely ignored them.

They came to a room which looked to be an infirmary. Immediately someone began cleaning her neck. She had bled quite a lot, she realised. Her shirt would likely be thrown out. The soldiers who had carried her here left. Prince Cul remained.

For a time he simply stood, allowing the nurse to dress her wound. When she had finished, she too left. Now it was just the two of them.

"Tell me about the soldiers." He began coldly.

"Which soldiers?" She asked, her voice weak and crackled.

"The soldiers from South Harbour." He barked.

"What do you wish to know? I have not spoken to them since they arrived, although they have tried to speak to me."

"So, you knew they were soldiers?" He questioned further.

"Something they said to me yesterday made me think so." She answered honestly, exhaustion erasing all but complete honesty. "Something about being ready."

"Ready for what?" His tone was growing colder.

"I don't know…" Tears began to well as a fear in her grew. "I did not even know they had hidden those swords in our room. I would never - I - it is too close to Tamra…"

"Your sister."

"Yes!" She said, suddenly desperate. "I must keep her safe from the fights, the battles. I want to be away from war. I must be, for her."

Cul sighed. Another slave girl entered the room with a pot of tea and some cups.

"My Prince." She began. "I was ordered to bring you… Assara?"

She sat up in bed before remembering her neck wound. It ached terribly. It was, however, worth it to see who had spoken her name.

"Jasmine!"

"Assara!" She wept, nearly dropping the tray on the table as she rushed to the bed. Through a rough embrace and the odd sob, Jasmine's questions began.

"What happened? Are you alright? Where is Tamra?"

Cul cleared his throat.

"Oh, my Prince!" Jasmine stammered, composing herself. "My apologies."

"You know each other from your homeland?" He asked, arms folded.

"We met on the slaver." Assara answered. "Jasmine kept us safe on our journey."

"You." He rounded on her sharply, causing her to jump. "Tell me about the soldiers."

Jasmine looked to Assara who pleaded honesty with a desperate look. "We have nothing to do with them, my Prince. They have tried to speak to me but I ignored them. You must believe me! I don't want to go back!"

"Go back?" Cul asked, his posture relaxing.

"They said Fauld would take us back." She paused, and when Cul didn't respond she added "I hated it there. I'll never go back."

"Please, Prince Cul." Assara added, grunting as she sat. "We are happy here, happier than we have ever been. We don't want war. We want to stay with you."

A knock interrupted them, followed by a soldier who spilled a very brief report. Cul glanced at Jasmine, then Assara.

"Rest. When you are ready, my men will escort you back." His tone was hard to read. He left then, and Jasmine embraced Assara once more.

"How did you get here?" Assara asked, grimacing and smiling.

"It's hard to explain. There was a man, a powerful man, in Safar who had a vessel. When he found out where I was from and where I was going, he decided to intercept our ship and take the slaves for himself. We came after you but ended up attacking the wrong slaver. All we found was a ship load of soldiers. He was killed and I ended up here, anyway. I have been searching for you for days."

Assara fought a wave of guilt at not looking harder for her friend. "I thought I would never see you again. I wasn't sure you would want to see me after..."

"No, no, it's alright. You were right not to follow me. Safar was terrible, even worse than home."

"Really?" Assara remembered Jonah. "Did you see any Banji soldiers, like the soldiers from Bandarat, while you were there?"

"No... why do you ask?"

"I, kind of, know one. He was there the night you escaped."

"Wait, you... you know someone from here? I thought you had never been here before?"

Assara filled in some blanks, as best she could. Jasmine's expression was hard to read.

"What do you think?" She asked.

Jasmine shrugged her shoulders. "It all sounds strange, passing messages in the spirit to someone you have never met."

"I know... oh, I better get back to Tamra, she will be worried about me. I will tell her you are here."

"Be safe." Jasmine smiled, embracing her one last time. As they left the room, they found two guards waiting to escort Assara back to her house. Cul watched from the shadows, but they did not notice.

*   *   *

"I still don't think we should leave the rifles." Rahim was saying. "Something tells me we'll be on the wrong side of them very soon."

"You're probably right, but it's the rifles Fauld wants, not us. If we leave without them, he will not come after us." Jonah replied, his eyes fixed on the dark horizon.

"You sure about that?"

"No."

A call in the form of a night bird's 'caw' signalled that the men were all present and accounted for, meaning the prisoners, including Bayern, had been sprung from their temporary cells. Jonah moved quietly off, hugging the rise as he went, leading the first group north into the dark hills. Rahim waited behind, leading the second group, to stagger the departure. The night was fiercely cool, which meant thick fog had formed between the hills. Jonah jogged when he could, mindful that at any time he may stumble on scouts from the Four Families army.

After an hour of marching through farm and pasture he ordered a head count, then went down the line to find their new ally. Though he was panting hard, the old man's eyes were no less sharp for it.

"You will come front?" Jonah requested. "We see Four Families soldiers soon?"

"I would expect so. If you will allow me to lead? I have spoken to Bayern. There is an old farmer's distress signal they use, which should hopefully ensure we are not shot at before we are spoken to."

Sivvel walked, with a slight limp, to the head of the column. Once there he produced a match and a mirror. Striking the match, being careful to hide the flare so as to protect his night vision, he held the mirror between himself and the flame. Twisting the mirror side to side sent flashes into the night, some fast, some slow. After only a few seconds he doused the match, then continued on. Jonah and his men followed.

They hastened on another fifteen minutes or so into the dark countryside, then again Sivvel flashed his message into the murk. This process went on for another hour. Hills grew from rolling to undulating. Meadows became sparse woods. The wind grew a voice.

Finally, as Sivvel doused his match after yet another signal to the night, a response came - from a tall rise to the left, flashes in a definite sequence.

"Friends?" Jonah asked their guide.

"We will see." Sivvel replied, still nervous.

"We will leave Banji here, first, yes?"

"Good idea."

Jonah sent for Rahim. "I take it that flashing was for us?" He queried when he arrived.

"Yes, my friend." Sivvel answered. "Time to meet the enemy.

Jonah motioned for Sivvel to move on ahead. The local was struggling at this point, especially up hill. Consequently, it took another half hour or so to reach the crest where the signal had come from. Finally silhouettes emerged from the receding night.

"You called for aid?" Someone spoke.

"I did." Sivvel responded. "My name is Sivvel. My allies and I are seeking representatives of the Four Families. It is a matter of some urgency."

"And what matter would that be?" A second voice asked.

"Defection." Sivvel replied.

A third party emerged. He had been hiding behind the other two. "I was hoping you would say that." He spoke.

Rahim stepped forward. "I know you. We spoke at the inn. You are Jehan?"

"Yes." Thick, heavy arms crossed in front of a wide chest. "You almost killed me yesterday."

"We saved your life." Jonah cut in. "We led the assault so that no deaths would occur."

Jehan did not answer.

"It's true." Sivvel offered. "I have been slave to the barracks in Hamtel for over a week now. Trust me, these men mean you no harm."

"We have over seventy able-bodied warriors ten minutes away, and six of your men taken prisoner last night."

"We are aware." Jehan interrupted. "We have been following you for over an hour. We wanted to bring some reinforcements in case your intentions proved to be hostile." The staunch man looked to Jonah to gauge his reaction.

"Understood. I do the same." Jonah said in nonchalant fashion.

"Would do the same, he means, were he in your place." Rahim added.

Jehan grunted. His expression spoke contempt. "The rifles, the portable cannons which have of late been poking holes in my farm. How many do you have?"

"We have none." Rahim answered, smiling.

"I am not a fool." Jehan's gaze travelled slowly from Jonah to his cousin.

"I should hope not. A strong fool walks blindly over peace."

Jehan raised an eyebrow.

"It is true." Sivvel said, stepping forward. "They carry bows and sabres. That is all."

The three scouts shared a look. Jehan turned, then stepped close to Jonah. He was a head taller, and an arm wider, than the young Banji captain.

"Signal your troop to follow, and release the prisoners. Know this: you are well into the realm of the Four Families. Our army lies everywhere. If you so much as spit wrong you will be killed."

Jonah remained nonchalant. "Okay."

Sivvel flashed a message into the night and shortly thereafter some seventy Banji riflemen emerged at a run from the lifting dark, encouraging a wary Bayern and his companions ahead. Jehan grunted and turned from the hilltop. It seemed as much of an invitation as they were going to get.

The wood thickened and the pace quickened. Their guides began to trot, then jog along well concealed trails. Jonah picked Sivvel up and piggy-backed him when he started to fall behind. Mossy ferns ringed mighty trunks of red and brown. Occasionally some foraging animal scampered startled through the brush as they passed.

The sun was well on the rise by the time the party slowed. Sivvel, now riding on Rahim's back, tapped his intentions and slipped off. Bayern, having joined Jehan's lead, produced a whistle. A series of blasts echoed through the morning cool. It wasn't long before armed men appeared to welcome them.

"Ho." Bayern called. "Are the matriarchs up? I need a meeting."

"Yes, my lord." Came the answer. "I will run ahead, tell them you are coming."

"Good lad. You, and you. Lead these men to the stables and keep them there. They will give you no trouble." Bayern looked to

Jonah as he finished. Jonah nodded, then ordered his warriors to follow suit.

"You three." Bayern spoke in a deep voice as he began walking north. "Come with me."

*   *   *

Tamra found her rest quickly, but whimpered and murmured in her sleep. She had been very quiet all day, reluctant to speak of the events of the previous night. No child should have to see death close up, particularly in such horrific fashion. Assara pulled her close.

Despite everything that had happened, Assara was feeling relief. Cul had been reasonable, listening and believing her when she had pleaded ignorance about the threats to his rule. He had been cold, sure, but that was hardly a surprise. Then, to discover Jasmine living at the palace! It had been the best news she had received in a long time. She no longer felt alone. Jasmine was clever and resourceful. She and her sister were safer with her around.

As it was, she fell asleep quickly. For once the spirit seemed stable. She stood, rising from her body, then walked around the room to test it out. The spirit was more stable than it had been in weeks! Finally…

Jonah, she thought. The world blurred, rushing by in a silent gale. Tall trees appeared all around. There, just a few steps away… there he was…

Sivvel? Sivvel was with him! She nearly dropped in amazement! Tamra had said he was in the castle, but that was before the king died and Fauld had taken over. Sivvel must have fled. But to be walking beside Jonah and his cousin…

It couldn't be coincidence. She leapt over to the old man who had been her guide and protector and threw her ghostly arms around him. He walked straight through but she didn't care. He was safe and well.

Now, where were they safe and well? A tall, heavyset fellow
was leading them into a village in the woods. Jonah looked confident,
but then he always did. His hair had grown quite long, hanging nearly
to his chin at the front and well down his neck at the back. She
fantasised about cutting it. The thought made her warm. There was
something, though, a clue as to his wariness. Assara walked beside
him, her feet passing through the underbrush alongside the forest trail.
Jonah's eyes moved constantly, his hand just about his sword hilt. He
was uncomfortable, though he was doing his best to hide it.

Quite suddenly the trees broke to reveal a substantial collection
of buildings, some two or three storeys tall. The trail became a
cobblestone road. People appeared everywhere. She had never seen
anything like this. The city consisted of many buildings, natural timber
with stone pressed hard against each other, sprouting from the ground
to the sun above. This place was wood and warmth, open arms
receiving every sliver of the sunrise.

As the party neared a large hall soldiers appeared in number
from all around. The click of weapons being readied carried an echo of
the ephemeral to Assara's spirit; the chatter of demons before a feast.
Her pulse quickened. The spirit began to wane, buildings at the edge of
her visions wobbling and dissolving.

Not yet, she pleaded.

The party stopped at an entrance way. Guards murmured
messages, then disappeared inside to convey them. She slipped through
a wall to see what awaited Jonah. Inside she found an enormously long
wooden table. At the head sat four women of various ages, obviously
people of some importance. Time for Jonah to plead his case, it
seemed.

Assara suddenly noticed a large wooden cross behind the
waiting party. Was that always there, she thought? She was on a
balcony, looking to the entrance where Jonah would soon appear,
though she did not remember how it came to be. The four women were

pointing at her, and though Assara knew they should not be able to see her, the realisation was distant. Her eyes remained on the door.

Jonah entered behind the wide shouldered man. A large hound, nose to the ground, sniffed at his feet like a loyal protector. Its eyes were the spark before a wildfire. Jonah was a boar, his nose tusked and his broad shoulders brown and sprouting fur.

The last image startled her awake. Tamra murmured next to her then sat up.

"What is it?" She said, slightly panicked.

"Nothing, I'm sorry. Something I saw in my sleep gave me a fright, that's all."

"Oh… Assara?" Her sister questioned quietly.

"Yes?"

"Do you like the prince?"

Surprise stalled a response. "Like him? I suppose so… he seems nice for someone who owns us now. Why do you ask? Do you not like him?"

"I, I think he is… he's scary."

Assara pulled Tamra close. "Did you see him in your sleep?"

"Yes." Came the soft reply. "He chased me with his sword."

"Sister." Assara sighed, stroking her hair. "You need not worry about him. He protected us, and I am sure he will keep protecting us."

"And Jasmine?"

"And Jasmine."

"Can I see her soon?" Tamra asked, her mood lightened.

"I don't know. We will try." Thinking of Cul of late certainly did bring Assara a sense of safety. She felt, with no small amount of surprise, that she was owned by someone whom she could trust. Trust to keep her and her sister safe.

"He better protect Jasmine." Tamra grumbled as she closed her eyes. Assara smiled.

＊　　＊　　＊

At the head of an exquisitely carved oak table, four women rose from their seats. Two of them were past middle aged, dressed in flowing robes pinched at the waist, long hair arranged ornately over the ears into twisting buns atop proud heads. The third was closer to Jonah's age, although definitely older, the fourth surprisingly young. All four, through posture and gaze, conveyed the same message: influence, and power.

Bayern led Jonah and his cousin to one side of the table, taking a seat between them and the two older women. It was hard to gage the mood. Jonah was expecting mistrust, sure. However, the confidence he sensed from the representatives of the four families left little room for anything else.

"What are your names?" One of the elder two spoke.

"I am Jonah, of the Northern Banji. This is Rahim, my cousin."

Rahim nodded politely. Jonah relaxed a little, glad for his cousin's politeness. It was never guaranteed.

"We are the First Ladies of the Four Families, and together we manage the northern districts of this nation." She continued. "You may state your business."

Jonah nodded to Rahim. "My men and I were traded as part of a bargain between your late king and our late shareef, our leader." He began. "We have since learned of a plot by Fauld which resulted in the assassination of both parties, resulting in his coronation. At that point we deemed our obligations to him fulfilled."

"A man named Sivvel who is travelling to us, he told of you, and we decided. We cannot fight for Fauld." Jonah added. "Fauld must not allowed to rule. We fight him, with or without you."

"But we would prefer, with." Rahim finished.

"Sivvel is a slave who ran from a post in Hamtel. He will be outlawed by now." Bayern said softly. "Do you wish to speak with him?"

"That won't be necessary." Came the reply. The youngest lady, across the table, had joined the conversation. "How many men are with you?"

"Seventy-three, sabres all." Jonah replied, impressed. The youth was intelligent, and authoritative.

"The rifles, Fauld's new weapons. They came with you?" Another asked.

"Most. Some were here already."

"You brought some?"

"No."

"Can you replicate the construction?"

"Yes." Rahim answered.

"The spirit." The youngest spoke again. "It is becoming changed. The dream is spreading. What do you know of this?"

"Only that it is affecting all without discrimination." Rahim leaned across the table, inviting further engagement with the young woman. "Our men speak of the same difficulties, and of their families in Bandarat suffering as we do."

They thought maybe we had something to do with it, Jonah realised. The timing probably would look suspicious.

"How do your people seal a contract?" The middle aged one asked.

"Our word is our bond." Rahim answered curtly.

"Very well. Swear to serve the Four Families, to destroy the false monarchy, and we will accept your service."

"We swear it will be done."

Jonah had expected to be feeling relief. Instead he felt a sudden wash of panic, like being trapped. Fighting a war here could take a long time. He had not realised until now how badly he wanted to go home, to get to Bandarat and Assara. The women stood, and as Bayern stood to bow Jonah and Rahim naturally followed suit. Bayern then turned to him.

"I will escort you to your men. You will be given time to rest while we adjust plans to make use of you."

"With respect Bayern, I would be involved with the plans." Jonah replied as politely as he could manage. "You know this place, but I know my men. We will be more effective this way."

Bayern grunted. "I will ask."

Sivvel waited just outside the door. "Good news, I hope?"

"As good as it gets." Rahim answered. "They have decided not to shoot us, but to let Fauld shoot us instead."

"I suppose that is about all we could have hoped for." Sivvel sighed as he limped alongside.

"Those women." Jonah queried. "Are they elected?"

"They lead by birthright." Bayern answered. "Their bloodline is their claim. They govern as a committee, so as to be a just form of rule for the people."

"Four rulers at once?" Rahim chuckled. "How do they get anything done?"

Bayern glanced daggers at him.

"Sorry, I meant no offense."

Away from the village proper was a more rudimentary collection of buildings and huts surrounding a field. Jonah's men stood to greet him and his cousin.

"Food." Bayern barked, pointing to one hut, then another. "Sleep. We will call on you soon."

A look passed between the three as their reluctant guide walked away.

"I still like him better than Falan." Rahim remarked. Jonah laughed. "Come Sivvel, eat with us before we rest. Tell us more about these people before we end up on the wrong side of the sword. Again."

*   *   *

Though the dining room was immense and the table within quite small, Fauld filled the room with his ominous presence. Since his coronation even the queen had become subdued around him. She sat opposite him, eating quietly. Yes, she had broken much faster than he had expected. The arrogance which once held centre stage in her marvellous brown eyes was now diminished.

"How is your quail, my queen?" He asked in a low tone. Lithe fingers jerked atop a silver fork.

A messenger strode into the room just far enough to be noticed. He faced the king but did not make eye contact. Fauld felt his pride swell. Finally, he was being treated with the respect deserving of one such as himself.

"Speak, scribe." He called.

"A pigeon arrived from the Hamtel barracks, my King. The Banji soldiers have disappeared."

"Did they take rifles with them?"

"No, my King. All rifles have been accounted for."

"Very well. You may leave."

A bow and a turn very nearly qualifying as magnificent punctuated the scribe's departure. Fauld continued eating. It was then he noticed the queen had stopped.

"Do not worry, my queen." He said without looking up. His fork dropped food as it waved about. "Those savages are nothing without their mighty rifles, and those mighty rifles are now mine. This changes nothing. I had, in fact, expected such treachery from these 'wild' men." His knife wobbled toward her plate. She nodded meekly, and returned to her food.

"Perhaps…" Fauld continued his monologue and his chewing. "Yes. Let this be the catalyst." His fingers wobbled above his head, calling an attendant over. "Send word. Begin the march to fortify Hamtel. Time to take back what the Four Families have claimed. Also, send word to our forces north of Bandarat. Begin moving into the city, twenty men at a time. I want to uproot this young prince sooner rather than later."

The attendant bowed and hurried away.

"In a little over a month, my queen, I will present to you the entire civilised world. Would you like that?"

She almost spoke, but the words seemed to catch in her throat. She managed to lift one corner of her mouth in what resulted in a crooked, sickly look. Fauld continued his meal.

    *   *   *

Assara awoke to the servant's call the next morning, her heart still full of the warmth of seeing Jonah. Tamra stirred next to her, grumbling beneath balled fists that rubbed at her eyes.

"How did you sleep?" She asked. Tamra shrugged and yawned in reply.

Donning the days apparel drew her eyes to her bunkmates, revealing the mood of the room. The women clearly shared her feelings of security. She could see it in the way they greeted each other, the lightness with which they performed menial tasks. No one had expected after being abducted from the Holds and streets of South Harbour that a better life awaited them all here. Indeed, none had really admitted to themselves that they were happier here until their own countrymen had spoken a violent promise of a return home. The scene had brought with it a welcome realisation, one that had united these once separate prisoners under a single banner.

Prince Cul's.

The day progressed as usual after that, sights and smells from the city ever more familiar. Tamra hummed atop the laundry cart, weaving small flowers into a chain. A cool breeze reminded Assara that this was technically winter. It was still far warmer than the land she had left behind.

At the palace she and Tamra looked eagerly for Jasmine but her friend was not around. Assara could not wait to see her again, but was not going to risk their fragile comfort by asking for favours just yet. Exiting the palace courtyard revealed Cul rounding a corner.

Without warning Tamra ran towards him. Assara dropped the cart in a slight panic. Cul noticed the small girl trot near and turned to face her, halting Tamra quite suddenly.

"Are you scary?" Tamra asked with all the innocence of youth. Assara hurried over.

"Prince, ah, my Prince -" She began. Cul cut her off with a raised hand. He knelt in front of Tamra, who in turn regarded him from beneath a furrowed brow.

"You tell me, little one. Am I scary?"

Assara was more than a little panicked, but somehow managed to hold her tongue.

Tamra swayed left and right at the hips as she studied the prince, meeting his steely gaze. "I think you're alright. You saved my sister." She leapt forward, wrapping her arms around his lean neck. Cul's face dropped.

"Ah, you're welcome. I, protect my, property." He stammered. Tamra released him, running back to Assara's side.

"Apologies, my prince." Assara said blushing.

"Please, think nothing of it." Cul said, brushing dust from his trousers as he stood. "Back to your duties now."

"Yes, my Prince. Ah, my Prince?" Assara called as he turned.

"Yes?"

"It was nice to see you."

Cul stifled a smile, nodded, and walked away.

As the two sisters returned to their cart, Tamra skipped and said, "He is alright. He is not scary."

"He is a little scary." Assara returned, giggling.

Tamra laughed. "He is a little scary."

That evening as the sun neared the horizon, Assara and Tamra were helping clean plates from the evening meal when the mistress called them from the room. With no small amount of trepidation Assara followed her outside and across the street, Tamra innocently in tow. Immediately she saw Cul, surrounded by guards. Her trepidation grew.

There, at a table on the street in front of a cookery, sat Jasmine watching her approach. Her friend was smiling warmly. What on earth was this about?

The mistress bowed when they drew near, so Assara copied. Even Tamra managed something resembling a bow.

"You have one hour, and one meal each." Cul spoke. He turned to leave.

"My Prince?" Assara bravely called. The mistress scowled openly at her. When he turned, she continued. "Would you, do us the, honour? Of joining us?"

Cul smiled ever so slightly. "It is not done." With that he left, taking his guards and the mistress with him.

Tamra acted first, running to Jasmine for a hug. Assara did not wait, joining the embrace.

"How are you here?" she asked, grinning widely.

"I don't know!" Jasmine exclaimed as she sat. "There has been no service today, just secret meetings between Prince Cul, his generals and advisors. I was resting in my room when I was called out and escorted here." A woman emerged carrying plates brimming with stewed meat and rice. "I had hoped this was the reason I was here but I didn't really believe it until I saw you. Both of you!" Tamra grinned as she began shovelling food into her mouth. "How did you convince Prince Cul to allow this?"

Assara savoured the warm meat a second before replying through a full mouth. "I don't know?" Came the shoulder mirrored reply. "I always thought Cul, Prince Cul, was being nice in some way so I just made sure to be nice back. After he saved me from the South Harbour soldier, I really wanted to thank him, which I guess I did a lot."

"I thanked him too." Tamra interjected, not wanting to be left out.

"Actually I think that is what Cul, ah bother, Prince Cul, likes most. Her."

Tamra beamed, strings of goat hanging proudly between her teeth.

"So we have your charm to thank for this wonderful meal, my little peach!" Jasmine said cheerfully.

"Maybe he will have dinner with us next time." Tamra commented more than asked. Assara and Jasmine shared a look, deciding in unison to let that slide.

"How is it in the palace? Is your room really nice?" Assara asked.

"The room is nice, but it is lonely. I am the only one from South Harbour serving there, so no one speaks with me. They are nice enough, the other servers. They smile at me, help me to learn what to do. They just speak to each other in their own language when we are not working." Jasmine's fork spun in her rice.

"Maybe C-, Prince Cul, will let you come to the bunkhouse with us?"

Tamra's face lightened at the proposal, but Jasmine's hands quickly doused her enthusiasm.

"I know that you both are feeling good about the prince right now, but we mustn't be too bold. He is still a prince, and can be ruthless. Besides which, sometimes powerful men only treat you well so that, well…"

"So that what Jasmine?" Tamra pressed.

"So that when they come for you, you will be more, obliging…"

"Oh…" Assara's face dropped.

"Listen," Jasmine went on, "I do not think that Prince Cul is that sort of man, for many reasons." Jasmine raised an eyebrow, but the meaning escaped Assara. "Still, favour like this always comes with a price. I think we should be careful how much we court it."

"Cul is nice. He will give me what I ask for." Tamra returned to her meal.

"Jasmine, you're right. We should be careful."

They returned to their meal, and before long the mood once again became light. When the soldiers came to return them to their rooms, they happily obliged.

*   *   *

Jonah wandered the moody streets of Bandarat in the spirit, revelling in the most stable sleep he had had in days. Perhaps it was because of his clear sense of purpose, his moral compass having returned to a solid heading. Perhaps it was seeing Assara and her sister laugh and smile as they worked their laundry route. Either way he wasn't complaining.

He had been told of a scuffle here between some soldiers posing as slaves and Prince Cul's new regime. Some of his men had received word from the families by way of notes left in the spirit. Jonah knew he wouldn't discover much from a visit during his sleep, but sometimes it was the subtle clues about a place, about the people there, that warned you of events to come.

At first, he skirted the blocks and alleys along Assara's route to the palace, reluctant to stray too far from her. The city bustled along as it always had, hawkers hawking, farriers 'farry-ing', if that was what it was called. He had to admit, Cul's leadership so far seemed stable. Or the people were so tired of war that with the coming cold they were more inclined to accept any rule that allowed their way of life to continue. He resolved himself to further reconnaissance, and with more than a little regret bid his love a temporary farewell.

There was little real traffic coming in or out of the docks. If Fauld was going to make another play for Bandarat, it wouldn't come from here. Cul would see it coming, now. More out of routine than suspicion he flitted toward the city gates to check on the situation there.

Again, the scene there seemed normal. Though the gates were open they were well patrolled, with all coming through questioned. Still, Jonah felt compelled to linger.

A cart arrived pulled by a donkey and with three men driving. Through the blurred specifics of the spirit Jonah thought he noticed a peculiar wave from the lead fellow. The cart meandered through the entrance way. It was not searched.

He leapt from the rooftop which had been his vantage point to peer through the cart covering. More men rode behind the cart's coverings. More compelling still, was their fair complexion.

So Fauld was still bringing men into the city. He was not done with this place yet.

It was then that Jonah felt a familiar sensation, one of being watched. Not a feeling one would normally experience in their sleep. He scanned the street, seeking the source.

At first all he saw was a crowd quite indifferent to his presence. The gateway was busy, and many people passed through him as they went about their business. He was so certain though...

A small boy climbed atop a crate, standing to make himself visible. Jonah recognised him immediately: the boy had probably saved his life all those months ago when Jonah had first taken Bandarat. His warning had been the difference between running into a wall of gunfire and completely routing his enemies. And yet... did the boy actually see him?

Jonah approached slowly, in case the child was easily startled. Indeed, it seemed as if the boy's eyes were about to depart from his face. As Jonah approached though he found his gaze held. He became ever more convinced.

"Can you see me?" Jonah asked, his voice sounding like an echo of itself.

The boy nodded.

"What is your name?"

"Marema-moie." He replied without smiling.

"My name is Jonah. You saved my life, didn't you?"

Marema-moie nodded, but still looked wary.

"Do you see what is happening here? The bad men that are coming into the city?"

The boy nodded again.

"Can you warn someone?"

"Warn her?" Marema-moie's head cocked to the side. "The one you are connected to?"

Jonah started. "What, wait, what did you say?"

Bandarat faded slightly. Jonah felt his body start to wake.

"Wait, ah, Marema-moie, are you talking about Assara?"

Marema-moie suddenly looked left to right. His shoulders shrugged. Hopping down off the crate, he wandered into the street to disappear among legs and beasts.

"Wait!" Jonah called, but his words were mist under a noon sun. He woke, back in his body in a tent far from home.

"Damn it!"

"What now, cousin? Miss the end of a domestic? Or were you cuddling up to your distant paramour?" Rahim stretched, obviously woken by Jonah's stirring.

"Did you dream last night?" Jonah asked.

"No, thank the Pitts. I was able to go home. I was even able to stay long enough to warm a fresh batch of curses for you for ever having brought me to this backwards country. Would you like one?"

"You visited Bandarat? Did you notice anything strange?"

"I did. Prince Cul has no Sleep Walkers. Listened to him and his general's talk strategy for hours. Although it is possible they were using coded speech, some of it made absolutely no sense. You?"

"I visited Bandarat as well. I am certain Fauld is bringing soldiers in. I think he has bribed the gate guard."

"We may have to wait another night to warn them."

"I think I already did. I met a child, a sleepwalker. I spoke to him of westerners, armed, coming into the city. He said he knew and would warn, someone."

"You met a sleepwalker? You're certain?" Rahim sounded a little jealous.

"How could I mistake such a thing?"

"You may have dreamed him. Remember that 'dream' thing that has good men leaping from boats in the middle of the night?"

Jonah sighed. "Ok, it is possible I dreamed him. At any rate, let us not wait until tonight to warn Bandarat. Order the men to post messages in the sleeping quarters. Fauld will attack again, from inside the walls. They must be ready."

"The enemy of my enemy, huh…" Rahim stated in a mumble. Jonah let it slide.

A solid knock announced Bayern's arrival moments before the door opened. "Is everything alright?" He asked, instantly noticing the serious look in the greeting eyes.

"Fauld, he is planning an assault in Bandarat." Rahim answered in Engsam.

"Where is that?" Bayern replied, instantly losing interest.

"Our country. He must have, more troops landed somewhere north." Jonah continued.

"Well, you both are here, and so is Fauld. It's time to talk strategy, so get your minds right. You cannot get home to help there until you finish it here."

"You don't need to tell us what we already know, Bayern." Rahim intoned, rolling his eyes.

"Come, Rahim." Jonah spoke as he stood. "We know what we must do. Let us be about it."

Bayern paused, then nodded a little reluctantly. He turned, stepping out into the cold morning. Jonah and Rahim layered clothing as quickly as they could, then pursued.

The mood was as chill as the air. As such, it was a silent march back toward the meeting house where they had met the heads of the Four Families the previous night. Guards at the large wooden house searched them for weapons, taking a knife off Jonah and two off Rahim before allowing them inside. The door opened revealing a well warmed room and a table covered with food. Three of the four representatives were present, eating in an overly dignified manner. Jonah felt suddenly unprepared. Rahim clapped once loudly.

"Well, now we are meeting like civilised people. Morning's blessings be on you all, my Ladies." Rahim punctuated the greeting with a flourishing bow, then immediately began filling a plate.

"My Ladies." Jonah spoke politely, awaiting an invitation.

The youngest, seeming somewhat taken with Rahim's boldness, smiled into her tea. However, the oldest was again the first to speak.

"Jonah, Rahim. Please sit. Eat." The words came wryly from the corner of her mouth.

"Thank you, first of your house." Jonah replied. Rahim nodded, not taking his eyes from a bowl of sweet breads.

"Please, you may call me Lady Jocelyn. This is Lady June." A nod singled out the more middle-aged woman, the quietest of the group so far. "This is Lady Serong." She was the youngest, definitely younger than Assara, Jonah decided. Though she worked to appear composed, her wave carried some of the enthusiasm of youth. "Lady May conveys her apologies. She could not be present."

"Thank you, Lady Jocelyn."

"Please, eat. The food will warm you, and I imagine you are finding our climate difficult."

Rahim looked up. He was about to say something. He changed his mind, returning to his well laden plate.

"Troops have left South Harbour." Lady Jocelyn began, reaching for her tea. "The highway is full of them, all heading north. If we march now, we should meet them at Hamtel. It seems Fauld's attack has begun."

Jonah nodded, mind beginning to whir. "You are committed to meeting him in battle in the village then?"

"Hamtel is the largest urban area for many miles, save for the city itself." Young Lady Serong had joined the discussion. "We dare not face Fauld in the field or those rifles he has will have too strong an advantage over our infantry. If we retreat to the next town, it will be too small to afford a decent defensive advantage. The next town large enough to hold him for any amount of time is over a hundred moles north. We may as well swear allegiance now rather than hand him that much territory uncontested."

Rahim had stopped eating. He was staring openly at the young heiress. She noticed, and smiled.

"You know strategy." He asked her.

"We have known war for many generations." She replied. A look passed between her and Lady June. Their peace was one of necessity.

"What about these woods?" Jonah continued. "Those weapons wouldn't count for much here."

"There is no strategic value in taking the woods." Lady Jocelyn answered. "No major supply routes or roads. We have no way of bringing Fauld's army in."

"How many men can you have in Hamtel when the time comes?" Rahim asked Lady Serong.

"Three thousand, with another two about three days behind."

"And Fauld? What has he committed so far?"

"Last night's count placed his force at somewhere around nine." The Lady Jocelyn was staunch, she didn't flinch as she delivered the crushing report.

Rahim leaned back into his chair, then regarded Jonah seriously. Jonah shrugged his shoulders. "Outnumbered, outgunned, and with the weather favouring your enemy and his resources."

Jonah reiterated. "If you Fauld in the field meet, you will lose."

"Not to mention the people of Hamtel who will be caught in the crossfire." Rahim added.

"Hamtel has already been abandoned." It was Lady June's turn to speak. "They have seen the approaching battle, watched the troops in the spirit."

"Almost the entire village has taken refuge here." Lady Serong added.

At that moment an unmistakable call of panic came from just outside. Jonah and Rahim were at their feet in an instant, reaching for weapons that were not there. Mere moments after the yelling began, the door burst open. Three men in cloaks burst in.

"For the king!" One yelled, then threw a knife down the table at the defenceless women.

Rahim grabbed a silver platter, flicking it up just in time to catch the knife mid-flight. No sooner had it dropped to the table Jonah picked it up and flicked it back to the first intruder. It plunged deep into his chest.

Ruthlessly another ripped the knife free and again threw it, this time at Rahim. Again, the platter deflected the attack and as the two cousins rushed their assailants, Rahim frisbee'd the heavy plate into a veiled face moments before Jonah's boot took him from his feet. The third turned to run but was quickly run through by guards attracted by the commotion.

In moments the room was full of armed men, but the threat had passed. The one survivor was removed quickly, leaving Jonah and Rahim to return to the three ladies.

"Maybe we should have a look at your patrol situation." Jonah suggested.

"I don't understand…" Lady June began. "We have men posted in the spirit at all times. They should never have gotten so close."

"My Ladies!" Came a call from a guard rushing forward.

"What is it, man?" Asked Lady Jocelyn.

"Two more men apprehended at the city's edge. One has been identified as the king's sleepwalker."

"But, why?" Lady June exclaimed, still a little panicked.

"Of course. With a sleepwalker present they could have mapped out your defences, both waking and sleeping. That's how they could get so close without being discovered." Jonah explained.

"Big gamble for Fauld." Rahim mused aloud. "That is a big asset to lose."

"But a worthwhile gamble." Lady Serong answered. "With us gone the Northern Provinces would be uncontested. It is just well for us that you were here."

Rahim winked at her, producing a definite blush.

"There must be a way we can use this to our advantage." Lady Jocelyn spoke, her voice trembling despite her efforts to remain composed. "As far as we know Fauld has lost his only sleepwalker." She turned to Jonah. "Shall we return to the table?"

Jonah nodded. Rahim grabbed another sweetbread.

*   *   *

Assara hated seeing Jonah fight, but something about her connection to him became stronger when he was in danger, so long as she kept calm enough to not wake. She had found herself chasing Tamra and Jasmine through a dark forest, surrounded by ghostly eyes, until in an instant the large room had appeared around her, Jonah at her side. She was certain her desire to keep him safe pulled her in, however ridiculous a notion it was. What could she do to protect him in such a situation?

It was hard to follow the conversation that followed between him and the important looking women he was meeting with. The spirit was holding, but was not as clear as the previous evening. Only one word was unmistakable:

Sleepwalker.

Those individuals to whom the spirit was not so restricted, who could see others in the spirit. So rare as to be nearly a thing of myth. Certainly the only reason Assara would have believed in such a thing was that in South Harbour it was one of the rumored reasons no-one spied on the palace during their sleep. Then she had met the local boy who had most assuredly seen her in her sleep, but as far as she was aware that meant there were two in the entire world.

Or, perhaps now, one.

A body was brought into the meeting, one of the attackers. Again, the word emerged from the mist of conversation: sleepwalker. Would this be an advantage to them? Could Jonah use this to help overthrow Fauld?

Her eyes felt heavy, she was beginning to wake. She moved once more to Jonah's side, placing a filmy hand against his chest in farewell.

Don't die, she thought.

Her eyes opened, affirming what her ears were hearing. The day had begun in usual fashion. Clothes were being donned, beds made, water shared. Tamra gave her a lacklustre smile before falling into the routine. Assara's was more genuine.

The local people had taken to wearing cloaks and shawls. She, and the majority of the other slaves from South Harbour, strolled comfortably about in long sleeve shirts, not yet acclimatised to the warmer winter. The day was grey, but Tamra sang cheerfully as they began their daily task of wheeling the cart toward the palace.

Almost straight away she spotted Marema-moie sitting against a wall just up the street. He noticed her too and immediately stood, heading in her direction. She had no idea how to react to the child. He seemed nice enough, at least he seemed to mean her no harm. He was just so odd. Even as he walked towards them he would slow, then speed up, looking suddenly left, then focused once more on his feet. Assara dropped the cart and waited for him to approach.

"Hello." Tamra said casually.

"Heello." He replied, his accent thick.

"Is everything alright? Do you need something?" Assara asked, crouching down.

"He says to warn you. He says more men coming into city."

"He? Who he?"

"The man. The man to you are, tied." His eyes darted, then met hers.

"Tied? Like, with a rope? I'm not sure I understand. Who am I tied to? You don't mean…. Are you talking about Jonah? Did you see him?"

"Jonah. Yes."

"When did you see him? Did you speak to him?" Her hands found his shoulders of their own accord. He seemed not to notice.

"Yesterday. I wait till this morning, you wake. He sees the men, like me sees the men. Men with swords and guns." His eyes traced some invisible thing that washed over her hand.

"Men with swords and guns? More men who, who look like me?"

"What men, Assara?" Tamra hopped down off the cart, keen to be involved.

Assara's back started to itch. Suddenly she became aware of all the other people in the street.

"Marema-moie, don't speak of this to anyone, ok?"

He nodded, still with that same nonchalant set to his eyes. Then, without another word, he turned and left.

"Bye Moie." Tamra waved cheerfully.

"Come sister." Assara said as she lifted Tamra back into the cart. "We need to get to the palace."

Everything seemed as it should. The same local peddlers hawked the same wares on the same corners. The same children played and the same mothers watched. Assara's route up the slight incline to the city's central point appeared completely unchanged from yesterday, but her instincts told her otherwise.

They reached the laundry room where their load was delivered.

"Please." She asked the first face she saw. "I must speak with Prince Cul."

Either the woman did not understand or did not care. Either way her request was ignored.

"Stay with the cart until I get back." She pleaded to Tamra.

"No. Prince Cul likes me. I'm coming too."

"Fine." She exclaimed in exasperation. "Come on."

In the kitchens behind the laundry there were more workers, but they reacted the same way. Cooks, maids, a palace guard, no-one paid her any attention.

"You, laundry server!" A familiar voice called out, female and very authoritative. Finally. "What is this I 'her' about you calling on the prince?"

"Mistress, thank you! I must speak-"

A firm slap cut her off mid-sentence.

"You do not call on the prince! Slaves do not call on a prince! You have been treated too well. You will remember your place."

Tamra quickly cradled her cheek. With a grateful nod, Assara gently pushed her small hands away.

"Mistress," she began, "there are armed men, soldiers coming into the city. Westerners, who mean to lead a rebellion against Prince Cul. Please, you must warn him."

She was panting from the exertion of running about. Her cheek blazed atop her hanging jaw. The mistress regarded her coldly.

"How do you know this?"

"A… boy, mistress…" She decided against using the term sleepwalker for little Moie's sake. "He has seen men, maybe soldiers, hiding in carts. Coming in through the gates."

Again, the imposing slave master paused, letting the heat of her gaze boil any untruth to the surface. When it became clear there was none, she dismissed them.

"Return to your duties. I will carry the matter further."

Assara slumped, letting Tamra rub her cheek.

"Ow, that sounded hurtful." She hissed.

Assara nodded. "We better get back to work."

Aside from a few sideways looks, the rest of the day was a quiet one. Having passed the news on, Assara began to relax, letting routine ease her anxieties. Meal time came and went. Before long she and Tamra were settling down to sleep.

"Psst."

Assara's eyes opened. She scanned the dark room.

"Pssst."

Where was that coming from? She looked to the window expecting to scan the street and almost yelled in alarm when she discovered Jasmine's face pressed to the glass.

As she climbed out of bed, Tamra stirred.

"Where are you going?" She asked.

"To the bathroom."

Tamra rolled back over.

Outside Jasmine waved to her from the corner of a nearby building. Assara skulked over, embracing her friend when she came near.

"Should you be here?" She whispered. Jasmine rolled her eyes. "Oh, of course. Why did you come?"

"I had to make sure you were ok. I heard some other servants speak your name in the palace. I had no idea why though. Why are they talking about you?"

"I, well it's kind of a long story. First of all, did you know there is a sleepwalker here in Bandarat?"

"A sleepwalker? Really?"

"Yes, a boy named Marema-moie. I met him months ago in my sleep, long before I even came here. He brought me a message today from Jonah."

"Jonah? That man with whom you are, well, that man who is in South Harbour right now?"

"Yes. They say there are more soldiers, Westerners, coming into the city in secret."

"For another attack you mean?"

"Yes, I think so. I tried to tell Prince Cul but I got slapped for asking to see him."

"Who slapped you?" Jasmine's eyes showed fire.

"The mistress."

Jasmine sighed. "I told you not to push the friendship with the prince. He is still a prince and we are still slaves."

"I know. You were right." Assara admitted.

"Did you get the message through?"

"I told the mistress. She said she would handle it."

"Alright…." Jasmine's eyes went distant. "So, Jonah comes here in his sleep?"

"I think lots of his men do. This is their home after all." Assara realised she hadn't been back to visit the Hold once. The very thought made her shiver.

"You don't care that he stalks you?" Jasmine asked, suspicion heavy on her voice.

"Stalks me?" Assara answered, surprised. "I want him to visit me. I also watch over him, so if he is stalking me, then I too must be stalking him!"

Jasmine didn't look convinced. "You watch over him? What has he been doing?"

"He and his men are preparing for war." She could not hide the sadness in her tone. "The new king in my country is marching an army north, to attack the free people who live there. Jonah and his men have joined with the opposing force, despite the fact that they are outnumbered and outgunned."

"He sounds foolish. I hope he is at least handsome."

Assara smiled, blushing deeply.

"I see!" Jasmine very nearly broke into a smile. "For your sake then I hope he does not die." Strange though the sentiment was, it was genuine.

"There is hope. Last night they killed the king's only sleepwalker, or I think that's what happened. With the spirit being so unstable these days they will at least be able to move more secretly."

"Perhaps. It is still impossible to move an entire army when your enemy can find you when they sleep. The only way to move in true secrecy is to stop your enemy sleeping."

"Sure, if only that were possible." Assara sighed.

"It's possible. Have you never heard of poppy seed?"

"Poppy seeds?" Assara asked.

Jasmine sighed. "Of course you haven't. There is a process men do to poppy seed which makes it into a drug. When you ingest it, normally by sniffing it, it makes you feel extra strong and energetic. It also keeps you up all night."

"So you can't sleep at all?"

"Not even if you wanted to."

Assara's eyes went distant. "Maybe that can help them?"

Jasmine giggled. "To stop an army? You would need a hundred barrels full."

Assara's expression did not change.

"You don't understand." Jasmine went on. "With that much poppy seed you could just about buy your enemy. Forget the fighting."

"Oh." Still her eyes carried heavy thought.

"I had better go, they will miss me at the palace soon. I am glad you are safe, but heed my words next time."

"I will."

With one last embrace they parted ways. Assara slinked back into the room, but before she lay her head she wrote two words on some paper and placed it next to her pillow.

Poppy seed.

*   *   *

She was on his mind like sand on a dune. Through talk of strategy, breaks for meals, training his men. Always, she was on his mind.

She was safe, but for how long? Had his message gotten through? Was she even as aware of him as he had thought? Maybe he should ask for a message from the boy, the sleepwalker. He could tell him.

"How old do you suppose Lady Serong is?" Rahim was delaying taking his rest, leaning against the window instead. "She is a clever one. She has seen conflict before."

"She is a wet snake in winter, cousin. I would warn caution if I believed you would heed it."

"You lost your privilege to advise me about women when you fell for perhaps *the* most unavailable woman on the planet."

"They say imitation is a form of flattery." Jonah retorted through a wry grin.

"Shouldn't you be rushing off to sleep so that you may moon over your distant love?" Rahim's hands clenched in mock sincerity.

"And who will you be mooning over while you sleep?" Jonah chuckled as he climbed into bed. Rahim snorted in response.

Candles were dimmed and gradually the bunk room became silent. Soon even Rahim reluctantly accepted sleep, allowing Jonah to drift off.

The dream was returning, one element at a time. Some were complaining that since the onset of dreaming, they could no longer return home to visit their families, so strong were the visions that came for them each night. As for Jonah, so far he had found focusing on Assara would hold the spirit stable for a while. It was becoming increasingly difficult though.

He drifted off picturing her face. Before he knew it he was in Bandarat. The scene before him was ever more ephemeral, were that possible. Familiar streets shifted beyond his perception, buildings becoming one thing and then another. He could still tell the difference between people who were really there, and those images that were part of the encroaching dream, but only just.

Assara, he concentrated. Where are you today?

He checked her bunk room cautiously. They were private women's quarters after all. Empty. She must already be on her way to the palace. He decided to walk to maintain as much clarity in the spirit as possible. He could catch her easily if she was pushing her cart, which if she wasn't here then she would likely be doing.

Sure enough, a few blocks up the already bustling street, he spied the cart. As always Assara pushed while her sister rode. It concerned her how much she coddled her sister. Tamra would eventually have to learn to stand on her own two feet. Jonah did not want the child to break should their situation suddenly change.

As he approached, he assessed every inch of her for clues as to how she was feeling. She was not slouching much, which was a good sign, but her shoulders seemed stiff. She was anxious, and yet she had a calm look about her, no frown adorned her face. Her eyes though… they darted just a little. She was definitely on the lookout. Probably for Fauld's men. It must be hard for her, knowing that at any moment an all-out war for the city could break out.

She stopped, dropping the cart to wipe sweat from her brow. Tamra produced a skin with some water, and Assara drank. It was wonderful how they cared for each other. The things they had both been through… They had, through the strength of their bond, held on to sanity, to hope. Without that support… Well, Jonah knew things could have turned out very different for both of them.

Slowly he became aware that the city had changed. The few buildings that remained around them were now swamped in trees. The dream was beginning to take over. Assara reached into a pocket and produced a note. That was new....

Poppy seed? Is that what it said? What on earth could that mean...

Tamra turned and spoke, but Jonah heard nothing. Even when the spirit was stable it could be hard to make out words. He had only moments before he became once again taken by the dream. Assara shared her sister's attention, also speaking wordlessly. Someone they knew was approaching.

Little Marema-moie! He appeared suddenly from where a tree was struggling to take form. The boy looked about to say something, then started, jumping nearly out of his skin.

"Man is here." Moie said. He can see me!

"Marema-moie, you see me?" He said at the same time as Assara spoke to him. The boy's eyes darted from him to her in confusion.

"You both talk at same time. I can't hear." He apologised. The landscape behind him warped from brown to blue to bright green.

Jonah began to speak but already Assara was at his feet, showing him the note. He still could not hear anything she said.

"She says poppy seed, make something that stop men sleeping." Moie spoke without taking his eyes from her. "She says hide you while you sneak past?"

"Poppy seed... powder. The drug, keeps men awake. I think I understand."

"Ok, he says good now." Moie kept his eyes on her still. She spoke again, then her fingers went to her mouth. The boy's gaze locked on his. Slight fingers raised up until pointed level at his chest.

Assara stood, turning to face Jonah. His heart began to pound. She waved shyly, and Jonah repeated the gesture.

"He wave too." Moie said, rather indifferently. Tamra watched on in confusion.

Assara's lips moved. "She say, I don't know what to say." Moie translated.

"Tell her, tell her I understand. Tell her I will see her soon, I will get to her soon."

"He says, it ok. He come soon."

Assara smiled widely. The snake around her neck reared and hissed. Wait, Jonah thought… snake?

Moie's eyes went wide.

The snake turned its head slightly, allowing the sunlight to illuminate its sparkling eyes which were made of clear diamonds. Assara was speaking, but Moie had stopped translating, so transfixed on the image he was.

"No more, please…" He said, crouching low and rubbing his eyes. Both he and Assara leaned down to console him. Jonah slipped through the melting street.

The sudden sensation of falling startled him awake. He glanced at the moon-cast shadow coming in through the window. He hadn't been asleep long. Maybe if he returned to Bandarat he could find her again. He lay back, slowing his breathing and relaxing his muscles with compression and flexing exercises. In minutes he again found sleep, but therein found only the dream.

*   *   *

"I'll be here, waiting for you…" Assara was saying. The words barely escaped her clenching throat. When Moie did not repeat, she glanced down to press him when he dropped to the ground, pressing his hands to his eyes.

"Please, no more." He said, sounding genuinely distressed.

"Moie, what is it?" Assara said as Tamra jumped to his side.

"It is too much… too much to see… people here, people spirit, visions…"

"Oh Moie…" Assara swept him up in a hug. "You see it all don't you? The people in the spirit, and the visions they are having. It must be chaos."

He began to sob against her chest.

"What's wrong with him?" Tamra asked.

"He isn't well." Assara answered. "Come, we'll take you with us."

"I'll take care of him." Tamra said sincerely as she climbed back into the cart. Assara placed the boy, his eyes still firmly shut, into her sister's arms. She turned then to wave, not sure if Jonah could still see her or not.

Moie's sobbing subsided as Tamra stroked his hair. Assara fell back into her usual rhythm. A smile came upon her that no amount of guilt or concern could erase. He had come for her, he would come for her. He was faithful, and loyal. How had Moie put it? Connected? It certainly seemed so. Tamra hummed quietly. Amazingly Moie soon fell asleep. What were his spirit hours like, she thought? Were they as traumatic as his waking sight?

At the palace the scene was much as it was every day. If the prince was preparing for battle, he was doing so quietly. Constantly her eyes sought a glimpse of Jasmine, but she was not nearby, and Assara did not want to again deviate from her regular route.

No-one questioned the children riding in the cart. Tamra and her charge barely occasioned a sideways glance as dirty laundry got stacked around them. It must be common for women to have to keep their children close, Assara mused. Slaves have to work, families or no.

Fully loaded, and then some, the small party again left the palace grounds. There, coming up the street, was the prince. Surrounded as he was by guards it was almost hard to spy him. She did though, as he also saw her.

She no longer knew how to react around him, but caution advised as much respect as she could muster. She stopped the cart, then dropped into a curtsy. Cul noticed, but did not respond. The large group passed, leaving her and her two passengers alone in the dusty street.

"Is Prince Cul angry with us?" Tamra asked.

"I don't know." She paused only a moment longer. "Come on, we have work to do."

*   *   *

Many visions assailed Jonah in his sleep that night. Assara was a prisoner, shackles binding her painfully to a dirty cell floor. He dreamed Rahim was a wolf who, despite Jonah's efforts, ran down Assara's sister and killed her. There was more, but as Jonah tried to remember single aspects they melted from his memory.

Quietly he and his men rose and began to prepare for the day. The mood was quiet, many had seen dreams last night. Perhaps it was time to say something. He called his men out into the cool morning for an impromptu drill to clear some heads.

Though the grass was muddy in places from the mix of dew and foot traffic, Jonah worked his troop as he always did. He could see in their eyes, as much as he could feel in himself, the routine bleed some of the confusion away. Finally, as his men stretched, he broached the subject.

"Men, soldiers of the Banji nation, a strange time is upon us. For the first time in our history we find ourselves in a strange land lending swords, sweat and blood to a people not our own. We also are fighting a new enemy, one that springs from inside. An enemy of doubt. Fear of the unknown. By now you have all experienced what is being called 'the dream'. These visions, which can be confusing and painful, which are taking the spirit hours from us, are affecting one and all, young and old alike. We do not know why they have come or when it will end. All I know is, like all trials, they must be endured. Like the 'ritual of war' which you all braved to wear the 'band of the warrior'. Like the trials of combat which you all survived to be here, with me, today. Like many more trials which will come, you, warrior clan Banji, will endure. We do not fear the blade, and we will not fear the dream. We will return to our families before their faces change, as victorious conquerors of the lands across the seas. Now, practise your sword. Ready your body, and your mind. Gird yourselves for war."

His men did not applaud, but as they turned to move into sword drills with each other they stood taller, fear and uncertainty washed from their eyes. Rahim clasped his shoulder as he came near.

"Thank you, brother. I think I needed that." He spoke genuinely.

"I think I did too. Come, I have something I must discuss with the war council."

He was feeling bold this morning and he knew why. He had told her he was coming for her. He had always planned to come for her, but actually saying it to her had made it real, placed an imagined time frame in place. He had a new motivation:

Don't let her down.

The council had not yet arrived in the hall but breakfast was laid out, affording Jonah some time to discuss his plan with Rahim as they ate and waited. One bowl of hot oats and a spiced tea later, all four Ladies arrived together, entering the room in order from oldest to youngest.

Jonah stood casually, reminding Rahim to do the same. Lady Serong had an almost imperceptible smile for Rahim, which he gladly returned.

"With respect, Ladies." Jonah began as he waited for them all to sit. "I have more to, ah, talk about, about our plans for, battle."

"I had hoped that you might after we abandoned Hamtel uncontested." Lady Jocelyn replied. "Please, begin."

"The spirit is becoming more and more, unavailable. In the past it has been the armies' greatest... greatest..."

"Ally." Rahim finished for him.

"Chances are Fauld's generals will still, act, as if it is." Jonah continued.

"Meaning?" The grand old woman pressed.

Rahim took over. "Meaning our plans should revolve around doing what could not be done before. Moving large parties in secret to confuse our enemy and rob them of sound strategy."

Lady Serong leaned in, receiving a nod of approval before joining the discussion. "It sounds as if you have something in mind already."

"We do, my lady." Rahim answered, very nearly bowing in his chair. "We will march our entire army south, past Hamtel and Fauld's army on its eastern flank. We will use cover of night to slip past unseen. When Fauld's men march on further north from Hamtel, a defensive detachment will enter Hamtel from the south, while the bulk of your army moves into the city of South Harbour."

"South Harbour will not be empty." Lady Serong countered. "Our depleted forces may yet not be enough to gain entry."

"We think we may be able to draw out Fauld's remaining forces. If we can get a foothold in Hamtel, we should be able to hold Fauld's northern troop long enough for him to send reinforcements. He will assume he has us surrounded, and will surely send forces north from South Harbour to attack us on two fronts. When that happens, and the gates open, you move into the city. From there your defensive position should be strong enough to hold against a larger force."

"If Fauld takes the bait." Lady Jocelyn was on board, Jonah could tell.

"All this hinges on being able to move an entire army unseen." Lady Serong was on the fence. "We know the spirit is unpredictable lately, but it would only take one soldier, with a clear sleep one night, to spot us."

"We had an idea for that too…" Rahim glanced with uncertainty at his cousin. "Do you have access to poppy seed powder here?"

For some reason three of the ladies looked toward the fourth. Lady Serong locked eyes defiantly with Jonah.

"Why do you ask?" She answered proudly.

"If we laced Fauld's armies' drinking water with it, his army would not sleep. It could buy us a full two days and nights to march south unseen."

Lady June screwed her mouth tightly against some imagined sour taste. Lady Serong noticed, smiling ever so slightly. "It can be done."

"You have access to that much powder?" Rahim questioned boldly.

"I do."

Some of the complications in their relationships are becoming clearer, Jonah thought. "We need to act quickly. Our best chance to spoil their stores is now, before they march north from Hamtel."

"I can have two barrels here in two hours." Lady Serong said confidently. This time Lady June openly balked, mouth agape. It was not very becoming.

"Good." Rahim went on. "We will take a small party to the town border today. I will need men who know the place well. When night falls, we will move in. Whether the army marches tonight or not, they will not sleep, so we must be moving toward South Harbour as soon as possible."

"Are we perhaps forgetting…" Lady June had finally been goaded into discussion. "An army inadvertently ingesting poppy seed powder will be more aggressive, more energetic, bolder…"

"Also, more erratic." Rahim interrupted. "Stupider. More predictable, after a fashion."

"With respect, Lady June." Jonah spoke politely. "Rahim is right. Every advantage the drug gives a soldier comes with a twofold cost. Generals have, in the past, tried drugging their armies. It has never ended well."

Placated, barely, Lady June reclined in her chair, eyes rolling.

Lady Jocelyn stood. "I will give the order to break camp. By tonight we will begin the march, whether we are being watched or no. Pray the dream is strong."

You pray, Jonah thought. I can't dream. Not yet.

*   *   *

The first sign Assara got that the attack was beginning was footsteps, running down the street outside. At first it was only two or three, but quickly it became ten, then twenty. Night had fallen, but she had not yet found sleep.

The bunk house roused quickly, the women there ever fearful of this very event. Distant shouts became clanging swords. It had begun.

Tamra woke quickly. Little Moie, who had not left her side all day, was already peering out a window. Without prompting, they all gathered what few possessions they had and waited behind the door, should they have to leave in a hurry.

Tense minutes passed. The fighting seemed to drift further away, towards the palace. Slowly the mood in the room began to lift.

"Psst!"

Assara leapt to the window. Jasmine was there, beckoning her outside. Instead, Assara beckoned her in.

"What's happening?" Assara whispered as Jasmine slinked in through the door.

"Many men are attacking the palace. I left as soon as I heard soldiers assembling. Assara, there are hundreds, maybe more, all with swords and guns, all calling for Prince Cul's head. Not just westerners either. Locals are with them."

"What are you saying? Is Cul going to be ok?"

Jasmine paused. "I… I don't know…"

"We have to help him!" Tamra pleaded. "He is our friend!"

Jasmine and Assara shared a look, a look that said we agree but we are powerless. The door opened at the far end of the bunk house. Soldiers, westerners, entered.

Jasmine went pale. "Run!" She whispered, already making for the door. Assara wanted to protest but had learned to respect Jasmine's instincts. She grabbed Tamra's hand, who in turn grabbed Moie's. Into filmy rain and a windy night they ran.

Jasmine frantically searched for a place to hide. Being out in the streets revealed groups of men everywhere, some locals, some showing the pale skin of South Harbour. Whenever one looked their way Jasmine veered into a side street or alley, dragging her panicked party behind. The drizzle soaked Assara's clothes. She was cold for the first time since getting off the boat.

"We have to find Cul!" Tamra called as they stopped to catch their breath.

"It's too dangerous, Tamra. Those men are all looking for him. We just need to hide until –"

"Until they find him? They'll hurt him!" Tamra looked to her sister for support. Assara genuinely wanted to help, but her words would not come.

"We have to keep moving!" Jasmine hissed, dragging the party behind her.

It was eerie in the quiet alleys. It was happening, wasn't it? Was it all too far away to hear or had Cul already squashed this second attempt at unseating him? Huddled in a corner behind some barrels Assara was just about ready to go back to bed. Jasmine was a cornered cat, senses awaiting the fight for life at any moment. The drizzling rain had all but soaked everyone's clothes. It was time to head back.

"Jasmine!" Assara nearly hissed. "Tamra and Moie are getting cold. We can't stay out in this much longer.

Jasmine did not respond. She didn't even turn her head. She scampered down another street, and Assara was forced to follow.

A dark figure emerged ahead, sword in hand. His posture was that of desperation, hunched to minimise his profile and yet running almost blindly into the open. The party hit the wall, seeking shadows to hide them. He was coming their way.

He spotted them as they recognised him. It was Prince Cul, sweating and with a bloodied shirt.

Assara wanted to say something but the look in his eyes was that of pure bloodlust. His blade was pointed at her chest.

Yelling drew their attention back up toward the alley from which he had appeared. Three more men, obviously in pursuit, spotted the embattled prince. They sprinted at him without a word.

Cul responded in turn, advancing aggressively on his assailants. Though they all attempted to attack at once, Cul did not wait for them to surround him. A parry became a left lunge, then a right slice. Three men fell unable to scream as they bled life into the muddy street.

Tamra, whimpering audibly, ran to Cul. She embraced his leg, leaving him to stare completely vexed at the child now firmly attached.

Her sister's exposure finally brought words through Assara's clenched throat. "Prince Cul. Are you alright?" She asked, approaching warily. He did not answer.

"Come!" Jasmine called. "We need to find a place to hide!"

"No!" Cul retorted, breaking his silence. "We need to leave! Lord Fauld's soldiers have joined with those still loyal to the Shareef. A man called Falan is leading them. None of us are safe here."

"You are not safe here. We will still be slaves tomorrow, regardless of who sits on the throne." Jasmine fired up. Assara found herself envying her bravery.

"You should come with me, now. You do not want to be a part of that rule."

"And go where? Into the wilderness?"

"To my villages, East." Cul's eyes darted. He was about to go, escort or no escort.

"Assara, we should stay. Tomorrow things will return to normal, you will see."

She looked at her sister, still clutching Cul's torn leggings. Tamra said nothing, but spoke volumes.

"We're staying with Cul."

He nodded and immediately moved off. Tamra followed him, and Moie followed Tamra. Jasmine shot Assara a glance but did not protest.

"The gate is that way." Jasmine whispered in a tone full of contempt.

"The gate will be guarded." Cul responded. "We will leave by way of the damaged wall. I know where repairs have gone the slowest."

Assara suddenly noticed how tired she had become. Moie began to fall behind so Jasmine, showing no signs of fatigue, picked him up. Moving through the city brought them close to more armed patrols but they managed to remain unseen. Sure enough, Cul led them to a wall still broken from the assault that had brought Jonah here months before, a gap through which his men had gained entry, now facilitating their escape.

Outside the city, free of the buildings and walls, the wind blew strong against the clear grounds that marked the city's borders. They had only what they had thought to put on before leaving the bunkhouse, and that wasn't much. Tamra clung to Cul's chest as he pressed forward into the dark countryside. Jasmine and Assara huddled around Moie, sharing the burden of his weight.

"I hope you know what you're doing." Jasmine called over the wind. Assara looked over, but did not respond.

*   *   *

"So do you think anyone who knows, I mean anyone who is familiar with the powder will warn their generals when they become aware?"

"Not at first." Rahim smirked. He wiped the accumulated moisture from the end of the looking glass, then returned it to the town ahead. "A grunt soldier, marching to war, always tired, always hungry… even if he was responsible enough to speak out, his fellow soldiers might stab him before he made it to the captain's quarters."

Twenty minutes ago, Bayern and two other men had snuck into town wearing the uniforms of the crown's army. Their plan was to hide in plain sight, as there was really no way to roll three barrels around a town under military occupation unnoticed. Soldiers moving water in preparation for a march however would not be given any thought.

Hopefully.

"Look." Rahim pointed, then passed the looking glass over. "The advance party is moving already."

Jonah raised the glass, careful to shield the end against any reflected light. Sure enough, a large group of men in armour was visible on the road heading north.

"I thought for sure he would wait till daybreak."

"Fauld is impatient." Jonah mused aloud. "An impatient foe falls quickly into the hands of his enemies."

"Huh." Rahim smiled. "You sound just like our Shareef."

Jonah lowered the glass, suddenly melancholy. "We really haven't stopped to grieve, have we?"

"We will. Once we are back home, and we have chased Cul back into the rabbit hole he calls a nation, we will."

Jonah sighed. "On to another war."

"You sound sad, cousin! Where would you be without someone to stab? You never speak of wintering by a fire instead of a fight."

"Even I would like to see an end to it. I need to find out who I am once the swords are laid down."

"You and me both, cousin."

An hour passed, then another. Black turned to blue overhead, causing the two onlookers to retreat to a secondary rally point behind the tree line.

"It's not looking good. We're going to have to head back soon." Rahim observed, still scanning the fields for signs of their comrades.

"And say what? We still don't know if they managed to spoil the water."

"Well, we can go and have a look, but I don't fancy our chances of getting in and out unseen during the day."

"No, there's no point. Whether they got caught before or after spoiling the water, the plan must remain. Fauld's army is still marching north." Jonah's gaze travelled to the road where for the last three hours group after group had been exiting Hamtel. "If they're still going north, then whether our men have been captured or killed, they mustn't have been alerted to our plan. Come on, let's get back."

Under a clear, crisp, and brutally cold sun they marched for camp. When they returned they found nearly everyone already heading south, save only for their compatriots. Lady Serong, last of the noblewoman to break camp, approached with her escort.

"Report." She was certainly used to authority, Jonah thought.

"The crown's army marches north. Bayern and his men did not return." He answered.

"So we don't know whether their mission was a success?"

"No."

The young princess sighed, her eyes drifting south. "Very well. We are committed now either way. I have placed a hundred swords under your command to assist in taking Hamtel once we are in position."

"Many thanks, Lady Serong." Rahim replied genuinely.

"Don't thank me, rifleman." She remarked, meeting his eyes. "Just don't lose."

Rahim flashed her his most charming smile as she departed with a slight inclination of her delicate chin. Once she was out of earshot he said quietly, "I may just beat you to the altar of marriage, Jonah."

"Cousin," Jonah replied with a laugh, "I would pay to see that!"

*   *   *

After marching into the hills for a couple of hours Cul had ordered rest in a dugout. At first it seemed like a natural formation, until from nearby the prince produced a covering made from woven leaves and sticks and huddled them all together underneath for some rest. Whatever this thing was, he had used it before.

She didn't sleep much. In fact, only Tamra and Moie seemed to get any real rest. Assara watched Cul from half closed eyelids. He was changed outside of the city. Every sound, every whisper or crack caused him to peer carefully around. Jasmine seemed intent on ignoring everyone, she was obviously upset. Assara rested as much as she could.

A whistle caused Cul to break cover. He pushed the covering back, allowing the cool wind to rush in. Several armed men surrounded them.

"My Prince." They spoke in unison, bowing heads to the ground. One shuffled forward. "We got your signal."

Signal? When did he do that?

"We are returning to Apandabarret. We leave at once. My slaves are hungry, give them food for the journey."

Dried meat, fruit and water appeared as well as cloaks. Cul immediately headed off, even as Tamra and Moie were still rubbing the sleep from their eyes.

"More walking, huh?" Jasmine said sarcastically. Assara sighed in relief. She was still talking to her.

"I guess so." Food entered hungry mouths and the march began anew. "What do you suppose this Apan, Apande, this new place will be like?"

"Hopefully much like Bandarat." Moie climbed into Jasmine's arms.

"It is huts." He said, barely audible over the wind. "Huts in the hills. I have seen it."

"Is it nice there?" Tamra asked him grabbing Assara's hand. Moie shrugged his shoulders.

"What happened last night anyway?" Tamra asked, tugging her sister's arm for an answer.

"Lord – I mean, King Fauld, from South Harbour, sent men to take over from Prince Cul." She answered.

"Why?" Tamra pressed.

"I, I really don't know. Jasmine, what do you think?"

"King's conquer, that is all I know." She called back nonchalantly. "Who can say why? Never happy with what they have? Men always want more."

"Prince Cul would have been a good king." Tamra said honestly. He didn't hear, leading the group as he was.

"Maybe." Jasmine answered, though she didn't sound convinced.

"He will look after us." Tamra looked up at her sister. It was a statement of faith, not a question.

"He will look after us..." Assara repeated. This time it was a question.

*   *   *

Jonah hadn't slept much due to the sortie to and from Hamtel the previous night, so he decided to bed for a couple of hours before he and his men would join the march south. He was also eager to check on the state of the dream. If he could spirit himself into Hamtel to search for Bayern, Fauld's men could search him and his out and discover their movements also. It was a difficult situation.

It took him a good half an hour to find rest. Immediately he was presented with a thin veil of the spirit surrounded by cascading dream imagery. Better rush to Hamtel before I do anything, he decided.

Jonah's spirit leapt through his bunk room ceiling seeking the tree canopy nearby. Instead he found himself standing at the outskirts of the occupied town, feeling suddenly like the only man in existence. He pushed his feelings aside.

They will only lead me astray.

Placing one foot squarely in front of the next, he tried walking in the direction of the nearest building. Immediately the Shareef appeared a few paces ahead, wrapped head to toe in bandages. Clenching forces hit his chest.

Focus, he chided himself. Still, like a child, he longed to rush forward and free the Shareef from his bonds.

He took a second step. The figure was suddenly in his face. A bandaged arm became free, striking his jaw.

Jonah nearly woke. He could feel himself back in his resting body. Affected as he was by the vision, he took some solace in not being able to search Hamtel. Perhaps his allies could move unnoticed.

He forced himself to relax, forming a picture of Bandarat in his mind. All became rushing images and soundless wind. Assara's bunkhouse appeared before him.

Or was it? It had an odd feel to it, despite the scene holding fairly solid around him. He leapt inside, passing through the outer wall.

The room was empty. A formidable feeling of being abandoned washed over him. The room seemed fairly together, although beds were not made. Was this reality, or more visions? He focused his feelings on Assara, brought memories of her face to the forefront of his mind.

Something grabbed at his hand, pulling him out of the city in a blur. Assara burst from the mist of the spirit, reaching down to pull him up a steep stair. He followed the movement without thought.

Her friend Jasmine passed through him. It was she who Assara had been reaching out to, helping up. Where were they?

His mind reeled; he was losing his grip. Foothills, outside the city… Tamra was here, was Moie? Then he noticed Cul. Armed guards were also around. What had happened?

The scene fell away in a flurry of cascading images. To his alarm, the clearest of which was a scene of two people quite definitely making love. It shocked him fully awake.

He woke with no small sense of relief, despite the confusing scene he had discovered. He couldn't even be certain what he had seen was real, but it certainly appeared that Assara had left Bandarat with Cul. He had to find out if it were true, and if it were, why.

Rahim slept soundly across the room. Jonah checked the shadows on the floor, it looked as if he had been asleep for less than two hours. He dressed, allowing the noise to rouse his counterpart.

"Time already then?" Rahim called a little groggily.

"Yes. Did you get anywhere in the spirit?" He questioned immediately.

"I'm afraid not." He replied. He was perplexed, that much was obvious.

"What did you see?"

"Ah, the usual platter of oddities." He said with furrowed brow, already getting dressed. "I had a meeting with Lady Serong but I had a huge nose and boils. Palm trees surrounded us, like the ones on the coast back home. I remember seeing an island, I think, or the beach?"

He paused, realising how serious he sounded. "I think I need to start drinking!" He forced a laugh. "At any rate, I got nowhere near Hamtel, and didn't even think to check on the situation in Bandarat."

"I tried as well, but couldn't get in." His voice must have been heavy, by Rahim's reaction.

"I have been insensitive, cousin. The dream, it is severing your contact with Assara, isn't it?"

A well of emotion swept over Jonah, panic verging on despair. Powerlessness. Desperation. He really hadn't considered the full implications of what was happening. Now it had been said out loud it threatened to break him.

"It is becoming, harder..."

Rahim embraced him, making it harder to keep his eyes dry. "We know what country she is in. That will be clue enough once we are home."

"I hope so. I think I saw her outside the city, heading East with Prince Cul."

Rahim's smile dropped. "Cul has left Bandarat? Why?"

"I wish I knew. I will ask the men to try to visit the next time they rest."

"Of course."

They gathered their things and went to find the Banji soldiers, all rested and ready for the march. They would have some catch up to do but if it was one thing the Banji could do it was march.

March, and fight.

*   *   *

The sun finally began to rise, though due to the hills being between it and her it would be some time before Assara could bleed some energy from its rays. She sat, huddled with her small party, trying to rest after a steep climb. Damp clothes added to the coldest part of the morning was taking its toll.

Cul called the party up, which despite her exhaustion she was glad for. Moving meant warming.

The hills had sections of stairs carved into steeper inclines, though they were big for stairs. Like clockwork now, Assara picked Tamra up, placing her atop the next step, climbed up herself then offered a hand down for Jasmine. When Jasmine's damp hand was firmly in hers, she pulled...

... Jonah up.

Her gaze drifted, suddenly glassed over.

"What is it?" Jasmine asked, instantly aware of the change. "Are you feeling alright?"

"I thought I saw... for a moment there..."

"Look!" Tamra pulled on Assara's dress excitedly. "We're here!"

"What?" She peered past Jasmine's concern. Sure enough, filling a small plateau ahead, in front of a few cave openings, was a collection of huts. A watercourse ran from inside the cliff wall to a large garden area. Nearby some goats bleated from a small pen. Many people were already rushing out with cloaks and steaming drinks.

Suddenly they were surrounded with fussing women spilling garbled words over each other. Once covered in furs they were all four herded into a nearby room where a fire was going. Assara gladly accepted some oats, ensuring Tamra and Moie were eating also. They required little encouragement.

"Moie, do you know about this place?" Jasmine asked between mouthfuls.

He nodded. "Lord Fauld send me here sometimes to send message to Cul."

Assara dimly became aware of a complicated series of occurrences involving Fauld and her new owner. However, in her tired state, the thought was quickly dismissed.

Cul entered then, a weathered, powerful man at his side. All present immediately bowed low, pressing foreheads to hands laid flat to the floor. Jasmine, Assara and Moie followed suit. Tamra leapt up and hugged his leg.

The imposing man to Cul's left grunted aggressively but Cul waved him away, then beckoned all to rise. He spoke some sharp, confident words which were answered only with nodding.

Assara wanted to ask if he was ok but was afraid to make eye contact. Then he surprised her by asking the question.

"Are you all alright?"

"Yes, Prince Cul. Thank you." She replied, meeting his gaze for just a moment.

He nodded tersely, then left.

*   *   *

Jonah watched his oldest friend walk through the deepening night with his feet on the ground but his head most definitely in the clouds. It was a strange sight. So strange in fact that he couldn't help but laugh.

The sound broke Rahim's train of thought and brought a violent response.

"Ow! Apologies cousin, I had no idea one could dream while awake!"

"You are one to talk, Jonah. If there is one among us who is guilty of dreaming while waking, it is you."

"You're absolutely right." Jonah admitted, rubbing his shoulder. "It is just an odd thing to see on you. What were you thinking about?"

Rahim glanced over his shoulder. The men, following warily behind, were more or less out of earshot. "That Lady Serong has got me thinking."

"I noticed." He laughed again.

"Not just about that! More about home."

"Back east? What do you mean?"
The staunch captain sighed, his shoulders slumping. "I am ready for a wife. But if I take a wife here, especially a Lady, will I ever see our home again?"

"Wow, when you fall for a girl you fall hard."

"Like you are any different!" Rahim swung at Jonah's shoulder again, but he was ready for him this time.

"Oh, I have realised I am exactly that. I just thought you were not."

"Yeah..." Eyes glazed once more into the daydream. "So did I."

Forward scouts returned at a jog, calling out as they neared.

"Captains!" One said in Banji. "Skirmish ahead. We missed it."

They shared a look before ordering the men into a run. In less than a minute they crested a sparsely wooded hill top, revealing the fresh battle scene ahead. Wounded were being patched while those still able formed a defensive line to the groups western front. Jonah searched eagerly for any of the four Ladies. Heading for the largest collection of grouped soldiers revealed Lady Serong's guard with her at their center. As the youngest she would have to march behind the other three.

"Lady Serong! Are you alright?" Jonah called as her men moved to prevent his approach.

"Let them in, let them in! Yes, but we have been discovered. A scout party, not large but big enough to hurt. There is no chance we got them all."

"They will warn the troops heading north, yes?" Rahim stated the obvious. "Bring them back to Hamtel?"

"Almost certainly. Gentlemen, if you do not secure that town before Fauld's rifles do, they will tear you apart on the approach. I know we had planned to move on from the south to afford you protection, but that option is now lost to us."

Jonah nodded, bowed and left. Rahim paused only a moment longer, fishing for a little extra acknowledgement. Lady Serong held his gaze, so Rahim left her with a wink.

"Banji!" Jonah called loud enough for his men to hear. "Gird yourselves. We run!"

Swords were lashed to backs, canteens strapped hard to legs. Cloaks came off shoulders to be wrapped around waists. When the party again became still Jonah led them off without a word, westward toward Hamtel. At least they would hit the plains surrounding the town at the darkest part of the night, although if Fauld did have rifles in place, even the dark would not save them.

"How far to the town from here?" Jonah called over his frequent breaths.

"Hard to say. We had better be careful we don't run right past it. This isn't exactly familiar territory and I can't exactly see in the dark."

Jonah checked his bearings. If they headed west and slightly south, they would put more distance between them and the enemy. They might just hand them the battle uncontested too.

*   *   *

"Moie?" Assara asked, leaning up in the bed to spy him out.

"Yes sister?" He had taken to calling them all sister. Tamra was calling Jasmine sister and Moie little brother now as well.

"Do you think you can go see Jonah tonight? Tell him what happened?"

"Maybe, if dream isn't too loud."

"Thank you Moie." Beside her, Jasmine sighed.

"This bed is hard."

"Harder than the street?" Assara replied. "Cul likes us. He will look after us."

"Maybe." She admitted, reluctantly. "You may have a bigger problem though."

"What do you mean?"

"What if Jonah does come for you? His men are loyal to the Shareef, same as the ones who just chased Cul out of the city. They're enemies."

"I know…"

"What if he comes back and they go to war?"

"I will stop them." Assara did not look confident.

Jasmine began saying something, then changed her mind. "Sleep. It has been a long day."

She wanted to argue the point, convince her friend it would all work out. In her heart she knew it would, but she did not know how or why.

Sleep came quickly, a blissful escape from aching feet and legs. Pure exhaustion made reaching the spirit all but impossible. Images drowned her, submerged her consciousness in metaphorical nonsense. In her heart she still longed to see Jonah but in the midst of her tired mind it wasn't enough.

A grand hall formed around her with Cul at its head. Tamra appeared, curled up in a cradle. The room shrank as Cul rocked it gently. His eyes glowed burgundy. Opposite him, in an entirely dark blue half of the room, Jasmine cradled Moie. Assara felt excluded, desperate to engage with the scene if only to bring peace. When the room finished shrinking it had changed, no longer a grand palace but a simple hut. For a moment she found clarity, rejecting the vision. It blurred before her.

Again, her thoughts returned to Jonah. He appeared next to her, smiling with familiarity. He was running, reaching out to her. She took his hand, then realised it was bronze. Others appeared around her, also running. Her feet became heavy, she could not keep up. The race would be lost. Jonah's grip hardened, he would not let go. Her arm separated then, allowing Jonah to speed ahead.

"No!" She cried, but her words were little more than breath. Black storm clouds, flashing red lightning, boiled beneath.

"Sister."

Amid the maelstrom stood little Moie. As she held his gaze the cacophony subsided. He was there, he was real.

"Your vision is strange. Your arm fell off."

"It's back now. Thank you Moie." She rubbed her shoulder with a ghostly hand, watching the clouds vanish. The room where they were sleeping once again took form.

"Are you doing this? I haven't seen the spirit this clear in weeks."

"It is better for me, when I focus on one. Too many visions the other way."

"You see them all, don't you? The visions people have in their sleep?"

He nodded.

"Well, I'm glad you're here with me." She knelt in front of him, allowing her spirit knees to imagine the floor. "Can we go to Jonah? Can you take me to him?"

Moie nodded, extending his hand. Though neither could grab the others, when the line between each blurred the boy closed his eyes. The world shifted.

Moonlit plains appeared all around, pockets of trees the only discernible feature. Jonah's warriors were scattered about, all moving fast in the same direction.

"Stay close." Moie said. He stepped away, suddenly appearing on a nearby rise. Assara gave chase, not being as good at fast movement in the spirit.

Small sparks of light broke the dark to her right. Moie pointed left: Jonah had appeared from behind a small hill, Rahim as ever at his side.

"What's happening, Moie?"

He shrugged, his face as always a mask of emotional detachment.

More sparks in the distance caused all around to duck. It was gunfire, she realised in a panic. Why was he always running towards gunfire?

"Moie, who is shooting at them?"

Moie pointed nonchalantly toward the flashes of light.

"Take me there!"

Again, they reached hands out toward each other. The world blurred briefly. Seven, no eight soldiers dressed in the garb of the royal guard materialised around her.

"Moie, you have to stop them!"

"I cannot, sister."

"There must be something you can do?"

"They only see me in the spirit sister, like you."

"Try! Please, little brother, try something!"

He stared for a moment, that same frustratingly calm expression on his face. Then, without warning, he moved calmly toward one of the men nearest; a fellow in the middle of calling and waving his hands about.

Moie's little arms flapped and waved in a most unenthused fashion. The soldier passed right through him. He trotted back around, jumping and yelling. Still the soldier showed no signs of notice.

Moie began to yell anew then paused. He leaned forward, causing his head to disappear within the soldiers. His arms flexed with the force of the yell.

The soldier jumped in shock, standing suddenly then falling over backwards. He pressed his hands to his ears.

Moie smiled and clapped, a look completely foreign on the child's face. He ran playfully over to the beleaguered man. Again, he leaned inside the soldier's head. This time the man leapt up, screamed and ran. His compatriots, having witnessed the behaviour, ceased their fire.

"What did you say to him?!" Assara asked.

"I say, worms! Very loud!" Moie smiled and clapped again. It was new to Assara's eyes, but delightfully so. Moie found another soldier and repeated the process. When that soldier abandoned his weapon and took flight Moie laughed openly.

"Thank you, little brother, but can we follow Jonah now?" Despite the diminutive sleep walker's talents, the spirit was starting to fade. Horses had appeared at the edge of her vision, white and black running ahead of each other. She knew in her heart they weren't really there.

Little Moie saw them too. His expression washed serious as he trotted quickly over and extended his hand. In less than a breath they two appeared right beside Jonah, crouching behind a short stone wall outside the village.

"What is this place?" Assara asked the darkness.

"Don't know, sister."

Jonah stood cautiously, signalling his men as he moved. His form shimmered, his eyes a glowing red fire. Power rippled from his shoulders like heat. She was genuinely intimidated by him.

"Sister, come back."

"Huh?" Looking at Moie separated her focus. Jonah's eyes returned to normal. She had nearly been taken again into visions. "Thank you, I will focus."

A pop, reminiscent of a memory, sounded in the hills behind. A wall nearby, one side of a small house nestled into the village streets, exploded. Assara crouched instinctively, screaming as flame and debris flew by her. She glanced over at Jonah. Though he was standing already, his back was ablaze.

"No!" She screamed, leaping towards him.

"Sister, wait!" Moie appeared between her and him. The second her eyes found the boy, the fire on Jonah vanished. "It is vision."

"What…" The explosion was real. The wall was well and truly on fire, crumbling around the now giant hole. "I don't… I can't…"

Soldiers adorned in the crown's colours appeared in the street. Jonah and Rahim began fighting for their lives.

"Is this a vision?" Assara called.

Moie strode carelessly through the mêlée. "No." He vanished, suddenly appearing on the shoulder of a man attacking Jonah, effortlessly attached despite the lunging and jerking. Again, his head sunk inside the others. Again the man stiffened in fright. Jonah didn't even flinch. His sword pierced the man's heart and, already thirsting for more, pulled Jonah and his cousin down an alley toward other Banji.

Assara's hands flew to her mouth. The bloodshed, the heartless nature of the killing… she could never get used to it. She would not.

Dirt erupted around her. The street was being fired upon by those enormous rifles. They had to put a stop to this, but how? One soldier at a time? Already she could see ten to fifteen more men entering the village from the direction they had come.

"Sister, you coming?" Moie asked.

"We have to stop this! Moie, many more men will die. What can we do?"

"I don't know?"

Assara let her love for Jonah draw her to him. She ran, through fire and flying debris. He lay, only his sword to protect him, behind the stone corner of a building. It seemed he was trying to draw their fire.

"What are you doing?" She cried. "Moie, please! You have to make them stop!"

The child looked genuinely affected. His eyes welled and his hands clenched. "I don't know how."

"Try, little brother. Tell them all to stop. Please, Moie…"

He hesitated, then turned and vanished, appearing next to a soldier. Gingerly he reached his ghostly hands into the man's head. The soldier's small gun began to rise for another shot then suddenly became heavy, sagging back to the street. The wielder's eyes glazed, no longer focused on any one thing. Moie's eyes were closed, his teeth gritted. He turned, looking towards another, then another. Eyes went blank, one by one. Some men collapsed, others just regarded their trembling hands in abject confusion. Assara smiled.

She was about to call a shout of elation to her small friend when ahead she spied Jonah's Banji about to launch into slaughter.

"No, wait…. Jonah!" She called, her words without voice or breath. She rushed to his side, pressed her hands without form to the sides of his head. As her forehead met his, time seemed to slow. He went still as she thought more than spoke –

It is over… tell your men to lay down their weapons, please…

His misting breath passed through her. Distant eyes focused close, closer…

He yelled something, words she did not understand. From his side Assara sensed more than noticed Rahim's complaints. Jonah stood, passing through her to stand in the street. The gunfire had ceased.

Assara spied the lone figure speeding towards Jonah's back a half second before Rahim shoulder charged him to the street. The sword that was meant for Jonah drew a lightning fast slash across Rahim's chest as he struggled to recover. The cry from Jonah's lips would normally have been muffled to Assara's ears. Instead it assaulted her mind.

King Fauld squared, levelling his exquisite blade at Jonah's chest. Down the street the fighting erupted anew. Moie whimpered, cowering against a wall. The two men leapt in, their swords arcing fire in the beleaguered street.

"Moie, help him!" She cried, but the child was afraid, as only a child can be. Swords lusted for each other, desperate to be free of their master's embrace. Fauld was ablaze with black fire from sword to boot, a sentient thing which quickly engulfed the entire town and everything in it. Jonah was a being of pure bronze; the fire did not touch him, rather it caused him to glow and shimmer.

She fought to stay, she could not drift into vision now. She could not hold for much longer though, and the fight for life seemed to rage endlessly. Fauld's blade of black fiery death lunged again and again, exploding off Jonah's own in blinding blossoms of energy. All she could do was watch in horror, fearing what would come next.

A shoe bounced solidly off Fauld's head, unbalancing him for just a moment. Assara did not see Jonah's blade enter the King's chest. A great wind entered him, drawing with it every ounce of living fire from the town. Jonah ripped his blade free and Fauld exploded, fire and force throwing Assara skyward…

She and Moie sat up in bed simultaneously. Jasmine, woken by the sudden movement, squinted against the daylight.

"What is it?" She asked, groggily.

Moie leapt over to Assara's bed and embraced her, sobbing quietly. Tamra woke as well, shaken by his leaping out of bed.

"What's going on?"

"Moie," Assara began. "Moie, it's alright. He's gone now."

"Who's gone?" Jasmine asked.

"Fauld. King Fauld. We just saw him killed. Jonah killed him."

"You were there? In the spirit, just now?" Jasmine pressed.

"Yes. He is dead, I am certain of it."

"That is good… I think. What will it mean for us though?"

Assara sighed in relief. "I don't know, but I do know we must inform Prince Cul right away."

*　　*　　*

Hatred filled Fauld's eyes even as the life seeped from them. Jonah cleared his blade aggressively then fell to his knees as his men cheered victory from wherever they fought. Swords fell from hands, rifles dropped to the ground. This, on top of the mental assault only a minute before, was enough to force a surrender.

Rahim grunted as he struggled to roll over. Jonah half ran, half crawled to him, retrieving a field dressing as he approached.

"Nice throw, cousin!" He said, not managing to hide the concern in his voice.

"Glad you appreciated my input." Rahim replied through gritted teeth. "How bad is it?"

"Your coat limited the depth of the cut, but it will need a lot of stitches."

"When you say a lot…"

"As in you will appear to be the product of the city's worst tailor."

Rahim chuckled, then grimaced. "Don't make me laugh."

"Captains." Some Banji appeared at a run. "We are disarming and binding the enemy."

"Get them inside, and bring me Jan. He is good with stitches." As they departed, Rahim voiced the question on both their minds.

"So, I suppose this will alter the strategy of the Four Families some, yes?"

Jonah allowed his gaze to sweep over the abandoned town. "Yes, I believe it will."

"Captains!"

The call from down the cobbled street drew their eyes. In the distance, limping slightly, came Bayern leading some men.

"Well, that all went rather horribly didn't it?" The staunch man called when he neared. He was clutching one of his enormous shoulders.

"Bayern." Jonah stood, clutching his hand in a sincere shake. "I am happy to see, alive you."

Rahim sat up with no small amount of effort. "What happened? Did you succeed in spiking the water supply?"

"Yes, but we were questioned and discovered as we tried to escape. We have been held prisoner here since then. After all this…" His huge arm featured dismissively toward the body of the fallen king. "Was it even worth it?"

"Bayern, my friend…" Rahim said wryly, sharing a knowing smile with his cousin. "You have no idea. These soldiers have been all over the place. Some ran away screaming for no reason, others simply laid down their guns in the middle of shooting at us."

"What??" He chuckled, incredulous. "I had no idea it would be so effective!"

"Poppy seed, it cause the mind to be, more easily spoiled." Jonah explained. "Believe me, you helped."

"So, what now?" Bayern asked them both.

"Now…" Jonah answered, his eyes on Fauld's corpse. "There is something we need to take to the front line."

*   *   *

Assara pressed through the complaints of the other slave women, not entirely sure where she was going but determined nonetheless. There was one sure fire way she would find Cul's tent.

Sure enough, there was the group of guards. They spotted her immediately. Two rushed forward, spears lowered threateningly, harsh words spilling from their mouths.

"Please, I must speak with Prince Cul. Prince Cul, take me to him!"

Just when she could move no further without becoming far more intimate with a blade than she had ever been, Cul appeared from the nearby hut in search of the disturbance.

"Young miss!" He spoke in his remarkably good Engsam. "You risk much by seeking me out."

"Please my Prince, there is something I must tell you."

He hesitated for a while before silencing the commotion with a raised hand. "Speak."

"King Fauld is dead."

At first his expression did not change. "How do you know this?"

"I just saw it happen. He was killed in a sword fight by, ah, Banji warriors."

"How did you see this?" his expression became hard. Assara's pulse quickened.

"In the spirit, my Prince."

"The spirit is lost to us."

"Yes, but…" She stammered, unsure how much to divulge. "With difficulty, my prince, I managed to see…"

"Are you… no, wait… the child. Fauld's messenger. I know him to be a sleepwalker. He can still visit the spirit?"

Her fear grew. Cul could be trusted, couldn't he?

"Yes. Moie helped me, to see in the spirit. We were both there when…"

He spoke in his native tongue though his eyes never left hers. Two guards departed, headed in the direction of the servant's quarters.

So cold, those eyes… and yet there was something in them.

Victory.

*   *   *

A lone bell rang out over Hamtel for hours as the rising sun read rooftops like braille. Captains, leaders of the crown's military, entered the village from the north where their advance had halted. The bells could mean only one thing.

Bayern met them as they arrived with his grim message: Faults head on a pike. There now was no successor to the throne, save only for the queen herself. Arms would be laid down until a new peace, or declaration of war, was presented.

At the town's southern border, awaiting the arrival of Lady Serong and her entourage, sat Jonah and his cousin. A half empty bottle of rum, liberated from an abandoned inn, adorned the short brick wall behind them.

"So, what will you say when you see her?" Jonah asked as he admired the sunrise.

"I haven't decided yet. I am torn between, 'you ask for a village, Rahim gives you a nation', and 'will you marry me?'"

Jonah laughed. A tension had left him, but in its place an anxiety had appeared.

"What will you say when you see her?" Rahim regarded him in a very knowing fashion.

"I am torn. All I want to know is if she cares for me as much as I care for her. Can such a thing be asked?"

"Blunt and honest has always worked for me." Rahim took another drink.

A group of riders cantered ahead of the column, the Lady Serong at their centre.

"Does that bell mean what I think it means?" She asked as she dismounted.

"May the rum we have drunk be your answer, my lady." Rahim said as he stood, then bowed. Jonah did the same.

"Lady Serong. Fauld was in Hamtel. We, crossed swords as we, took the village. He is dead."

"His severed head is currently negotiating a tentative peace with those soldiers still on the town's northern border." Rahim winked.

Lays Serong was impressed, although she tried to hide it. She turned to her guards. "Set up a camp for the crowns army on the eastern meadow. We will hold Hamtel until control of them has been legitimised. Move everyone else into the town, including the displaced residents." She turned back to the two Banji captains. "You are men of your word. You have restored a balance to these lands. Will you leave now to return home?"

They shared a glance, then said in unison, "Soon."

"Well in the meantime I am certain your presence will be appreciated in South Harbour. Word of the king's death will bring panic and could lead to rioting."

"Very well, Lady Serong. We will leave Hamtel in your, capable hands." Rahim bowed, Jonah nodded. Lady Serong took once more to her mount, smiling wryly as she departed.

"You know she is going to fill this town with drugs, don't you?" Jonah said, after she had ridden away.

"Absolutely. There goes an opportunist if ever I saw one."

"Come on." He said, already walking. "The sooner we rally the men into the city, the sooner we can go home."

*   *   *

"I don't like this."

Jasmine paused from her pacing long enough to stare up at the large round hut where Moie had been taken. "What are they doing to him in there?"

"They're talking, probably." Assara didn't sound confident. "Cul will just ask Moie to show him some places in the spirit tonight. I'm sure it will be ok."

"Don't worry sister." Tamra joined, sounding far more confident. "Prince Cul is a good prince, you'll see."

"Have you been getting anywhere in the spirit lately?" Assara asked her still pacing friend in an attempt to change the mood.

"No, not for weeks now. There are so many visions I have trouble remembering them all. Sleep passes quickly. Although, I am feeling more rested lately, despite all this."

"Maybe you are happier now?" Assara asked in hope.

"No, that's not it." Jasmine replied dismissively.

Finally, the flap at the hut entrance opened and out trotted little Moie. Were it possible, his diminutive form seemed even more so. The three girls waited till he drew near, then began the questioning.

"What happened?"

"He ask, how I know things. What I see. He ask, what can I do. Then he say I take him to the town tonight, in sleep."

"To Bandarat?" Jasmine asked. Moie nodded stiffly. "I knew it. He will try again to take the city."

"Really? But he was chased out of there last time by all those soldiers. What will be different this time?" Assara asked. She did not want to be anywhere near more fighting.

"It doesn't matter. He wants this, all of this." Slim fingers spread wide in dramatic fashion. "I knew he would not stay here."

Tamra grabbed Assara's hand. "Will he leave us here?"

"I... I don't know..."

"Will Jonah be on his way back to Bandarat, now that Fauld is dead?" Jasmine asked innocently.

"I... well, I guess so..." It suddenly felt like a long time since they had passed a message to each other. Even that had only happened once or twice. "Surely his men, his cousin will want to return home?"

"If they do, it may be to Prince Cul's sword." Came Jasmine's thoughtful reply.

"I don't know, do I Jasmine! I don't know everything like you do!"

There was no reply this time.

"Jasmine, I'm sorry! I am tired of being moved from one bed to another. I'm tired of wondering when we will be running for our lives again!"

"And you're worried about never seeing him again, aren't you?"

Frustration turned to exasperation on her face. "You really do know everything, don't you?"

Women carrying trays of steaming food appeared from around the corner. Spiced, minted meat on the bone wafted tantalising aromas from a bed of steamed vegetables and sweet breads. Through the bizarre babble that passed for language here, the small group found themselves herded inside and into a meal.

"So, miss 'know it all'." Assara questioned wryly. "Why is Prince Cul doing all this for us then?"

"Believe me, sister. If a man does something for you, he wants something from you. The only thing that I know for sure, is he wants our little sleepwalker here." Moie did not look up from his handful of meat and mashed vegetables. "My guess is he wants us, or more importantly little brother here, to sleep."

She was right, Assara knew. Still, was there any malice in Cul's actions? Was it wrong of him to make use of the gifts Moie possessed?

Something inside her said yes.

*   *   *

Jonah and Rahim marched their men slowly south toward the city throughout the day. It had been a hard twenty-four hours and neither knew what they would find in South Harbour. A city suddenly freed from rule could be an absolute catastrophe. Could be a week-long celebration as well.

Another messenger galloped past carrying negotiations between the Four Families' contingents. It was a terribly inefficient means of communication, but now that the spirit was all but lost there was little in the way of alternatives. The two cousins shared a knowing glance.

"How much do you suppose Lady Serong is trying to get away with while this back and forth continues?" Jonah asked good-naturedly.

"By now I am sure half of these messages all say the same thing: don't do that! Which, by the time it arrives, will have given her plenty of time to do just that. She will own that town by the time the other family heads have even laid eyes on it again." Rahim replied, laughing.

"She would be a troublesome wife, that one." His raised eyebrow signalled the direct nature of the observation. Rahim was not fazed.

"Only to the weak, cousin. A strong man such as myself needs a worthy challenge, both at the table and in the bedroom!"

Movement down the wide road caught their attention. A contingent of soldiers with banners was approaching from the south.

"Is that Lady June?"

He stood, using Rahim's shoulder as a crutch. "Yes. Seems her entire contingent is with her."

"Are they going home, or into Hamtel before Lady Serong makes off with the entire town?"

He shrugged around a mischievous smile.

As Lady June's honour guard neared, Jonah ordered his men to a pause in respect. She offered a nod as she passed, but did not speak. The gesture was polite and very, very measured.

"She does not trust us."

"Nonsense." The manner in which his cousin clapped his shoulder displayed his insincerity. "She just hasn't worked out how to chain you to her bed yet. Shall I offer her a veil over which to bat her eyelids?"

Jonah withheld his cold retort. A prickle in his shoulders gave him pause, pulled his eyes to the horizon.

"What is it?"

"Something..." He sighed, forcing his shoulders to relax. "Call the men back to the march. We can cover a few more miles tonight before we make camp."

      *   *   *

The Banji captain's gaze passed right through him. Yes, there was a very good reason why this one was in command. He had instincts to rival Cul's own.

"This is the man who lead these here. He warn, when soldiers come to kill you." The child said, quite unnecessarily. Marema-moie's voice was a wisp on a soundless breeze, barely registering in the cacophony that surrounded them.

This was the man who would challenge him for possession of the city.

"Take me to Bandarat." Cul placed a filmy palm onto where the boy's shoulder should be. The world shifted. Day became night, meadow's dusty streets and laneways.

"The palace."

In less of a blur and more of a melt this time, walls bled from clay brick to columns. The courtyard was all he could see, beyond that the world of visions raged, consuming the horizon of the real world.

Cul walked toward a hallway. Marema-moie followed dutifully, fearfully. The hall led to a formal dining area, then the throne room. Sure enough, draped arrogantly over the unnecessarily wide throne, sat Falan. Representatives from South Harbour, still dressed in rather complicated fashion, reclined nearby.

This truce would easily be broken.

"Boy, we must tell these ones," he gestured to the foreigners at their table, "that their king is dead."

"I will find someone who is asleep, and speak to them."

Cul nodded. The child vanished, with what seemed a look of some relief. Marema-moie was afraid of him.

Good.

He paced slowly around Falan, watching him drink wine and regard the room with absolute arrogance. A cruel twist of fate that one such as this could rise to prominence, but even the foolish fell onto cushions sometimes. Then they fell again, and that time? That time would be different. Falan's nakedness was all of a sudden arousing to him. One of the many crocodiles in the room snapped at Cul, a ferocious growl gripping the young prince's heart with fear.

The fright was enough to wake him. He punched his bed hard, then leapt from it in search of clothes. He was outside, striding past the night watch less than a minute later.

The flaps about the servant's hut banged loudly as he burst through. All inside woke sharply, including Marema-moie.

"Is it done?" Cul barked.

"My prince, what is the matter?" Assara asked. Cul ignored her, striding to the bed where Moie and Tamra slept.

"Is it done?" He pressed again.

"I think, yes…" The boy stammered, obviously rattled. "I find two soldiers, and tell them. Then you wake me."

He realised suddenly how his impatience had gotten under his own feet. He was losing composure.

"Good, boy. More soldiers must be told. Continue till morning."

He left quickly, not wanting to bandy more with the foreign servants. Despite their lack of humility and proper decorum there was a loyalty there which he never questioned. It made him soft toward them, especially toward Tamra and Assara. The way they accepted him, treated him as if he were family… it was disarming. Intoxicating almost.

He must keep his distance.

*   *   *

As night fell later that evening Jonah quickly found his rest thanks mostly to the little sleep, and the long march, of the previous day and night. Plus, fighting for one's life generally involved some recovery. He ached to see Assara. They had barely communicated lately, plus it was becoming difficult to distinguish reality from the dream. Was she really outside of the city now? Was she still with Cul, and if so, why?

A familiar and yet puzzling dreamscape opened up before him. He was aware, and yet not aware that he slept. Thoughts of Assara brought him a mixture of comfort and longing but not, he realised dimly, a clear vision of her. Moie seemed to be the only one left who could still reach the spirit.

Moie. Maybe that was worth a try. Familiar landscapes formed that both were, and were not, his homeland to the east. In a small village in a clearing Moie and Prince Cul appeared, Moie as an infant and Cul as Jonah's own brother. He continued to focus on Moie. Cul's form melted away as Moie's became firmer, more familiar. He was no longer in a clearing but in a hut. Tamra took shape beside him, they were folding blankets together. No sign of Assara though.

Little Moie started ever so slightly, then rushed to where Jonah's spirit stood. "Man!" He said urgently. "The Prince, he look for you. He make me bring him to you in spirit."

Jonah knelt down, picturing his ghostly knees resting on the rug until it was so. "Cul is looking for me? Why?"

"He say you will be coming for Bannerat. He also want big town. He will fight you for it when you come back."

Ramifications stumbled one against the other in Jonah's sleep addled mind. Cul *had* been pushed out of Bandarat, and he wanted it back. More importantly though was the fact that regardless of Jonah being essentially on the other side of the world, Cul considered him to be his biggest threat.

"What of Assara, little one?" He questioned, but before Moie could answer Cul burst into the room, a beast with the body of a wolf and the head of a snake making threatening noises at his side. The prince's sudden appearance was rattling the spirit.
"To whom do you speak, Marema-moie? Tell me!"

Tamra instinctively stepped between the two. A vulture swooped upon them like a mother protecting its nest. Assara appeared at the doorway, her ample bosom showing from beneath a thin, copper shift.

"Bandarat is mine!" Cul yelled, his form already diminishing. "If you challenge me for it, you will die!"

Jonah spent the remainder of his rest hearing Assara call his name, though in reality, or as a dream, he couldn't be sure. The cold woke him, a harsh precursor to the azure sky that followed.

When Rahim woke about twenty minutes later, Jonah was searching the dawn for answers he had not yet formed questions for.

"I hate sleeping on the ground. It is cold enough to make ice angry."

"I have a fire going."

"You have kindling resisting death. Where is the blaze, cousin? We have no fear of attack, do we?"

"No." Came the very unsure reply. "No, we do not."

"Oh, I see." Falling logs punctuated the sarcasm. "What did she do? Or could you not see her? Hard to see my hand in front of my face in the spirit these days." The flames began to take. Other soldiers came to take braziers to fires of their own. "So," Rahim pressed, with a little more sincerity. "What happened?"

The young Banji leader sighed, then smiled. "I suppose I shouldn't be surprised. We are never far from the fire." Rahim gestured with his hands for a continuation. "I managed to visit the east in the spirit. I was having difficulty reaching Assara, so I searched for Marema-moie instead."

"The child sleepwalker?"

"Yes. When I found him he had a warning for me. He was forced to bring Prince Cul to me in the spirit."

"Prince Cul wanted to visit you in his sleep?"

"Yes."

"I would have thought he would be more interested in Bandarat. But, of course... those loyal to the Shareef hold the city."

Jonah nodded.

"And Cul still wants Bandarat for himself."

Again, he let his cousin find his own conclusions.

"So, when we get back... he thinks you will take charge. I thought Falan had taken power? Are you planning on killing him? Because you know I had claimed preference."

The jest was not lost on him, despite his mirth melting quickly away. "Cul appeared, he heard the warning. He threatened to kill me if I claimed the city for my own."

"I am at something of a loss." Rahim showed Jonah his backside, not as a gesture of dismissal but simply because his front was now too warm. "Were you also planning on proclaiming yourself king of the east, and forgot to mention it?"

Genuine laughter accompanied his response. "Believe me cousin, the thought had never occurred to me."

"Until now. But the truth is, if we kill Falan, which I fully intend to do…"

"Mine may just be the strongest claim."

"Huh." They both mused aloud.

"Unless of course we don't kill Falan, and let him rule…" Jonah pondered. Almost immediately they in unison agreed.

"Absolutely not."

"I am beginning to understand the state I discovered you in this morning." Each word brought Rahim closer, until at the last each had a hand on the other's shoulder. "We are in for a fight when we get home."

"So, we will return home then?" The question was for himself as much as it was for his faithful companion. "With what is left of our contingent to retake the city?"

"What else can we do?"

"I thought you had grand plans for you and the Lady Serong?"

"And what about your plans for Assara? No, cousin. It must be this way. It was always going to be this way. We must return home."

At that moment Jonah had a very clear sense of his cousin's devotion. Of his brother's devotion. Perhaps it was dreaming of having a brother that had caused a revelation. Here was one who was closer than family, deserving of the title.

"Thank you, brother."

A clap, reminiscent of an oncoming storm, stole their attention north.

"It can't be…." Jonah said, unconsciously stepping toward the sound.

A second, then a third followed. There was heavy cloud about, but it was not the sound of thunder. Jonah's men were dressing for battle.

"Fauld's men mounting a resistance?"

"Whoever it is, I believe our blades will be needed more in Hamtel than the city today."

"We sail for home tomorrow, then?" Rahim said as he gathered his sword belt around his waist. Jonah's only answer was a grim look.

  * * *

Again, Assara found herself bundled and herded into a march. Again, forced from civilisation into the wilderness.

"I'm still tired from walking here!" Tamra complained. With relief she saw that Cul was not around, so her sister's complaints would not be heard.

"Please Tamra. I know you're tired, but we mustn't cause a fuss."

"Listen to your sister, little peach." Jasmine crouched to add effect. "I will carry you if I need to."

"You better."

The party of slaves moved off, taking the first steps of the two-day journey back to Bandarat, soldiers ahead and behind.

"You think he can do it?" Assara asked Jasmine without looking over. Moie, ever at their side, glanced up but did not speak.

"He has a good advantage, being in possession of the only sleepwalker. No-one will see him coming. Cul can search their defences, numbers, even find where their leaders are sleeping and…"

Tamra was watching her so she left the remainder of the thought unspoken.

"I wonder whether Jonah is on his way here?" Jasmine asked casually.

"I am not sure what to hope for." She stumbled, her thoughts interrupting her footing. "After what Cul said in the hut last night…"

She waited for the harsh life lesson, the truth laid bare with forked tongue. In its place was a most sincere, "I am sure it will work out."

From Jasmine the sentiment sounded like a death sentence.

She looked down at Moie, her only contact with her distant paramour and now Cul's greatest weapon. His little eyes watched his small feet take step after step. Moie had always seemed sad, conflicted, always reflecting a forced submission somehow. He looked more a slave than ever. Defeated, and accepting of his fate.

"Moie?" She asked, helping him climb down the stairs made for giants. He looked up but did not speak. "You know we are family now, right? We will never leave you. You are safe with us."

The growing dark matched a gloom in the boy's eyes. Assara wished she had more to offer him.

"This man of yours. Jonah. How great a warrior is he?" Despite the question being obviously directed at her, Jasmine kept her eyes on the horizon.

"He has led his men to many victories, both with the rifle and the sword, both here and in my homeland."

"Hmmm."

When her friend did not continue, Assara pressed. "Are you thinking about who will win?"

"Yes."

Steps kept coming, and silence with them. "And?" She pressed again.

A heavy sigh precluded the answer. "It's not that I don't think Jonah could triumph over our prince here. It's just that Cul has the advantage. If Jonah could make it back to Bandarat before him, he could double his forces. He is, however, more than a month away. By then Cul will have removed Jonah's allies, he will know exactly where Jonah is coming from thanks to our little brother here, and will have the defences of the city walls as well."

Assara didn't answer. More steps punctuated the silence.

"Maybe… maybe you should tell him not to come back."

She stopped then, giving Jasmine a look that defied description. Still she did not speak. What could she say in the face of such honesty?

Moie took her hand, then gently pulled her once again into the march. Whatever lay at the end, standing still could prevent nothing.

*   *   *

Jonah ran his men hard back up the miles they had just walked. They were ragged by the time they reached the battle line. Well away from danger, in an impressively large tent, was the Lady June and her honour guard. He was admitted entry, but was painfully aware of swords leaving scabbards as he entered.

"My Lady June." He said as respectfully as he could. "We heard gunfire, explosions. Has the late king's army mounted a resistance?"

She studied him in place of reply, her expression grave and threatening. He glanced at the men to his left and right. They held their blades flat, ready to strike.

"When we left, the Lady Serong was in the village. Have you had news from her?"

An eyebrow lifted, showing a mix of interest and insult. "The Lady Serong," she drawled, breaking at last her silence, "is in the village still."

"Is she safe? Does she require assistance?"

"Assistance?!" The snort took nothing from her regal demeanour. "Considering the rate at which she is firing those insane cannons at us, I would say she needs very little assistance, thank you."

"The, Lady Serong is –"

"Currently firing on us, yes."

Her eyes held his, studiously observing every twitch of his eye, every set of his limbs.

"You are waiting to see if we will take sides."

"Not waiting, so much as insisting." Those swords hadn't moved an inch.

Jonah paused, resetting his posture. He stood tall, but not proud, set his shoulders and clasped his hands before him comfortably. "I understand your, ah, situation, my lady. But please understand, we came here on oath, which we broke, after a fashion. Our task, done. The Lady Serong may hold Hamtel, for now, but real prize – South Harbour – hard fought and won. Release us. We will leave these shores. My men wish to shed no more of your noble blood."

"Hmmph. You speak well, outlander, considering ours is not your tongue. I will not, however, let you go." He made to interject but she spoke straight over him. "Your knowledge of the weapons she has turned on us is unmatched, your relationship with Serong can be exploited and you have just been battling in Hamtel so you have the best intelligence as to the state of the city. South Harbour will not be divided three ways while some child controls the greatest trade route into the north." Realising she was leaning forward in her chair, she forced herself to relax. "You will fight for me, my boy, like it or not. Though I suspect not."

Jonah's hands were now clenched at his sides, his breathing flaring his chest.

"Rest your men, I know you have run hard to be here. I will call on you later. Run, and you will be shot. I can have a pigeon with orders to keep you from a ship should you make it as far as the city, so trust me when I say you have no choice but to accept your fate. Return to your men, Jonah of the Banji."

He did leave, rather than speak the words forming on his breath. Rahim and a few others were waiting close by, crouched in a circle. They stood when they saw him approach.

"What is it?"

"Serong. She is using Fauld's rifles to take Hamtel for herself."

"Opportunist indeed!" Rahim actually smiled.

"Cousin, June is forcing us to remove her, or we will be killed."

"She wants us to attack Serong? Now they are at war with each other? Pitts and the pestilence! How does this keep happening?"

"Can we run, captain? Make it to a ship?" another asked.

"Even if we made it to the docks alive, we would have to take a vessel by force. None of us know how to sail."

"None of us know how to sail…" Rahim mimicked sarcastically. "By the mother's milk, I am about to start killing every single person in this fortune forsaken land, and name myself king!"

"What are your orders, captain?"

"Rest." His eyes sought the village. He would end this here, somehow. "Whatever happens next, we need to rest."

He would visit Assara in the spirit. Once he saw her, was reminded of where he was headed, the journey would matter less.

He just had to see her.

*   *   *

Prince Cul marched his fractured nation throughout the night, until all that stood between them and Bandarat was a few foothills and the flatland that had been the city's greatest ally for a hundred years.

Here he finally ordered all to rest, but no fires would be made in the hope of keeping his approach secret.

Nursing swollen feet and aching backs, Assara and her surrogate family crawled onto a bed mat under a low tent canopy. Tamra and Jasmine fell asleep in seconds, far more accepting of whatever fate lay ahead. She had little chance of relaxing. Her mind raced, struggling to find the answer to the conflict between her love, and her master.

In answer to her reverie, the young prince strode past her small party, pausing slightly as he glanced in. His eyes were seeking Moie, but found hers as well. As he moved away, she leapt up, defying the protests from her weary body. Moie watched dispassionately her departure.

"My prince..." She called quietly, prostrating herself to avoid retribution for calling on him. She heard, rather than saw, him stop and sigh.

"What is it?"

"Please my prince, you have nothing to fear from Jonah. If you will offer him a peaceful return -"

"I offered those loyal to the Shareef peace. It nearly cost me my life. It is not a mistake I will repeat."

She struggled to find words, but none came, only shallow breaths.

"How do you know him? When did you meet?"

"Ah, my prince..." She stammered. "It is, hard to explain."

"Try."

"Jonah and I, we met in the spirit."

He walked closer. "Are you also a sleepwalker?" His tone was suddenly dangerous.

"No, no my prince, I swear."

"Then how?"

"I, we just, followed each other. Our paths crossed in Safar, briefly… I don't know how else to describe it…"

"You are in love with this man?"

As the holding of a breath one longs to release, so came the word. "Yes."

Cul knelt down, raising her chin with a gentle hand. "I am truly sorry. I have no desire to hurt you, or your family. You have brought me luck at every turn, despite the fact that you are foreign to this place, to me. For this I show you favour. I cannot, however, let a snake into my bed for you."

He stood then, walking away without another word. Assara waited a moment, then returned to where Moie lay still fighting sleep.

"Sister." He said, ever in the emotionless manner which so personified him. "We will be ok."

She hugged him close, more to hide the welling of her eyes than anything. Sleep finally took them both.

The spirit was ablaze with wind, noise and fire. Assara turned her head from her sleeping form. Moie's ghostly figure was seated cross legged at the wall of their small tent, staring west.

"Moie?" She asked, her words barely more than a drop in a storm. He looked at her, then pointed towards the tent wall, and the city beyond.

Miles melted before them as the city rushed near. It caught fire, or was already on fire, she couldn't be sure. She was aware of the screams of people as they perished, as walls fell and flames consumed.

"It is a vision, nothing more."

Her head snapped in fright to reveal Cul, also in the spirit, watching the scene unfold.

"How do you know?" She yelled over the maelstrom. "How do you know it is not a warning?"

In answer to her fears an enormous cracking explosion sounded from over the ocean. Great plumes of fire and molten rock sprang forth. A great wave came next, smashing walls and toppling the towers of the palace. The sky boiled as at the worlds ending.

"Cul!" She yelled. Moie reached out to her.

"It a vision, nothing more!" Even the prince was yelling now.

Somehow, beyond conscious perception, Southharbour and Bandarat became one terrible visage of death and destruction. Her homeland, distant and dark, fell to wind, waves and fire. The heavens clawed at the earth. Everywhere people fell to the chaos.

"Cul, please!"

"Assara?"

Her breath caught so hard in her chest at first she couldn't move. When finally her form responded to her will, she saw him. Jonah, as clear as he had ever been, standing right in front of Cul.

"Jonah?"

"Banji captain!" Cul stepped to the side, his stance indicative of one bearing a sword. "Witness your death, warrior!"

Moie continued to watch the world end, his expression unchanging.

"Jonah, you must not return!" Assara stood before him, hands reaching in futility toward him.

"This is your sign, warrior!" Cul gestured to the scene before them with the sword that had appeared in his hand. "Your end awaits you."

Jonah all but ignored him. "No, prince. It is what awaits us all."

"What is this? What is happening? Jonah, are you really here?"

A woman appeared at Jonah's shoulder, young, lithe and pretty.

"Lady Serong? Yes, I am here!" He replied, to Assara's horror.

"Where are we? Who are these people? Why is my homeland being destroyed?"

Moie stood calmly, then took a step toward the vision ahead. "I have seen this dream, many share it. Common dream, common fear. It is on our mind all the time, and this is why we are making it."

"In the spirit." Cul yelled.

"No." he shook his head in response, but did not turn it. "In the flesh."

"What is he talking about?" Serong yelled.

"He's right!" Jonah turned, eyes on the horizon. "This is what we are creating with our actions, our war."

"You don't believe that!" Cul screamed.

"You do." Moie spoke gently, now looking back at him.

"I knew it!" the newcomer, the strange girl, exclaimed. "Somehow I knew it was too much, but I was greedy, and it was so easy… Jonah, please, you have to help me! What have I done?"

"Lady Serong?" He called back, but even as the words left his mouth her hands began to melt from her outstretched arms. She screamed as she vanished.

"Cowards!" Cul yelled to no-one in particular. His form shifted and warped, as each person's vision of him fought for prominence. "I will not yield." He too vanished, leaving only Moie, Jonah and herself.

"Assara!" He called. Despite her fears something soared in her, hearing her name on his voice.

"Jonah, you mustn't come…"

"I am coming. I am coming for you." He was close now.

"Cul will – "

"Cul cannot. Whatever force is bringing us together, it is bigger than Cul, bigger than his greed. Wait for me, Assara."

Moie cried out suddenly, small hands flying to his eyes.

"Wait for me…"

Again the small boy cried out. Assara woke in an instant, wrenched so suddenly from the spirit that her held felt clapped from each side. She gasped as she sat, waking all with her.

Jasmine, as always, reacted first. "What is it? Did you see something while you slept?"

"Ah, my head… I saw Jonah, and Cul and, someone I didn't recognise… what time is it?"

Moie groaned where he lay, alerting them to his condition. "My head hurts."

"I'm not surprised, poor thing!" Water was nearby, contained in a skin. She wet a part of a shirt and placed it against his temples. "Four people sharing a vision of the end of the world, must be hard on you."

"What did you see? Can you tell me?" Tamra queried.

"Some other time, sister." Sounds of activity, of swords and shields being readied, carried to them in the dark. Peering outside they discovered the last of the day giving in to the assault of night.

"What is happening? Are we marching again?"

"Cul." Her eyes were sad over the words. "Cul is attacking the city."

*   *   *

"Argh!" His temples fought to leave his head in both directions at once. The bitter cold of early morning here helped sooth the throbbing, but still the pain was unexpected. Rahim was already up and dressed.

"You seemed to be deep, so I decided to let you rest. Are you unwell?"

He paused a moment, then regarded his cousin seriously.

"Follow me."

In as little as he could afford to wear he burst from the tent, Rahim hot on his heels.

"Jonah! Where are we going?"

"Just follow me!"

He was unarmed so despite the panicked looks he received as he ran through the camp, none challenged his passing.

"We are headed for the village, yes?" Rahim yelled between breaths. "Did you see Lady Serong last night?"

"Yes." Over cook fires and horse lines they ran, ever nearing the killing ground between the two armies.

"Did you arrange something?"

"No, not exactly."

"So will she shoot at us?"

"I really do not know."

"Did I ever mention," Rahim went on, "how much I enjoy these little excursions?"
Finally, from the camp they were about to exit, an alarm bell sounded. Someone must have decided they were defecting. Jonah's back itched in thought of the shot that was minutes away.

They breached the firing line facing Hamtel, the open ground here now full of holes. The town itself lay not fifty feet away. All he could do now was hope that Serong's men did not automatically open fire.

Someone burst from behind cover, a petite form scrambling over stacked boxes and crates. Blonde hair flapped haphazardly from shoulder to shoulder as she ran, as fast as Jonah himself, from Hamtel toward them.

"Jonah!"

The lady Serong crashed clumsily into his arms mere moments later, much to the chagrin of Rahim. She sobbed softly, looking more a lost, confused child than the fierce tactician they had come to know.

"We're going to die, all of us... we're going to die..." Was all she said.

"No, no it's going to be fine. It can be fine. You must make peace though, otherwise... well, you saw..."

"Cousin, I don't mean to be rude, but an explanation would be appreciated..."

In answer Jonah passed her to him. She didn't complain. He led them back toward the front line of Lady June's army, to where Lady June herself, now roused by the alarm, was waiting.

"Would you care to tell me," The staunch, proud woman began before suddenly recognising the child in Rahim's arms. "By all the North. What did you do to her?"

Serong did her best to compose herself. "Lady June. I have seen... I have decided..."

For a moment all June did was stare, obviously weighing up the situation. When at last she spoke, her posture changed in an instant. "For heaven's sake girl." The words ventured through a sigh, the kind only disapproving mothers can do. "Let's get you cleaned up. You can tell me about it when you are yourself again."

Lady June all but stole Serong from Rahim's arms, giving him a look which said 'this must be your fault' as she did.

Rahim waited patiently for the women to leave before turning to Jonah with a look of genuine exasperation.

"Now, for the love of the mother, will you please tell me what just happened?"

*　　*　　*

Assara moved as quickly as she dared through the small camp in the direction of Cul's tent. As before, she just followed the swords. Still she feared retribution for stepping outside of her position. Cul was far more understanding than those loyal to him.

She was, however, too late. From a little hill she saw the line of men beginning their march toward battle. The prince glanced back, a leader governing his troops. As their eyes met, for a moment that grim determination, that fierce stubbornness, softened. Only for a moment. Then he turned and began the low, hunched run of a soldier racing fate.

"I do admire you, you know."

Jasmine appeared at her side, crouched low against the rise.

"Why?"

"You have a hope that does not fade. You seem to only see what people can become, whereas I see only what they are."

Assara sighed, her gaze tracking Cul's band until the night all but swallowed them.

"Come. Tamra and Moie will be missing us by now."

*   *   *

It happened thus: Cul's forces entered the city through the same broken wall which had facilitated his escape two nights past. Patrols, guarding the streets after dark, spotted them quickly. Most of the soldiers of the crown, the late King Fauld's military, had left or were leaving, having confirmed their liege, and by proxy their orders, were deceased. Cul pressed his advantage.

His prowess with the sword carried him almost to the palace where finally, in the dark and dusty street, he faced the man who had led this latest rebellion. Falan, of the Banji, was no match for him. He fell quickly to Cul's sword.

It was not, however, Cul's victory that was spelled in blood on the street that night. As is often the case in battle, remnants of the

Shareef's army, given time to mount a defence, opened fire on him now that he was in the open. Terrible apparatuses of destruction were the Shareef's mighty rifles. By the time the smoke cleared, there was nothing left of young Prince Cul.

His people waited through the night for the signal of victory. They waited through the next day. When again night began to fall, group by group they abandoned their camp to begin the trek back east to their huts and homes, acknowledging their fallen hero through silence.

The next morning, a full day and night since Cul had marched on the city, Assara woke hungry. Moie was sleeping so soundly his little snores sounded monstrous, so uncharacteristic were they from him.

She climbed from the small tent, rousing the others as she shuffled.

They were completely alone.

"They left us behind?" Her sister asked, peering out from her knees.

"I guess so."

"I'm hungry."

"Yeah, me too. Jasmine, why did they leave us?"

Her friend paced around, stretching the hard night from her back. "I don't know… maybe now that Cul is gone all bonds are broken… or maybe they are expecting us to return once we have finished grieving, however long that is?"

Assara looked west, toward the much contested Bandarat. "That is where we must go. That is where Jonah will look for me."

Jasmine didn't pause long before nodding in agreement. "Did you see him last night?"

"No, I didn't see the spirit at all. You?"

"Only visions."

"I saw a man with no face, coming from over the ocean." Now Tamra also looked west. "It was strange."

Assara's stomach rumbled noisily. "Whatever that means, the ocean is where we must go."

*   *   *

Four banners lined the road at the entrance to South Harbour, their graceful and lithe motion a stark opposite to the city's rigid doors. The four Ladies of the Four Families stood together, but still slightly apart. At least, Jonah mused, they weren't shooting at each other.

He and Rahim approached Lady Serong, naturally at the end of the order, leading their somewhat diminished band of warriors. Despite the breach of decorum she hugged Jonah warmly as he came near.

"Travel safe. I hope to see you again one day."

"Perhaps you will. May I ask a favour?"

"You may?" She replied, fully returned to her previous authority.

"Please pass this letter on to the man Sivvel, and treat him well. A large part of this victory belongs to him."

"I will see it done." Her look conveyed the seriousness with which she took the charge. She turned then to Rahim, who was blushing slightly. "And you. Take care of your cousin."

"Easier said than do- "a light kiss cut off the last word.

"You are always welcome in our kingdom, Banji." Lady Jocelyn announced regally, as Ladies May and June watched on.

"Thank you. I hope we can return soon. Something tells me trade will soon be busy between our nations."

"We hope so. These carriages will transport you to the dock where a ship awaits. Wools, silks and spices have been gifted in thanks for your service."

He nodded graciously. He hadn't been expecting a payment.

"It is a changed world, Jonah of the Banji." Jocelyn continued. "Why this thing called 'dreaming' has come none can say. It has placed a distance between us at a time when our peoples are closer than ever."

"Then let us new ways find, to communicate." Jonah replied.

"Well said. Travel well."

The looks that followed he and his men onto the carriages still spoke mostly of relief. It was a trust that could only be built with time, he realised. He would have to make efforts to keep the trade alive, preserving the friendship which had been so hard won. Tomorrow's problems.

"Are you ready to go home, cousin?" He asked, expecting an immediate reply.

After a pause, Rahim answered. "Yes. Yes, I am. Ready for that, and more."

"More?"

"Indeed, cousin!" Trademark joviality returned to Rahim's voice. "I am ready to be an uncle!"

Jonah would have protested, had laughter not drowned the words.

*   *   *

A strange mood had fallen over Bandarat. The constant attacks, changes in leadership, it had all taken a toll on the heart of the city. Perhaps it was the late winter winds speaking quiet uncertainty in the streets that huddled people in corners, or perhaps it was the lack of a clear ruler that fuelled anxiety. Perhaps it was all of it.

Whatever the cause, Assara and her party entered the city unchecked. No guards searched them, or asked about their allegiance. Everyone avoided everyone else.

Unsure where to find a bed or food, the group wandered along familiar streets, gravitating back toward the bunkhouse which had last been their refuge. Very few hawkers braved the melancholy day, and those that did sat quietly at their stalls. Assara tried to smile at them, but found only distrust in their eyes.

The three girls walked closer and closer together, the pall around them keeping conversation to a minimum. The only one immune was Moie, who for some reason all but skipped down the streets. When at last they neared the bunkhouse, a meeting of some sort was happening on the street outside, people coming and going in groups. A few local men were issuing direction between bouts of serious discussion.

They were near enough that words became clear. Unfortunately, those words were not Engsam.

"Moie, what are they saying?"

"They are telling people where to go, giving them jobs."

"Can you ask them if we can work for food?"

He moved easily into the dissipating crowd, quickly gaining the attention of a few leaders. As the conversation progressed Moie pointed at the girls, the bunkhouse and the palace. Assara even thought she heard Jonah's name mentioned. Finally, with a surprisingly charming nod, little Moie finished his negotiation and returned.

"The man say there is food inside." He pointed to their recently abandoned room. "He also say to go back to what you were doing before, that they try to put Bandarat back together."

Tamra and Assara both turned to Jasmine. "Let's just pretend you were here, on the laundry cart with us, this whole time."

"Agreed."

In the bunkhouse, filling the space where the building expanded left for closets, a table was filled with pots containing soup and plates of rolls. Moie led the way, his bizarre new carefree attitude carrying him skipping to the food, much to the delight of those attending it. The two women there clapped their hands and soothed his greasy hair like doting aunts as they filled a plate of food for him. They also said much to Jasmine and Assara, none of which was understood. Their affection then moved to Tamra, who smiled warmly under the attention.

"What are they saying, Moie?"

He didn't stop eating to reply. "They say things like adorable, we look hungry, they look after us, poor children."

"Poor children!" Jasmine barked, her voice brimming indignation.

"Jasmine, we are safe. We are fed. Let us be gracious."

They approached again, already offering seconds. Though they directed questions at the girls, Moie answered.

"I say, we work the laundry cart. She recognise us. She will bring it for us tomorrow. She say men moving into palace. Men taking charge of city."

"Are they nice men, Moie?" Tamra asked.

"They are Banji, like Jonah."

"What does that mean?" She pressed, looking up at her big sister.

"It means," Assara replied with a burgeoning hope, "that Jonah can safely come home."

*   *   *

Four weeks later Assara still struggled to communicate in the local tongue, despite exhausting herself through practice.

"Hello." She said clumsily. Her grasp of the language was still terrible. It didn't help that even those who tried to teach her still spoke faster than her mind could decipher.

"Hello, Assara." The server answered, then asked her something about the food that she missed. She nodded, held out her deep rimmed plate and hoped for the best. A slop of oats spread quickly to the edges, followed by a ladle of milk and some drizzled honey.

"Ooh good!" Tamra exclaimed next to her. "I love oats and honey."

"Where is the bacon?" Moie protested, then apparently repeated the question in Banji. The server just laughed and scuffed his hair. Jasmine, standing behind him, smoothly requested a hot drink. With a sincere nod of approval, it was provided.

"How do you do that?" She was genuinely frustrated.

"Don't worry sister, you will get it. You just need more practice."

"My tongue is still tired from last night's practice. Speaking should not be such hard work."

"I like it." Tamra was already seated and stuffing her face. "Everything sounds funny here, even food!"

"You are very clever, my little peach!" A nuzzling as Jasmine sat next to her brought a squeal of delight. "You will be announcing kings and queens in the city centre before long, I am sure!"

A few minutes passed as the four filled empty bellies. "What is it, Assara?" Jasmine asked. "You have seemed a little, well, off lately?"

"Off? No, no I'm fine."

"Are you sure? Are you a bit tired of the laundry cart?"

"No, I like the cart."

"Because we can talk to the captains, they seem quite open to people's requests?"

"No, really. I like the cart."

"It is the man." Moie joined. "She hasn't heard from the man, Jonah."

Assara didn't answer, but she didn't have to. Jasmine tried her best to look sympathetic.

"Oh. Because the spirit is gone. Assara, I'm sorry."

"You still haven't seen him, Moie?" She asked, already knowing the answer.

"No, sister. Spirit is gone, gone since we watch the world end."

She nodded.

"Sister, it will be alright. Let's get to work. Afterwards, we will go to the square and watch the dancing, maybe even try a few steps."

"Yes." She said, faking relief at the suggestion. "I would like that."

It was a long day that day. The sun was high, but the season bled some warmth, which made for a perfect temperature. The city was experiencing a feeling of freedom that shone from the eyes and spilled from the mouths of all they saw. All Assara saw, however, was him: in every face, around every corner, every time she turned her head.

It was the end of the week, which meant there would be celebrations in the square into the evening. Their duties fulfilled, they four wandered into the cacophony, Tamra and Moie immediately joining the dance. Assara couldn't help but smile. For the first time, she felt that her family, now bigger than ever, could relax. Finally, they were safe.

The music stopped abruptly. All around hushed and pointed. As usual, she had no idea what was being said. Instinctively she gathered Tamra and Moie close to her.

"What is it, Moie? What are they saying?"

"Someone is here." He replied, his tone unreadable.

Crowds gathered around them, preventing them from seeing who, or what, was coming. No-one seemed panicked, which should have comforted her.

It did not.

*   *   *

After a week at sea, Jonah stood comfortably on the deck despite the rolling ocean. Though the morning sun was now over the horizon, it as yet struggled to lift the chill from the air. He couldn't wait to be back in his homeland under a brutal and blazing red sky. Thoughts of Assara, always at the edge of his mind, swamped his concentration. Would she be there waiting for him still?

"Good morning." His cousin handed him a warm 'tea', a drink he had all but become addicted to lately. If his countrymen enjoyed it half as much as he did, his on-board stores, gifted to him from the four families would bring a considerable income.

"Did you reach the spirit last night?" He asked before sipping gingerly on the hot, spiced drink.

"No. I checked with the men as well, it is the same for them. It has been weeks for some."

"So now there is only dreaming."

"It certainly seems that way." Rahim's tea was heaped with cinnamon and cloves, so much so that the aroma beat the salt from the air at times. "It is a big part of life to lose. I lie awake at night sometimes wondering what happened to the spirit, who took it from us, and why."

"At least you made the most of the spirit hours while they were here, learning languages and bettering yourself. What did I do?" An unplanned harrumph signalled his displeasure with himself.

"Well, you met 'her'. Time will tell who made better use of the spirit."

"What do you think they are for? Dreams?" Leaning against the railing gave him a rest from balancing on the deck, and turned him to see his cousin's reaction.

"Dreams? If what I have seen so far is anything to go off, they are some higher being making life infinitely more confusing than it already was. Perhaps for his own amusement."

It may have been a morose observation, but Jonah laughed all the same, so light was his heart of late.

"And you, my captain? What meaning have you assigned to these visions named 'dreams'?"

"I don't know. They must serve some purpose. They have in the past."

"One time."

"Ok, one time so far." They both laughed. "Still, although I can't quite figure it out, there is something to the things I have seen, some hidden meaning, I am sure of it. We just haven't had time to figure it out yet."

"Maybe." Both gazes returned to the featureless ocean. "So, we have no way of knowing who will greet us when we make port in Bandarat; Cul, or Falan?"

"No." Jonah answered. "Personally though, I am hoping it will be Falan. Killing him will be so much easier than killing Cul."

"Have you begun to sympathise with the Prince who had a hand in the Shareef's death?" Rahim's reply bordered on incredulous.

"Maybe... but mainly I don't want to fight him because I think I will lose. Have you seen him with a sword? He is an artisan."

"Do not concern yourself."

Jonah turned to read his cousin's expression.

"I have purchased another boot." He very nearly looked serious.

"You are the very definition of humour, Rahim." Jonah rolled his eyes, letting them again find the horizon.

"Decided yet what you'll say to her?"

"No idea. Figured I would just improvise, you know. Wait till the moment."

"Good plan." Rahim said sarcastically.

"Feel free to give me some ideas?"

"Sorry, cousin." A dismissive hand mirrored the tone as he turned and left the deck. "When it comes to you two, I feel it best to stay out of the way."

"Where would I be without you?" Jonah called after him. He had hoped for a little help. The real truth was he had no clue what Assara and Cul's relationship was like. It was possible that she was just property to him, but he had sensed something more. Perhaps not a romantic something, but something. When he imagined killing Cul he was brought back to the docks at Safar, and the first time he had laid eyes on her. She had not liked seeing him take a life.

What would she think if he took Cul's?

One problem at a time, he thought. Get to Bandarat, don't get killed getting off the boat, find Assara.

Find her.

Another week passed in the agonising monotony of life at sea. He, in unison with the captain of the vessel, had decided not to make port in Safar. No point in tempting fate any further. The straight-line voyage then was entirely without incident. Jonah began hoping for pirates.

A third week of waiting with no word from Bandarat or South Harbour had all on board, on edge. People were still getting used to the absence of the spirit, which meant they hadn't yet learned to cope with the isolation of not being able to 'visit' home each night. The captains put their heads together, devising games and changes to the routine in an attempt to stave off cabin fever. Some initiatives worked better than others. Friendly sword play contests turned out to be a little one sided, so the crew were ordered to teach the Banji how to sail, to balance the ego-scales somewhat. A series of harmless pranks began, starting with noses being painted black during sleep. The crew retaliated by changing the Banji's flask water to salt water. The crew also started teaching the Banji some basic Engsam, and in turn the warrior tribe taught the sailors how to fight without weapons. The camaraderie between them grew.

Week four, Jonah's final week at sea, naturally took the longest. Personal rivalries became conflicts, which he found himself breaking up more and more. His men were beginning to lighten now their journey was nearing its end, whereas the westerners were becoming more disgruntled with every nautical mile added between them and their home. Their captain added duties to keep them as busy as possible.

Jonah and Rahim began talking of their plans for the future, although it was difficult, due to their not knowing who was controlling Bandarat. Through the discussions of living arrangements and hopes for what might come next Jonah started to notice the subtle changes in his cousin. He had always joked about having a large family. It was becoming increasingly clear that those jokes were a mask for a very real desire. It caused him to face some scary realisations of his own: children, homes not huts, things maybe not far from his future as well.

Would Assara be thinking the same thoughts, he wondered? She seemed younger than he. In truth he did not know how old she was. Perhaps she was too young to want children, or she might not want them at all. Or she could not have them…

So, the 'not knowing' bred anxiety, and the days on the ocean gave room for more 'not knowing', and again, more anxiety. As a result, when the call finally came that land had been seen; when Jonah's eyes once again rested on his homeland, it was less elation, and more terror, that overwhelmed him.

He had arrived.

*   *   *

Ahead, somewhere in the throng, noises emerged. Cries, squeals and even some weeping, was spreading on the other side of the wall of bodies. Assara looked to Jasmine for guidance, for a clue as to how to react. Standing on tip-toes, trying to see over heads much taller than her own, Jasmine was preoccupied. At least she wasn't running.

A murmur rose. Despite it seeming joyous, Assara was still panicked. So many months of running, fearing for her safety and the safety of her sister. In her heart she was preparing to leave the crowd. Whatever had come, they could witness it from a safe distance. She found Tamra's hand.

Those nearest her finally parted enough to reveal the source of their attention. They were welcoming Banji warriors, patting them on the shoulder, hugging them and congratulating them. Some women were draped joyfully around the shoulders of some, while others were wailing and being commiserated.

Assara's heart stopped.

"Sister..." Jasmine said, a moment before a parting of heads revealed Jonah's face.

He saw her a split second after she saw him. He was smiling politely, but there was an anxiety in his eyes, a searching. Her free hand rushed to her mouth. Her shoulders began to shake as sobs came, though she was unaware that she was crying. Carefully, gingerly, Jonah stepped through those between them, hands guiding shoulders gently left and right. She wanted to rush to him, but her legs would not move. Tamra grabbed her leg, her sister's display unsettling her. When finally he was near it seemed the entire crowd fell silent.

"Assara." He spoke.

*   *   *

The ship had made port that afternoon, Jonah releasing his men to their homes and families immediately. Attendants working the dock had communicated the state of the city before they could even embark. Though Falan was dead, Cul, who had been the cause of his death, had also fallen. The Banji had regained control of the city.

Arriving at port at the end of the week, to the celebrations of the weekly festival… it was as good an omen as his men had ever had. He followed his men toward the square, toward where their friends and families would likely be waiting. He wanted to share in their joy. Rahim, for once, was strangely quiet. Even he seemed overcome with the feeling of finally coming home.

More and more people recognised them the nearer they came to the square. The square itself, already crowded with those celebrating weeks end, suddenly swarmed as wives discovered husbands and children found fathers. Even as the losses were conveyed, and some began their mourning, the feeling was one of triumph.

Jonah warmly accepted hands and congratulations as he passed, the crowd thickening with every step. Still, a fist grew around his heart. Always his eyes searched, face after face, seeking the one.

A space appeared in front of him despite the crowd. There, clutching her sisters hand, she appeared. He had hoped, beyond hoping, that she would be here. Her hand flew to her mouth, bringing with it sobs. He wanted to rush, but her reaction slowed him. That, and his head was swimming. He moved slowly past his men, caught in the embraces of their loved ones, until he was close enough to speak.

"Assara." He managed without sounding too broken.

For a moment, at once brief and at the same time an eternity, all she did was stand and stare. It seemed as if the crowd had fallen silent, as if everyone on earth was paused in wait for what came next. Then, as if drawn in by the forces that had so long ago brought them together, she fell into his arms.

A cheer grew, at first close by then shared by all within earshot. Warriors had come home. Victory had been won, homes assured, livelihoods protected. Through the cheers, and cries of victory that escalated louder and louder still, she sobbed quietly into his neck. For the first time Jonah breathed deeply her scent, tightening his arms as he did.

"Jonah." She managed, finally. He melted to hear his name on her voice. "Are you really here?"

"Yes, yes I am here."

He pulled back enough to smooth her hair, to wipe her tears. However, no sooner had their eyes met, that their lips pulled together, every power in the universe overcoming conscious thought. He was beyond rational. He was emotion: powerful, pure and honest, their kiss conveying all that could not be formed in words. The crowd cheered anew.

Assara's tears turned to laughter. Jonah felt a hand on his shoulder.

"Ahem." Rahim said.

"Assara, this is – "

"Hello, Rahim." She said, cutting him off. She left Jonah's arms long enough to offer Rahim a hug. Her departure created an emptiness that bordered on physical pain.

"To say I have heard a lot about you would be the understatement to end all understatements."

Jonah rolled his eyes, but any annoyance he felt melted as she returned to his arms.

"Jonah, Rahim, I want you to meet my sister. Tamra."

Tamra looked uncertainly up from Jasmine's leg, which she was again clutching.

"I recognise you, from the spirit." Jonah said warmly. She did not reply, but he understood why.

"Hello, man." Moie strolled casually over. Jonah released an arm from Assara's waist and scooped the boy up.

"Little one. I owe you everything." He said.

Moie smiled warmly. "I am glad to see you."

"Jasmine, come." Assara called, not releasing Jonah. "Don't you want to meet him?"

She approached, and seemed to force a smile. "So, you made it?"

"Jasmine. I am glad to meet you."

She all but harrumphed.

"I know you have cared for Assara and her sister, kept them safe. I can never say how much I appreciate what you have done for me."

She softened a little. It would have to do, for now. "Of course." She replied, sceptical to the last.

Rahim stepped in closer, extending a hand. "My cousin mentioned you, Jasmine, during our travels and our battles. He spoke of your name, and of your heart, but not of your beauty."

Jasmine snorted at him, but shook his hand. Awkwardly. A knowing glance passed between the two men which made Jonah laugh.

"Captains!" A call came. "Jonah! Rahim!"

Three men pushed through the still celebrating crowd. Jonah recognised them as other leaders of the Shareef's army.

"Welcome back!" One commended. "How was your mission, the Shareef's last?"

"As everything that he turned his eye to, a success." Jonah answered proudly. The specifics could wait. "You are managing the city?"

"Yes, just. You are here to help, I trust?"

"We are." He said, although his sardonic look, mirrored by Rahim, belied his noble words. "We also have new trade arrangements to show you, and treasures from the west."

"One last mighty victory!" The captain yelled. "To honour our Shareef! Hail, the fallen!" He called.

"Hail, the fallen!" Those nearest repeated.

"Hail, the fallen!" The square shouted, in a voice so loud as to reach the lands of the dead, and those now residing there.

Jonah let the crowd take up the chant. His lips had far more important matters to attend to.